Jack, Be Nimble

Jack, Be Nimble

R. H. Peake

Writers Club Press
New York Lincoln Shanghai

Jack, Be Nimble

All Rights Reserved © 2003 by Richard H. Peake

No part of this book may be reproduced or transmitted in any form or by any means, graphic, electronic, or mechanical, including photocopying, recording, taping, or by any information storage retrieval system, without the written permission of the publisher.

Writers Club Press
an imprint of iUniverse, Inc.

For information address:
iUniverse, Inc.
2021 Pine Lake Road, Suite 100
Lincoln, NE 68512
www.iuniverse.com

ISBN: 0-595-26710-6

Printed in the United States of America

"A little learning is a dangerous thing"

—Alexander Pope
Essay on Man

Contents

The Opening Gambit...1
   The Charge.. 1
   The Leader.. 9
   The Youthful Professor 14
   The Frenchman 19
   The Provost and the Dean.................................... 23

The Battle Is Joined 27
   Fall Entertainments... 27
   Meeting of Rustic Faculty 34
   Belle's Bottom... 38
   Supporters of the President 43

Attempted Murder and Mayhem 49
   Failing Brakes 49
   Jaykyll's Marriage 54
   Library Trouble 61
   Malmuth and the Church 65

Explorations 68
   Another Session 68
   Malmuth Summons Jaykyll................................... 79
   The Festival 84
   Childhood Memories.. 91

Learning Experiences..99
   Sherri and Jason... 99
   Senior Faculty Meet with Malmuth 104

    Donnybrook at Student Life Council *108*
    Hike to White Rocks *112*
    Poetry in Arms *117*

Jay Relives the Past 120

    Philwaggen Explores Again *120*
    Poison *126*
    A Little Learning *130*
    Students Beware *137*
    Comedy Not Divine *142*

The Winter of Discontent 145

    Malmuth Winter *145*
    Suspected Unethical Behavior *150*
    Malmuth Winter Ends *156*

Lovers' Revels 164

    Exploring Karen Cleaver *164*
    Duvant Asks Belle: Finances *171*
    RAU Work *174*
    Messerand Unmasks Samp *176*
    Malmuth and Melissa: Louisville *180*
    Ambush *186*
    Malmuth Attacks faculty *189*
    Malmuth Plays Golf *193*
    Karen Again *197*

Malmuth Schemes 206

    Malmuth and Melissa: Memphis *206*
    Belle Pumps Hiram *210*
    Administrative Changes *212*
    Last Session *218*

Malmuth Wins and Loses 220

    Sherri's Evidence *220*
    Malmuth and Melissa: Galveston *224*
    The Shooting *229*
    Messerand Strikes *232*
    No Confidence *235*

Melissa Dumps Malmuth *237*
Jaykyll Emerges Victorious 240
RAU confronts Malmuth and Bottleby............................ *240*
Duvant and Belle.. *243*
RAU Parties.. *246*

The Opening Gambit

The Charge

For weeks John "Jay" Jaykyll had resisted Sarah's pleas that he seek help. "Nonsense," he had told her. "The only thing wrong with me is an overly active sense of duty that leads to overwork compounded by a sense of guilt that never lets me be satisfied with what I've accomplished."

When the time came, however, John kept the appointment that Sarah had made for him with her friend Dr. Emma Clauswomb. The opening discussions did not go very well even though Emma looked and acted quite professional. Antiseptically dressed in a white coat, she tried to work with her skeptical patient. Both John and Emma felt uneasy about a professional relationship after having known each other socially for many years. After a couple of unproductive sessions, Emma told John that she was transferring him to Dr. Philip Philwaggen.

"Jay, we're getting absolutely nowhere. I don't wish to be sexist, but I think you'll open up more to a male psychiatrist. I propose to transfer you to Phil. Today. He's waiting for you."

John had to admit that the change made sense, so he readily acquiesced. A short walk down the hall brought them to Philwaggen's office. Emma knocked.

"Come in, Emma. The door's open."

John was impressed favorably by the scene that greeted him. A bust of Goethe stood on one side of the room. On the other side, a bust of Sigmund Freud gazed across the small room at the great author. Prints of Delacroix, Munch, and Van Gogh adorned the walls of the office. John noticed approvingly that Munch's "The Cry" occupied the most prominent spot. "I can really sympathize with that fellow," he thought. The unruly mop of red hair that spread above Philwaggen's long, somber face caused Jaykyll to feel right away that the psychiatrist approached life with a serious though somewhat sybaritic attitude. Philwaggen smiled disarmingly as he shook Jaykyll's hand.

"Dr. Clauswomb tells me that your case has some very interesting features, Dr. Jaykyll. I am delighted I'm to have the opportunity to work with you."

"Thanks, but I really don't think my case is very exciting."

"Jay, you're too modest. I'll leave you two alone. I hope you have better success than I have had, Phil."

After she had left, John expressed his doubts about the need for treatment. "I think you'll be disappointed, Dr. Philwaggen. I'm not really convinced I need help. I seem to be functioning quite well. I get my teaching and administrative duties done despite my conflicts with upper administration."

"I'm told you've been exhibiting some rather bizarre behavior, Dr. Jaykyll. May I call you Jay?"

John nodded acceptance. "Bizarre is in the eyes of the beholder. College professors should be a bit eccentric."

Several sessions and Rohrschach tests later, Jaykyll had become more trusting of Philwaggen and no longer argued that he needed no help. His trances, or whatever they were, had become worse, or at least more embarrassing.

"Jay, could you tell me what the Dean said about the reception?"

"It was not a confrontational meeting. Dean Grudger had called me in for a talk. He claimed I had begun to make strange noises next to the punch bowl at the reception for new faculty...."

Jaykyll's mind slipped back to the meeting. "John," Grudger had begun, "You really frightened that new young sociologist, Julie Cabot. She came to me next day, threatening to resign if we don't keep you away from her, even though she has no prospects for another job. There you were, according to her, offering her a glass of punch in a very debonair and scholarly fashion, discussing the erotic imagery of Keats, when suddenly you began grunting and stamping. She said that all she did was say that she much preferred Shelley to Keats. She saw a wild look in your eye as you began to stamp your feet and make sounds like a bull about to charge. You looked to her as if you were a predator eying prey to be devoured. She thinks the only thing that saved her was the arrival of Professor Webbot, who concurs that you looked quite strange. We can't have this. You have to get help."

Jaykyll had been relieved at that moment to be able to tell Grudger that he already was in therapy. Grudger was relieved as well. "I don't need another problem in your department, John. Young Duvant is problem enough...."

Philwaggen brought Jaykyll back to the present. "Jay, that's a good beginning. I think you have a problem dealing with conflict. We'll have to explore in detail, but I think that all we have to do is get some of your past experiences out in the open. We'll work on that theory for awhile."

From that time on, John talked to Philwaggen more freely. He was now willing to admit that he had a problem. Dr. Philwaggen explained Jay's problems might be stemming from what is commonly known as a mid-life crisis, although John thought that he had been through that ten years earlier.

"Nothing to be ashamed of, Jay. I see men every day, successful men, many of whom are displaying weird behaviors. It seems to be a result of the pressures of modern life. The years between forty-five and fifty present great difficulties for the modern American male, but for some the reaction arrives as late as fifty-five or even sixty.

"After all, we have a cult of youth. Nobody knows how to grow old gracefully any more. Ambitious men who have devoted their energies to their careers begin to wonder what they have missed when they reach forty or so. At first they try to hide from themselves with various defensive mechanisms—young women become very tempting, for example—but as their sense of desolation increases, their behavior often becomes more bizarre than simple philandering."

John was mildly reassured to know that he was not alone. "Misery does love company as the adage goes, I suppose, but I can't see how that is going to help me."

"First of all, you need to tell me what you can remember. I could put you under hypnosis, but I don't think that will be necessary for you. Just try to relax, drift off, and tell me what comes into your mind."

Jaykyll relaxed and thought about what had happened a few weeks earlier....

The short drive to school had given John time to prepare for the coming conversation with Dean Grudger, who had summoned Jaykyll to discuss what the Dean had termed personnel matters within Jaykyll's department. When Jaykyll arrived at Grudger's office, he found that the Dean had gathered several other faculty and administratiors to discuss whatever the matter was. Moving across Grudger's dark carpet, Jaykyll was surprised to see that none of these people were members of his department. After Jay had greeted everyone and sat down, Grudger began.

"Sexual harrassment of students is something we must guard against. I think all of us can agree on that."

Everyone murmured polite agreement. Encouraged, Grudger went on. "The harassment of female students by male faculty is especially deplorable." Jaykyll had reservations about this proposition and noted that the two female administrators winced slightly at the obviously sexist emphasis. Jean Bright, the Dean of Students, objected with as much mildness as she could muster.

"I think we should take any sexual harassment seriously, whether it's by male teachers or somebody else."

"Well, yes, of course, Dean Bright, but you know that boys will be boys."

"That may be true, Dean Grudger, but these days girls may also be girls. Some even feel compelled to consider it their duty to prove that they are emancipated. These girls don't wait for someone else to make a move."

After a pause to regain his composure, Grudger continued. "We have a charge brought against a male faculty member in the Department of English."

"Damn," thought Jaykyll, "now I know why I'm here." Aloud, he merely joked, "Well, Dean, I hope I'm not the guilty party."

Grudger had never appreciated Jaykyll's humor. Only a brief twitch of his lips in irritation betrayed his dislike of this example. "Of course not, John. The charge has been brought against Roger Duvant. A co-ed has accused him of making an advance to her in the hall after class."

"I find that difficult to believe, Dean. Roger may be a bit randy, but he certainly is not desperate. He receives plenty of unsolicited attention. He doesn't need to seek it out. Just what led this young woman to think that Roger had made a pass at her?" Jaykyll was beginning to put this meeting together with something that he had overheard in his optometrist's office a few days before. An obese young woman across the room from him had been regaling an elderly lady and her husband with a tale of harassment by a professor. At the time Jaykyll had wondered who could have been desperate enough to make an advance to the mountain of flesh whose voice he was overhearing. The girl was apparently so starved for a fantasy life that she had transformed solicitude about poor performance in class into a sexual encounter with her professor. Jaykyll had quickly dismissed the incident and had forgotten it until now.

"Well, in confidence, I will tell you that she says Professor Duvant put his hand on her shoulder and made suggestive remarks to her."

"Have you asked Roger about this? What does he say?" Jaykyll was aware, even as he asked the question, that Grudger would not have faced Duvant immediately. That wasn't his style.

"Well, no, I wanted to consult with all of you before doing anything."

"Then I suggest that you talk to him and get his side of the story. If it seems that there is anything to the girl's story, then I'll talk to Roger," Jaykyll offered. "I'm sure that whatever happened was misinterpreted by the young woman. I suggest that you consider whether the young woman in question is attractive or whether she is an unattractive girl creating a fantasy world in which she is desirable."

"As a matter of fact, the young woman in question is not very attractive."

Jaykyll fought to keep from sliding into the grayness. Obviously Grudger had judged Roger guilty without making any attempt to explore alternatives. There wasn't any presumption of innocence in Grudger's court. "Then I think her interpretation of events is quite likely wrong. If nothing else, Roger has high standards—in feminine beauty as well as in judging student work. Have you explored the possibility that the student may be disgruntled over the way Roger has judged some of her work?"

"Not yet."

"I think you should. This is a very serious charge. We agree on that." The discussion continued, but Jaykyll began to lose track of what was being said after he had come to Roger's defense. He felt very strange. A grayness seemed to envelop him, and he found himself in a gray outdoors—

A small meadow animal scurried across the upland sand, headed for a pool of water, seemingly so bent on slaking its thirst that it did not pay attention to the great bird of prey circling above it. The small animal was oblivious to the ornate hawk-eagle's grace as it soared ever higher, evidently soaring for the simple pleasure of riding the thermals, not looking for food—

Jaykyll was barely aware of the bird's loud, piercing scream and a hand touching his arm. "Oh, I didn't mean to upset you, Dr. Jaykyll," Jean Bright was saying. "Don't you agree with me?"

"Well, yes, I think so," Jay agreed hesitantly, assuming anything she suggested would be more sensible than what Grudger would bring forth.

"Then it is agreed," Grudger said in a relieved tone. "I'll talk to Duvant and get back in touch with Dr. Jaykyll."

John Jaykyll escaped into the sunlight and breathed the warm September air deeply. Glad to be away from his confrontation with Hiram Grudger, he walked to his office, entered, and closed the door behind him. For a long time he sat at his desk. Why should Roger be called on the carpet just because a disturbed co-ed had accused him of an imaginary instance of what everyone else seemed to be doing in actuality. Jaykyll didn't object to their breaking the code so much as he did their sanctimonious way of attacking others less powerful and less discreet. It was common gossip around campus that Hiram Grudger had married Rauncibelle only after she had bedded him and then threatened to expose his love of perverse pleasures unless he married her and confined his perversities to their marriage bed. Hiram had not been all that bad a Dean despite his love of calm on campus, but he should be careful about throwing stones at others. And it was rumored that Sherri Whetman was going to bed with Jason Malmuth and that Provost Bottleby had his eyes set on Raunci-belle Grudger. Jay antiicpated unpleasant battles ahead. Lapsing into grayness, Jaykyll found himself in a barren landscape—

Below the clouds an eagle screams at another large bird intruding on its space as it soars above the snow-covered mountains. Circling high above the parched landscape a condor searches for carrion. Mile upon mile of rock and sparsely vegetated earth stretches below the two huge birds. Stalked by a jaguar, a large rodent wanders about seeking water. As the shadow of the large bird passes over them again and again, the cat lifts its head and snarls defiance. Then, stepping up its pace, it gains on the rodent pausing at a mountain stream to drink thirstily. As it drinks, the panther pounces upon it. Cries of pain rise from the parched landscape toward the condor and eagle as they continue to circle expectantly—

At this point Dr. Philwaggen called Jaykyll back to the present. "That's all for today. We seem to be making some progress. Your case interests me greatly, Jay. You are too modest about its features. I'll see you again next week at this time, if that fits your schedule."

"That's quite convenient. I must admit I feel a little better already."

"Don't get your hopes up too soon. It will take several sessions before we can be certain of any real progress. I have some theories about your problem. I believe that you have had great difficulty dealing with conflict. If that's the case, we must explore the reasons why conflict is so frightening for you."

The Leader

Set in a verdant valley abutting the Cumberland Mountains, Pine-Mountain College added greatly to the intellectual life of the community of Pine Mountain, a town that owed its origins to the opening of the Appalachian coal industry in the 1890's. There was little in the town or at the College to remind students and faculty of this historical background, because the coal beds rested miles away from the green valley harboring the College and town. Except for those who provided services at the hospital and in the courthouse or at other government institutions and a small merchant class of Jackson County, Kentucky, the townsfolk worked either in the mining industry or at the College. The President of the College therefore assumed a very important presence in the larger community as well as in the campus community. He needed to be aware of the needs and values of the larger community surrounding the College. The language of Pine Mountain was the language of creek and hill and hollow and ridge. Pine Mountain folk tended to model their formal utterances on the language of the King James Bible or sermons that they heard on Sundays. This speech and the flowing pace of their utterances reminded knowledgeable listeners of the Keltic as well as the Anglo-Saxon elements in the heritage of Appalachians. Many nuances of mountain dialect hearkened back to the British Isles before and just after the Norman Conquest. Although the search committee that had sought a new president had tried to make this need to be attuned to the idiosyncrasies of the region clear to the candidates, Jason Malmuth tended to ignore this part of his introduction to the College. Instead, he focused almost exclusively on the evident desire of both communities to have a first-rate liberal arts college. He managed to conceal from everyone who interviewed him that he was a mountain boy who had, in the mountain phraseology, "got above his raising." Unfortunately for many people including Jason Malmuth, his tunnel vision did not become apparent until after he had taken up his duties at Pine Mountain College. Unfortunately, also, Malmuth's perception of what constitutes a first-rate liberal arts college consisted largely of image and much less of intellectual substance.

Besides his tall, lanky frame, the chief physical characteristics about Jason Malmuth were his prominent nose and narrow, projecting chin. Those who dealt in verbal cliches described him as hawk-like, although admirers of raptors preferred to talk about his predatory countenance. Nevertheless, the chief epithet used by women to describe Jason was handsome. Those who had the pleasure of his handshake could not, however, help detecting a limpness to it that belied the masculinely handsome, aggressive face. Their confusion tended to work in Malmuth's favor in the beginning, because people could not decide whether to admire, fear, or loathe him. Taking advantage of this indecision, he was able to persuade many weak-minded persons to do exactly as he wished.

Jason Malmuth felt that he would be able to put his mark on Pine Mountain College in short order. He could hardly believe the lack of effort that the previous administration had made to project a truly collegiate image. His predecessor had simply accepted the glorification of rusticity that he found in place when he came to Pine Mountain. Malmuth was already at work changing that complacent acceptance of traditional ways. He would see to it that his school shed rusticity in short order. The signs that would delineate each building's name with the college emblem in blue and gold were already ordered, and he had signed a contract with a local nursery to give the college campus a much-needed facelift. Some of the other problems that he perceived were less tractable. He would have to make do with Dean Hiram Grudger. He, after all, had had experience at some major universities; but Malmuth was bringing in a new Provost, Jeremy Bottleby, who gave promise of being willing to help Malmuth rid the college of the mountain rusticity that he judged its greatest handicap. The new president wanted to present the school as the epitome of a sophisticated institution of higher learning, not the foremost bastion of Davy Crockett and Daniel Boone studies. Malmuth thought some of the faculty were major impediments to his plans. Some of these professors had the misguided notion that they were supposed to honor and support the mountain heritage of their local students. They also seemed to have the misguided idea that they were the ones to decide what goals the school should pursue.

Malmuth had found a competent and enthusiastic ally in Sherri Widderbee Whetman, his secretary. He had shifted the former president's secretary to Student Services and brought in Sherri from the business office, where anyone could plainly see her talents had been wasted. Sherri was from the bluegrass and spoke with an acceptably cultivated southern accent. She was sophisticated, vivacious, and well groomed—not to mention her having a classically beautiful face and a splendid figure. She had proved to be invaluable to him because she knew so much about the politics of the College and was on good terms with all of the faculty members, who told her all the rumors floating about the school. She then passed on to him just what the professors were thinking. Her information had enabled him to develop a list of faculty who were likely to oppose his plans. John Jaykyll's name occupied a prominent position on this list. Sherri had also warned him about Rauncibelle Grudger, who—rumor had it—had a habit of seducing administration and faculty and then using their weakness as material for blackmail. In fact, Sherri had told Malmuth, Rauncibelle's methods had made it possible for her to become Mrs. Grudger. She was also rumored to be responsible for the resignation of one of Malmuth's presidential predecessors.

No matter what other problems he perceived, Malmuth considered his most immediate concern to be eliminating the rustic image the College had acquired. As far as Malmuth was concerned, it was an image the College had actually reveled in, citing its beginnings on a shoestring budget in buildings that had previously housed the county poor farm and the county home for wayward women of Jackson County, Kentucky. Whenever the College's origins were recalled, the story of how local businessmen had gone to the president of the state university in Lexington to beg his help in starting a college was sure to be told. As the story went, the benefactor had agreed to begin an outreach program if the local people would provide the land and buildings to house the program. The men and women who had formed the early faculty of the College had ever since been proclaiming its origins with a sense of prideful ownership. They practically deified its rustic beginnings and an era they apparently viewed as an Edenic time of bucolic bliss. When they spoke about the college's beginnings, one could almost envision pastoral shepherds from antique paintings frolicking over the fields with shepherdesses while sheep grazed contentedly around. The truth was far more rustic, Malmuth knew. Those who eulogized Davy Crockett killing bear and Danel Boone fleeing Indians to save his scalp, these were closer to the truth. But they too presented these times as heroic and Edenic. Even those who should know better, professors from the bluegrass or from out of state, aided and abetted this deification and promulgation of communal origins. They had even created a group to worship at the altar of the school's humble origins, The Pore Folks Frolic. Every year they got together and ate corn bread, soup beans, and turnip greens in a ritual celebration of the humble beginnings of the College. He would put a stop to that if he could. At the very least he would hide their activities from the outside world. Perhaps a name change would help. Maybe Malmuth College…that had a pleasantly collegiate ring to it, he thought. Very sophisticated.

The first step to achieve the necessary new image would be to eliminate or render ineffectual those faculty who sought to preserve the mountain heritage. High on the list that he had compiled with Sherri's help was Jonathan Large. Professor Large had been with the school almost since its inception, having been sent there by the administration in Lexington because of his mountain background.

He taught the classics, philosophy, and some history. His wife Lavender taught history and sociology. Also on the list were Nathaniel Boone, Daniel Crockett, Pauline Hauptman, John Jaykyll and Roger Duvant. Unfortunately, from Malmuth's perspective, all were tenured faculty except Duvant.

After mulling over his course of action for several weeks, Malmuth sat in his office composing his thoughts. His office was decorated with objects and paintings that suggested a desire to be correctly modern. A number of prints of paintings by Salvadore Dali and Pablo Picasso hung on his walls, which were painted an icy blue. A few delicate figures of glass here and there contributed to the coldness of the room, to an overall effect of restraint, of emotions under control, yet some of the art suggested a dark underside to the control.

"Mrs. Whetman, please bring your pad in for dictation."

"Right away, President Malmuth."

When Sherri appeared, Malmuth took note of her becoming hairdo and outfit with an appraising glance. She certainly lived up to the image he wanted for his college—beautiful, sophisticated, and competent. Bringing his attention back to his mission, he asked her to take a memorandum to faculty teaching in the Appalachian program. Sherri dutifully took down the message and sent copies to all those teaching Appalachian courses. Loud were the groans and curses of unhappy faculty when these memoranda were received.

"The man has no idea of what he is doing," Jonathan Large told his wife Lavender when he received his copy. "Malmuth says that he appreciates the time and effort that we have spent over the years working on this program, but he thinks we should consider turning our efforts into more mainstream academic areas. Lavender, we are going to have trouble with this fellow."

"Yes, Jonathan, but I do believe we should turn our efforts in a new direction, as President Malmuth suggests. I think we should put our efforts toward figuring out how to get rid of the man."

The Youthful Professor

Anybody who saw Roger Duvant immediately noticed his shock of blond hair above his handsome face. They found the gaze of his blue eyes compelling. He was often compared favorably to Paul Newman or Robert Redford by his female students. Roger was old enough to have obtained a Ph.D. in American Studies and to have begun a family with his wife Betty, but he was still young enough to induce palpitations in the breasts of impressionable young co-eds. Though he enjoyed basking in the adulation of his admiring throng, Roger viewed himself as a happily married man—fortunate in having found Elizabeth Pomeroy and having had the good luck to persuade her to marry him.

Since accepting a joint appointment in the Departments of History and English, Duvant had established himself as a valuable member of the collegiate community. He was director of the Appalachian Studies Program during the regular terms and Coordinator of the Boone Institute during the summer terms. His course in Appalachian folklore was particularly popular. Roger and Betty had spent a number of enjoyable years at Pine Mountain College before Jason Malmuth arrived. They had fallen in love with the mountains, and Duvant was well on his way toward achieving tenure. They were looking forward to buying a house and moving out of the faculty housing, although this housing had been a godsend when they first moved to the small mountain community of Pine Mountain. The arrival of Malmuth had had a somewhat unsettling effect on what had appeared to be the Duvants' idyllic life. By the time classes opened in late August, Roger Duvant had begun to suspect that what he had considered his secure place at Pine Mountain College might be in jeopardy.

The late summer evening brought cooler air to soften the hot early September day. After supper with Betty and the children, Roger looked out at the evening glow and decided that it was the perfect time for a jog. Katydids were calling and fireflies were beginning to glow. Duvant liked to stay in good physical condition. He regularly engaged in a jog around the campus, down Arthur Drive, up Tornado Highway, around the government low-income housing for the elderly, then back to Arthur Drive and the campus. He jogged this route two or three times a week except when the weather urged against it. Roger wished to stay fit, not catch pneumonia. He wasn't obsessed with exercise like that Spanish professor, Mickey Moriarity.

Tonight his jog proceeded uneventfully until he reached the narrow lane in front of the low-income housing complex. The traffic had been rather heavy on the highway portion of his jog, but he was always careful to stay alert and out of the roadway whenever traffic approached. After the right turn onto Meadow Lane, he could relax, as there was rarely any vehicle using this route. Tonight he was pondering the words of Provost Bottleby at the afternoon's faculty meeting. When Dean Grudger had introduced the new Provost, the man was greeted with polite applause by the faculty.

Bottleby was obviously Malmuth's man, and that fact alone caused a certain amount of trepidation about how to deal with him. The new provost had begun pleasantly enough, telling them how pleased he was to be joining them here in these beautiful mountains. Their beauty was undeniable, he asserted, but this beauty brought with it a negative quality of rusticity.

"President Malmuth and I have discussed this matter at some length, and we have concluded that Pine Mountain College must shed its rustic image. With your help, ladies and gentlemen, we will project the image of a sophisticated citadel of higher learning."

Bottleby's succeeding remarks were perfunctory, but these few words had been sufficient to stir unease among those faculty who had endeavored to foster respect for mountain traditions even as they sought to prepare their students to compete in contemporary American society. During the queston-and-answer period that followed Bottleby's prepared remarks, Duvant had had the temerity to ask the Provost how he viewed the Appalachian Studies program.

"Do you and President Malmuth feel that teaching Appalachian studies sullies the image of the College, Provost Bottleby?"

Taken aback by the bluntness of Duvant's query, Bottleby paused, glowered at Duvant, and looked out the window a moment before answering.

"No, no. Not at all. But we do not believe that they should receive major attention. They should not be what people think of when Pine Mountain College is mentioned."

Taken together with rumors about Malmuth's hostility to anything that hinted at mountain traditions and his recent memorandum, these words were definitely a cause for concern. Thinking of the implications for his Appalachian folklore course, Duvant failed to notice a vehicle approaching him from the rear without any lights, creeping along. Suddenly it speeded up and veered to Duvant's side of the road. Luckily, it did not hit him full but grazed his left side, knocking him into the ditch as it sped off. When Roger again became aware of his surroundings, he felt a pain in his left ankle, his left side at the ribs, and in his left shoulder. Feeling his left side with his right hand, he could detect no broken bones. Apparently he had escaped with a sprained ankle, bruised ribs, and a dislocated shoulder. Dragging himself out of the ditch, he limped back to the campus and the faculty housing. Betty asked a neighbor to watch the children while she drove him to the emergency room of Pine Mountain Hospital. There he received care for his hurt body, but his mind kept trying to recall the moments before what might have been an accident but could well have been a deliberate attempt to run him down. It was difficult to remember in the hubbub of the emergency room. Though Pine Mountain Hospital was relatively small, it served a large area. It tended to be constantly active, especially in the evenings and on weekends. Like many small hospitals in comparatively remote regions, its emergency room staff had been drawn from the corners of the world and their English had a quality that rendered it difficult for the majority of their patients to understand. The staff had similar difficulty with the southern mountain dialect of many of their patients. The famous movie line uttered by Paul Newman applied here. What the doctors and patients had was a "problem to communicate." The intensity of the emergency room situation caused the problems of communication to increase exponentially. Coupled with the drastic and very pressing needs of some of the people who claimed the services of the emergency room, the language barrier added to the noise and tension. The staff were glad to deal with a case as simple as Roger's. His treatment involved some pain, which Roger managed to deal with admirably because his mind was occupied with the evening's events. Roger's mind kept going back to the question, "Who would wish to harm him?" He had no enemies—at least none he knew. Surely he had not offended the administration that much. Surely it must have been an accident. That is what he told those at the College next day who inquired about what had happened to him when he appeared for his classes limping, his left arm in a sling. He did make a point of going to the mathematics department and asking Rufus Webbot whether he had been driving down the lane by the low-income housing the night before. Rufus had a reputation for poor driving. Since arriving at Pine Mountain, he had wrecked two cars totally and had put numerous dents in a third. Rufus denied having been the culprit. "I was grading papers all evening," he protested.

"You've got to be more careful when you go out jogging, Roger." Betty had told him as she drove him home from the emergency room. She patted his thigh, "You'll have to be a good boy."

Roger appreciated Betty's concern for his wellbeing.

She pampered him inordinately. She watched his diet and constantly sought new recipes that were both tasty and healthy. How she had time to take care of the children's needs and baby him amazed Duvant. In return he showed his appreciation of her loving care by praising her efforts and praising her beauty. They shared a love of the natural world and of hiking in woodland settings, so family outings and picnics occupied a great deal of their leisure time. "You take care of yourself and get well, Roger. In this condition you couldn't keep up with our children on a hike, much less keep up with me."

"Well, for the time being I'll just limp along behind and admire the beauty of your behind."

Laughing, Betty admonished him for being gross, although she enjoyed the compliment. "Sometimes you're outrageous. I think you see enough of that so that you don't have to concern yourself with it on our hikes."

Both Betty and Roger valued the camaraderie of their relationship. They remained enamored of each other after eleven years of marriage. Each thought the other very desirable. But their attraction for each other extended beyond the bedroom. They were comfortable with one another.

They would not have conceived being happy living day in and day out with another person.

The Frenchman

On the basis of a doctorate from the Sorbonne, Jacques Messerand had obtained his position as a lecturer in French at Pine Mountain College. His letter of acceptance provoked overwhelming consternation in Professor Wilhelm Bertrand, head of the foreign language department. In his consternation, Bertrand consulted John Jaykyll, whose advice he valued. Reading the letter Bertrand had handed to him, John was less concerned but equally taken aback.

"This man is mad."

"Ja. But there's nothing I can do now. We're stuck with the schmuck for at least a year."

Messerand arrived several weeks before the fall semester's beginning with his young wife Simone in tow. Simone was buxom, beautiful, and dutiful—apparently a French country girl awed by her husband's intellect. The object of her awe was a six-foot man in his fifties without much other than a few slivers of graying brown hair that appeared to need washing. Over his nose, there were rimless spectacles. Those who saw him for the first time might well guess that he was a scholar. His eccentricity was immediately apparent, as he habitually engaged himself in conversation, ignoring Simone and anyone else around him.

It soon became clear to those who had dealings with Professor Messerand during the ensuing weeks that his attention to French verb declensions was far more assiduous than his attention to personal hygiene. Perhaps for this reason rather than awe for his great intellect, people tended to keep a respectful distance from Monsieur Messerand. His boorish manners did not enhance his social acceptance, and both male faculty and male students, especially the younger ones, soon became aware of the professor's insecurity concerning his young wife. Messerand appeared to be insanely jealous of Simone. If she happened to speak to another man, either student or faculty—unless the man were obviously considerably older than

Messerand—the Frenchman assumed that this man was attempting an affair with Simone.

Messerand displayed an especially intense reaction to their neighbor on faculty row, young professor Roger Duvant, who had taken pity on Simone one day when she seemed particularly forlorn. Duvant had given her a ride to the grocery store and had helped her with her shopping. When he brought her home and began to help her unload the groceries, Messerand came rushing from the house brandishing a pistol, which he fired once in the air.

"Libidinous rascal," he yelled, "have you no shame. Leave my wife before I shoot. The next shot will be for you."

"Non, non, Jacques, mon cher. Monsieur Duvant, please leave quickly."

Duvant complied with her request as rapidly as possible and was soon out of sight. Later, discussing with Betty his encounter with the Frenchman, Roger laughed at what was, in retrospect, the obvious humor of the situation. Betty Duvant saw less of the humor than did her husband. "It's a shame we live next door to them. Roger, I want you to stay away from that man as much as is possible. He sounds dangerous to me." Although Roger pretended to think her fears exaggerated, secretly he agreed with her and resolved to follow her advice.

Not only young male faculty came under Messerand's jealous gaze. Male students whom he saw speaking to Simone were equally suspect. In fact one student in particular aroused his ire during their first week at Pine Mountain. Part of the College's student staff, this young man had been called upon to do some repairs in Messerand's faculty house. During the time scheduled for the repairs, Messerand was supposed to be in class, but the Frenchman arrived home just as the repairs were completed. Notwithstanding the fact that he had insisted that the repairs be done immediately, Messerand flew into a rage when he found the young, rather handsome repairman taking his leave of Simone. Rushing to the bedroom, the Frenchman grabbed his pistol and returned brandishing it at the departing young man. Chasing the youth down the walk to his truck, all the while uttering harsh verbal threats that included a rather gruesome ex-rated list of punishments to be meted out to the offender if he was ever seen again at Messerand's house, the Frenchman stood at the end of the parking area waving his gun triumphantly as his enemy hastily boarded the maintenance truck.

"Know you what a castrato is? Wish you to become one? The student ignored these parting words as he turned his truck away and left Messerand gesticulating to the heavens. Back at the maintenance office, Joe Walker parked the truck and went in to the office to file his work report.

"Don't send me to that house any more, Mrs. Banks," he told Selena Banks, the maintenance secretary.

"Why, Joe? What's wrong?"

"That Professor Messerand, he's crazy—threatened to kill me if I come around again."

"What did you do? Didn't you do the repairs?"

"I did the repairs. I was saying goodbye to his wife when he came home. First thing I knew, he was pointing a gun at me and chasing me. He threatened to castrate me."

"Well, I declare. I've heard he's strange. You're not the first man he's pulled a gun on. He did he same thing to Professor Duvant a few weeks ago."

"I sure do feel sorry for his wife. I wonder how she got hitched to that old geezer anyway."

"It must have been an arranged marriage. They still have those in France, I think. Her parents must have chosen him."

"Then her parents must be as crazy as he is."

Before many weeks had passed, the other faculty who dwelled on faculty row shared Joe Walker's opinion. The yells and screams that issued from the Messerand household from time to time unsettled his neighbors. Occasionally Simone's voice was the source of the noise, but more often than not the source of the sounds appeared to be the booming vocal apparatus of Jacques. It was well for the peace of mind of the neighborhood that the Messerands kept their blinds closed and their shades down. Had the activities that provoked the vocal outbursts been visible to the neighbors, their alarm would have been much more pronounced.

The Provost and the Dean

Jeremy Bottleby was the huge bulldog that waddled along behind Jason Malmuth in his peregrinations about the campus. With rapt attention, Bottleby imbibed the ideas of his president as he might drink his favorite disguised drink of bourbon-and-coke. Their shared interest in golf occupied a large portion of their conversations other than those concerned with the College. As chunky as Malmuth was lean, Bottleby seemed a huge, rectangular monolith topped by an equally rectangular head. His high forehead was beginning to show slightly the evidence of a receding hairline. His full jowls, large nose, and fleshy lips hinted at a man of crude but hugely sensuous appetites. He was by no means an ugly man. Some people might even term him handsome.

The Provost had listened to Malmuth's case for changing the image of the College. While he did not think the matter as important as his leader did, he saw that his most profitable course would be to wholeheartedly support a campaign against rusticity. To that end, soon after the faculty meeting that had upset Duvant, Bottleby arranged a conference with Hiram Grudger. As he was ushered into Grudger's office, he noted the very austere carpet and the rather unexciting examples of modern art on the walls. Aside from the Jackson Pollock prints, the office was functional and quite uninteresting. That pretty well summed up his first impression of Dean Hiram Grudger also.

Below a shock of thick gray hair, Grudger's blue eyes gave off a coldly calculating gaze that belied the sensual petulance of his lips. His unwillingness sometimes to look at people directly during conversation hinted at a bit of deviousness, but the set of his jaw suggested that at moments he might show great fortitude. His thin, sharp features presented a lean and hungry appearance, not what many men would call handsome, but suggesting a harsh masculinity that Grudger had found to be appealing to some women.

"Dean Grudger, as you know Jason and I have grave misgivings about the image that the College has been projecting. We need to change our image from that of a haven for rustics to a place where sophistication is as natural to our campus as its green grass."

"I'm not sure that I agree that Pine Mountain College is immersed in rusticity. After all, we don't milk cows here, nor do we raise pigs."

"I'm afraid Jason doesn't view this as a joking matter."

"Then I suppose that you and I cannot treat it with much levity either. I'll try to be more serious. What do you wish me to do?"

"The president has compiled a list of faculty whom he thinks contribute heavily to the rustic image of the College. The first step is to see that these faculty members are warned of the error of their ways. If they fail to change their ways, then we will have to use harsher methods of either obtaining their cooperation or—if need be—ridding our campus of them."

"What if these are tenured faculty?"

"They will pose a greater problem, but I'm sure that we can either neutralize them or get rid of them somehow. We'll have to deal with them on a case by case basis."

"This all sounds very unpleasant."

"All for the greater good, of course."

"For Malmuth's good, perhaps. I'm not so certain about the greater good."

"Well, any reservations that you have are best kept between us. Will you cooperate with us?"

"If I don't, I suppose my name goes to the top of the list."

"I think so, if I read Malmuth correctly."

"Then, being only a year or two from retirement, I suppose I must become a battler against the rustics among us. Where should I start?"

"I think that fellow, Duvant's the name, I believe, who asked about Appalachian studies at the faculty meeting—he might be a good place to begin. He's on the list."

"Roger has other difficulties than his support of rusticity. He might prove an excellent subject for an object lesson, especially since he doesn't yet have tenure."

"Good. Let me know if I can be of help."

At that moment, Rauncibelle Grudger appeared in the doorway to her husband's office. A tall woman with brown hair and dark eyes, she dressed her thin but well-curved figure very becomingly in a blue-and-red suit. Rauncibelle smiled at them.

"I hope I'm not interrupting anything important."

"I was just leaving, Mrs. Grudger." Bottleby rose politely from his chair and moved toward the door.

"Oh, don't go on my account, and please don't be so formal. Just call me Belle. May I call you Jeremy?"

"Of course, Belle. By the way, I need to come by to talk with you about our school's assessment activities. I understand that you are in charge of assessment."

"Any time, Jeremy. Probably some afternoon would be most convenient for me."

"I'll see you soon, then, Belle." As Bottleby's large form disappeared through the doorway, Belle gazed at his bulk like an automobile dealer appraising a used car.

"There certainly is a lot of him," she observed. "I wonder what's under the hood."

"You don't need to check."

"My, my. Do I detect a note of jealousy? Would you object even if it's to your advantage?"

"That man can be dangerous, Belle."

"I believe that I can take care of myself. Don't you worry, Hiram. I don't deprive you of what you want, do I?"

"No."

"Then don't you concern yourself with how I use what's left over. Now, why has he got you so worried?"

"He was here to enlist me in Malmuth's campaign against rusticity. Bottleby says the President has compiled an enemies list, and we are expected to attack those on the list or suffer unpleasant consequences. Roger Duvant is to be our first target."

"Too bad. He's such a handsome hunk. Maybe I could help. It could be fun."

"I don't want you mixed up with Duvant."

"Hiram, we just went through that. As long as I satisfy you, you should be content. I want the freedom to do as I please. You don't have enough energy to satisfy all my desires. Besides, I need the thrill of conquest."

"Please be careful."

"You know I am."

"Well, I don't want to be obvious in my approach to this. I think I'll call a meeting of faculty involved in the Appalachian Studies program. That way I won't seem to be singling out Duvant."

"You do that. I'll approach Roger my own way. I'll call him in to discuss assessment of the program."

The Battle Is Joined

Fall Entertainments

Very soon after arriving at the College, Jason Malmuth had begun listening carefully to the speech of the students at Pine Mountain College. At the faculty-staff picnic held toward the beginning of the fall term, Malmuth made it a point to hunt up Gentry Flowerpiercer. Shaking hands with Gentry, Jason undertook to enlist his support.

"I understand that you teach some of the speech courses at the College, Gentry."

"That's right, President Malmuth."

"Why don't you just call me Jason. From what I've heard since arriving, you have a difficult task."

"That depends."

"What do you mean?"

"Our students, especially our local students, can be very expressive. They've been exposed to an oral tradition. Many of them really know how to tell a story. They give interesting speeches."

"I see what you mean. I'm glad you can find something positive about our students' speech. I've been aghast when I've talked to our students."

"Why's that?"

"A large portion of them murder the King's English."

"Maybe they're aware that their ancestors helped defeat the King at the Battle of King's Mountain."

"I don't find it a subject for humor, Professor Flowerpiercer."

"Like our faculty in English, those of us who teach speech work very hard to inculcate proficiency in standard English usage, President Malmuth, but we don't want to do this in a way that will cause our students to deny their heritage. We want them to be able to compete in the national arena, not to deny their fathers and grandfathers."

Jason Malmuth had himself seen to it that his speech patterns denied those of his father and grandfather. He had decided that this course of action was necessary for advancing his career, so he had ruthlessly excised all mountain colloquialisms from his conversation. He thought he had made a good bargain not only in rooting out his non-standard forms of speech, but in denying his heritage altogether. "From what I have observed, you and your colleagues have been somewhat too squeamish about stamping out our local students' mountain dialect. I would like to see a more vigorous effort. I intend that we require an examination in speech for our entering students similar to the one that we demand of their writing. Those whose oral use of standard English has glaring deficiencies will have to take a remedial speech course."

"The Curriculum Committee would have to approve that requirement."

"If they don't, I'll create one that will."

A lengthy silence ensued. Gentry breathed more comfortably when John Jaykyll walked up and greeted them. "Good afternoon, President. Hello, Gentry."

"Hello, Dr. Jaykyll. I was just discussing with Professor Flowerpiercer the woeful state of our students' oral English." The tenseness of the situation revealed itself in Malmuth's tone. Jaykyll thought some humor might be conducive to social harmony.

"There's a story going about campus along those lines that might amuse you. One of our professors swears it's true. He had a student in class who had a problem using standard English. This student lived in the dorms but went home on weekends. On Monday mornings, he would be speaking a broad dialect. By Friday, he was speaking fairly standard English. For weeks the professor observed this phenomenon. Finally, one Monday he asked the young man just what caused his weekly lapse into non-standard English. The student replied that by Friday he could get his language under control, but when he got home speaking like that his pa became angry. His pa told him every Friday that if he was coming home talking that way an antidote had to be applied. 'I'm a-goin' to take you'uns out to the woodshed and whupp you,' his pa would tell him."

Before Jaykyll finished, Gentry was already laughing, but John could detect no sign of amusement on Malmuth's countenance. "I find our students' speech atrocious. I'm sorry that you find this problem a matter for joking," Jason Malmuth told them as he stalked off.

"I'm afraid you didn't win a friend, John."

The fall season at Pine Mountain offered other entertainments than the faculty-staff picnic. Waited for expectantly by the young and some of their elders, the county fair garnered a great deal of attention from the College faculty as well as the general public during late summer in the Pine Mountain area. The ferris wheels, the chamber of horrors and marvels, the famous singing groups, the horse show, and various other carnival attractions drew people from all around southeastern Kentucky. A downside to the fair's popularity was the amount of money it drained from parents just as the fall school session began, but no negative features could dampen the enthusiasm of the local populace for the Fair. Even the faculty of Pine Mountain College who did not teach in the Appalachian Studies program went to the Fair. It definitely had characteristics that Jason Malmuth would term rustic, but nobody who went to the Fair seemed to mind.

On a Friday night, Sarah and John Jaykyll and Betty and Roger Duvant decided to spend their evening at the Fair. They met at the entrance gate, bought their tickets, and proceeded to enjoy the entertainments, not the least of which were the people in the crowd. After the Duvant boys left to venture about on their own, John looked around among the booths for the table that the College always set up at the Fair to encourage prospective students to think about attending Pine Mountain College. He could not discover it. "Where is the College's table, I wonder?" he asked Roger.

"I heard from Lavender Large that Malmuth commanded that there be no table this year. He was afraid that an event like this would attract the wrong kind of student-the rustic type."

"I don't know what we're going to do for students if we confine ourselves to those that are clearly devoid of rusticity. We may have to stop recruiting in this region altogether."

After the fruitless search for a College booth, they took in the display of local art.

"There are some really good paintings here," said Sarah Jaykyll, who painted a little herself. "I really like that painting of the waterfall. I can almost see the water falling."

"It's by my barber, Jock Sinclair," Roger told her.

"He's certainly talented in a number of ways. I think he does a great job with your hair."

"Roger tells me he writes music, too," Betty added. He's hoping to get some of his songs recorded in Nashville."

They traversed the arts and crafts booths and then came to a booth where people bought chances at fifty cents a piece to throw a ball at some moving figures. If a ball-thrower hit one, he got a stuffed animal. "Roger, do you think you could win one for me?" Betty pleaded.

"I'll try. Give me two tickets," he told the barker.

Roger had no success with his first two chances, so he bought two more. He hit a figure with his next throw, but he missed again with his fourth. "Which animal do you want, honey?"

"That's a cute little cougar. I'll take that. After all, the Pine Mountain mascot is the mountain lion, even if we don't have cougars in our mountains any more."

"There are some people that say they've seen them around here. A fellow over at Big Lick got some money last year for some goats. He claimed were killed by a cougar. There are lots of mountain tales about painters killing animals and even people. Painter's another name for a panther. Those tales indicate there used to be plenty of cougars in these mountains."

"Your folklore knowledge comes in handy now and again, Roger." Jaykyll joked. "Be careful, though, those tales might scare off prospective students who aren't rustic."

"Well, my cougar's cute. He's certainly not rustic."

The four of them then proceeded to the grandstand in front of the stage where the musicians were performing. Sarah and Betty particularly wished to hear Loretta Lynn, the headliner of this year's entertainers. Though they both taught in the Appalachian Studies program, John and Roger were reluctantly dragged along. The two of them much preferred to hear someone like Jean Ritchie singing a cappela or with a dulcimer to accompany her. "You two are stick in the muds. You think you're into rusticity, but you're really just old fogies. If you truly want to be rustic, you need to listen to people like Loretta, Wayland Jennings, and Johnny Cash," Betty upbraided.

"Yes," Sarah added, "Don't forget Johnny Cash married June Carter. He's part of the Carter family. Remember, Roger, you dragged us over to Hiltons to the Carter Fold and thought all the music there was just great. I don't see why you get so unhappy when somebody uses a steel guitar or other electric instrument." So they all listened to Loretta do a set that included *A Coal Miner's Daughter*.

"I really feel rustic now, John. How about you?"

"Roger, if I were any more rustic, my shoes would be rusty."

Sarah and Betty then decided to go back to look more closely at the art and the arts and crafts. Left to their own devices, John and

Roger decided to view the Chamber of Horrors and Marvels. Inside they were drawn immediately to the show's Fat Woman. She seemed to be over six feet tall and must have weighed almost six hundred pounds.

"Why, she'd give Maybird Upshaw a run for her money," John told Roger.

"Who is Maybird Upshaw?"

She's a character in a James Still short story. Her relative got her a place in a carnival so that she could see the world. His wife wanted to get rid of her. She was a house guest who'd overstayed her welcome. She had become so big she couldn't get out the door. The carnival people had to cut a hole in the house to get Maybird out. Maybird's a character based on a real woman, a Melungeon woman, I've heard. They had to cut her house open to take her out to be buried when she died."

"I've heard about that woman. She ran a blind tiger on a ridge over in Tennessee. Her customers slipped their order and money under one side of the turntable window shutter and then the lady flipped the turntable and slipped out their liquor. Nobody saw who was buying or who was selling. She was a Melungeon. They say she sold good moonshine. I don't know that this woman here could compete with Maybird, John. Still, she's big. There's a lot there to love."

"True, but it would take a lot to feed her between lovings."

They went on to other marvels. A calf with two heads, a huge boa constrictor with two tails, and many others. The Horrors included a tableau entitled FORTY WHACKS depicting Lizzie Borden with a bloody ax standing over the dead and bloody corpses of her mother and father. The famous poem about the incident was set at the foot of the display case. They were properly appreciative of the literary merit of the exhibit. "Too bad Malmuth doesn't have a daughter," Roger observed.

Departing the Chamber of Horrors and Marvels, they went to the agricultural displays. As a dedicated gardener, John always enjoyed seeing what some of his neighbors were producing. There were champion crookneck and straightneck yellow squash as well as zucchini and patty pans. "My Dad used to call those white patty pan squash cimelins. I never knew how he came by that name," John told Roger. There were also champion tomatoes, beans, corn, and eggplants. "Those eggplants are hard to grow in our climate," Jay observed. Though he had no place on faculty row to garden, Roger appreciated seeing these evidences of folk activity. As they walked past all the sights, the two men congratulated themselves on thoroughly enjoying what was thoroughly rustic.

"We'd better enjoy it while we can, John. Next year President Malmuth may make the Fair off limits for Pine Mountain faculty. We might imbibe too much rusticity if we come here often."

Had Roger known about Malmuth's plans, he might have joked less.

Meeting of Rustic Faculty

Summoned by Hiram Grudger, John Jaykyll, Roger Duvant, Nathaniel Boone, Jonathan and Lavender Large, and Pauline Hauptman gathered in the conference room of the administration building on a warm autumn day when the leaves were beginning to turn. The beauty of the season was somewhat lost on the assembled faculty members. All of them were involved in the Appalachian Studies program, so after some discussion about why they had been asked to meet, they surmised that the meeting must have something to do with the comments about rusticity that had been rampant on the campus.

"After all, those of us gathered here by the great Grudger are in some way involved in the Appalachian program. We all received that damned memorandum. We're prime offenders, if I read Bottleby's words at the faculty meeting correctly," the geology professor, Daniel Crockett, guessed. "Of course, you may all say that I have rocks in my head."

"No, I think you're right, Dan," Roger Duvant said in a mournful tone as Dean Grudger entered the room three or so minutes after the appointed meeting time. He looked a bit flustered, Jay thought.

"Thank you for coming on short notice. President Malmuth has asked that the faculty review our academic program to determine whether or not our efforts are encouraging a truly collegiate atmosphere or whether they contribute to the College's image of rusticity. Provost Bottleby and I believe that we should begin an examination of the Appalachian Studies program without delay."

"Why the hurry?" asked Nathaniel Boone.

"President Malmuth has made changing the image of the College his top priority. He believes that the Appalachian Studies program may be contributing to the perception that this College is a haven for rustics."

John Jaykyll was a bit nonplussed by this statement. "Has anybody in the administration considered that a college in Appalachia has an obligation to offer courses dealing with this region? Would anybody question a course in colonial history taught at William & Mary?"

Nathaniel Boone also interjected his dismay. "It would be difficult for me to do any field ecology outside this area. Does President Malmuth propose to provide me with a research station in Florida? Or perhaps he thinks I should have a station in Frankfort or Lexington."

"As far as I'm concerned," Jonathan Large interjected, "the history of this area is just a subset of Kentucky history. Do you and President Malmuth propose that we cease teaching Kentucky history? How would the legislature regard that?"

Somewhat taken off guard by this vocal, reasoned opposition, Grudger tried to absolve himself of responsibility. "Don't blame me. I'm just the messenger for Provost Bottleby and President Malmuth."

"You appeared to be supporting them with vigor, if not enthusiasm," observed Lavender Large. Pauline Hauptman added, "Surely you can't expect us to abandon all of our investment of time and effort in this area? Does the administration have the funds to send me to New Guinea or Samoa to study the culture of Pacific Islanders? Come to think of it, I believe Margaret Mead and some others have done that."

Roger Duvant was pleased to see the determined support the Appalachian program was receiving. It emboldened him. "Dean Grudger, it is difficult for me to see how I could help refurbish the College's image as President Malmuth desires—at least insofar as the Appalachian Studies program is concerned. After all, my contribution to the program is the course in folklore. Folklore by definition is of the folk, therefore rustic. Are you suggesting that folklore should be removed from the curriculum?"

"What about geology? I don't see how I can avoid using rustic rocks," Daniel Crockett needled.

By this time Hiram Grudger had concluded that his calling this meeting had been a huge blunder. He had not really considered beforehand that he had been bullied into taking an intellectually absurd stance. Matters of image are really a matter of public relations, not academic endeavor, he belatedly realized. To make the situation worse, he had alienated a considerable portion of his constituency, the faculty. He decided to avoid further conflict. "These are legitimate concerns that you have voiced. I'll pass them on to the President."

"Please do," Jonathan Large requested. "Tell him that the academic program does not depend on the image of the College for its integrity. The image Malmuth thinks of is largely superficial. If he wants a better image of that kind, he should raise some money to beautify the campus, set up a public radio station to tell the public how collegiate we are, and promote more cultural activities and other entertainment for the students and the general community. Academic image comes from research that leads to reading papers and publishing articles. He should leave that to us. But he shouldn't ignore the fact that the first duty of a college faculty is to teach students, and each of us has a heavy teaching load."

Loud applause followed Large's diatribe. Grudger left the room as quickly and as quietly as possible. He was apprehensive about reporting this meeting to Bottleby and Malmuth. He had to admit the sensibleness of these faculty members' position, but he could not keep his deanship if he failed to satisfy Malmuth. Perhaps he could present the faculty views positively. The less friction between the administration and the faculty, the happier the Dean to Grudger's thinking. Maybe Rauncibelle's interest in Bottleby and Duvant would prove helpful. Accepting her help might be a sacrifice that he'd have to make in order to preserve his job. Escaping into the beautiful evening color outside, Grudger breathed in the autumn air with relief. He took a long walk over the campus to clear his head. The more he thought about his unpleasant situation, the more he saw himself as between Scylla and Charybdis, or, to put it in more rustic terms, between a rock and a hard place. "It's a helluva way to end my career. These last years are going to be pure hell. If I were a Democrat, I'd ask for a New Deal." Somehwat bouyed by these feeble witticisms, Hiram Grudger proceeded dejectedly to his office, cursing his luck at having drawn Jason Malmuth as his superior.

Belle's Bottom

For several weeks, Belle attempted to arrange a meeting with Roger Duvant to discuss assessment. Duvant did not consciously avoid an interview with Belle Grudger, because he was a reasonably popular teacher even though he actually insisted on teaching his students something and required high standards of them. He had little to fear from the actual assessment, he knew, but the rumors that circulated about what was jokingly referred to as Belle's Bottom caused him concern, as he was as yet untenured. According to the rumors, trips to Belle's Bottom had undone any number of young male faculty members. With some misgivings, then, Roger walked slowly toward Rauncibelle Grudger's office late one Wednesday afternoon. Except for one or two students the hallway was deserted when he reached her office door and knocked. "Come in, Roger," she said as she opened the door and ushered him in. The room was dimly lit. A maroon shag carpet covered the floor and the walls were painted a light pink. Adorning the walls were reproductions of various famous paintings that added to the sensuous tone of Belle's office. Botticelli's *Venus Rising from the Sea,* Guercino's *Susanna Bathing,* Titian's *Danae,* Manet's *Dejeuner sur l'herbe,* and Gauguin's *Tahitian Women* added to an atmosphere of subtle sensuousness created by an odor of gardenias. There were no lights on except for a floor lamp in the corner next to the sofa. It provided a suffused light for the entire office, though only the one corner was brightly lit and the rest of the office was in a dim halflight. The sensuous strains of Ravel's "Afternoon of the Faun" echoed faintly through the room.

"Have a seat on the sofa, Roger."

Collecting papers from her desk, Belle sat down on the sofa beside Duvant. He soon determined that a faint aroma of gardenias and roses was emanating from Belle, whose red and black outfit set off her figure very effectively. She proffered some papers to Roger, keeping copies.

"Roger, these are copies of the assessment report for the Appalachian Studies program. I think that we need to go over them together and determine what might be done to improve the effectiveness of the program. Perhaps we could just look on the same copy." As she said this, Belle eased closer to Roger and put her arm across the sofa behind him. As they discussed the program's assessment methods during the next half hour, Belle continued to edge closer to Roger.

He tried as surreptiously as possible to edge away. Duvant was exceedingly relieved when there was a knock at the door.

"Just a moment," Rauncibelle called to her visitor.

"Roger, I definitely think that the assessment methods described here could be improved, but I think we'll have to finish the rest of this discussion at a later time. We have lots to talk about. I believe that is Provost Bottleby. We had an appointment at five."

Quite relieved, Roger rose and went with Belle to the door. Roger greeted Bottleby and, saying a hasty goodbye to Belle, made his exit as quickly as possible. Belle ushered Bottleby to the sofa seat that Duvant had just relinquished.

"You're looking quite ravishing, Belle. That's my assessment," Bottleby joked.

"Thank you, Jeremy. That's the best thing I've heard today. To return the compliment, that's a handsome tie you have on. It goes so well with your suit."

"Thanks. I've come to ask your help. Your position as assessment officer puts you in an excellent position to help President Malmuth with his campaign against rusticity."

"How could I be of help?"

"The Appalachian Studies program seems to project the very essence of rusticity, and some negative assessments could enable President Malmuth to justify reducing the funding for those programs."

"The courses in that program are among the most popular we have."

"Perhaps, but reducing the enrollment in certain courses could make it easier for us to justify releasing certain faculty."

"You have Roger Duvant in mind, no doubt, as the rest of the faculty in that program are tenured."

"Well, yes, I suppose he is the first faculty member who would have to go."

"Something like that would take time, Jeremy. Why should I do it? I have no reason to dislike either the program or Roger Duvant."

"Consider that Dean Grudger's support of President Malmuth's campaign has been lukewarm at best. I suppose that you would like to see your husband retain his position. You could assure his being Dean until retirement year after next."

"I would need more reward than that for taking the risks involved in pleasing you by a false assessment report."

"Surely you value your husband's position."

"Yes, I definitely do like being the wife of the Dean. But you are asking me to do something that could cause severe repercussions. I barely know you, and here you are asking me to risk my whole career. Perhaps you're just setting a trap for me. I would like to please you and President Malmuth, but I don't wish to do something dishonest."

"There are other ways to please me, Belle." As he made this suggestion, Grudger eased himself closer to Belle, who responded to his hand on her leg by placing hers on his inner thigh.

Detecting the hugeness of his response, Belle suggested, "Jeremy, why don't we lock my office door. I think we could be more comfortable discussing these matters if we could be sure of not having an interruption."

"A splendid idea, Belle. I'll just get comfortable." Bottleby slipped off his suit jacket and undid his tie, hanging them on the office coat rack.

"It will be difficult to produce evidence that Roger is a poor teacher," Belle argued when they were again seated together on the couch. "I think that there might be other ways to get the result you want."

"What do you suggest?"

"Perhaps a charge of moral turpitude would prove more effective. That is sufficient to remove even tenured faculty."

"Yes. But how do we obtain that. I'm told that Duvant is a happily married man. A young woman has brought a charge against him, but it appears to be totally without merit."

"I have my ways, Jeremy. It's possible that evidence could be provided. Fake photography could be used if necessary. I think a fake photograph might be less dangerous than a fake assessment report."

"All right, then, I'll leave Duvant to you, although we hope to use him as part of our attack on John Jaykyll. Perhaps we should try to demonstrate a trend of declining effectiveness in his reports. We wouldn't want the shift in the reports to be so sudden as to be lacking credibility. If you can't accomplish that, then we can try other alternatives."

During their conversation, Bottleby and Belle had also engaged in tactile communication. "Jeremy, you are a large man!" Belle laughingly exclaimed. "You mentioned other ways to please you besides developing material damaging to Roger Duvant?"

"Are you woman enough to accommodate me, Belle?"

"Where there's a will, there's a way, Jeremy."

Very few people, if any, had ever accused Rauncibelle Grudger of lacking will power. Or charged her with lack of effort. Certainly none of the men who had visited Belle's Bottom had ever publicly or privately charged her with deficiencies in will power or energy.

It was a memorable experience for Jeremy. Had Bottleby known that all of their activities were being recorded on camera, however, he might well have enjoyed their liason less and understood better the many meanings of the popular title of this office. Belle's Bottom had not received its name solely because it was on the basement floor.

Supporters of the President

Jason Malmuth was not without supporters among the faculty and members of the Pine Mountain community. Other than junior faculty who feared the President's decisions on their tenure and some tenured faculty who sought advancement by currying his favor, Malmuth had support from a group of people dedicated to bringing experiences in the arts to Pine Mountain. Known as For the Arts or FORTS, this group was the creation of and ram-rodded by a small, rotund, persistent woman named Petunia Falta. She worked tirelessly to bring to Pine Mountain ballet and modern dance, opera, and classic drama such as Shakespeare's *Romeo & Juliet*. The only arts that Petunia did not seem to care for were those that traditionally had been handed down in the mountains. She had no problem bringing English country dancers from England to Pine Mountain, but she would not countenance calling English country dancing's Appalachian offspring, clogging and flatfooting—art forms popular in the mountains—culture worthy of attention. Like Jason Malmuth, Petunia viewed these local arts as unworthy of serious attention.

A woman who had lived almost all of her life in a bustling urban setting, Petunia could not find it within her to accept the rural environment into which she had been thrust by circumstance. She wanted her daughters to take part in the cultural activities that had been part of her youth: ballet, chamber music, opera, and lively popular music and dance. The community of Pine Mountain seemed to be lacking these activities that defined for Petunia what it meant to be civilized. She could not or would not make a connection between the arts of the mountain people among whom she found herself and the popular entertainments of her youth. She saw little worth in dulcimers and fiddles. They certainly lacked the excitement of the mariachi bands of her childhood, and the traditional songs that accompanied the dulcimer and fiddle music were for the most part, dreary and depressing—not lively and joyous like the songs she remembered. Petunia refused Roger Duvant's argument that the northern European tradition carried on by the local mountain folk had as noble a heritage as any of her Latin music. "Anglo-Saxon and Keltic artists had to contend with a much harsher environment than people to their south. It was often bleak and oppressive. Voltaire has spoken of the dark, damp days when the English hang themselves," he told her. To no avail. Petunia turned deaf ears. She wanted life and entertainment in vibrant reds and yellows, not somber blues and grays.

Petunia had conceived and brought into being a festival of the arts on the Pine Mountain College campus. It had an international flavor—Taiwanese dancers vied with Peruvian musicians playing the music of the Andes on native instruments. Russian balalaika competed with Swan Lake performed by students from the local school of ballet. The throbbing sounds of the Caribbean competed with the guitar music and castanets of Spain. In short, art endeavors from all parts of the world were welcome, except for the dancing, dulcimers and ballads of the Appalachians.

Another trait that Petunia had in common with Jason Malmuth was a dislike for any ideas other than her own. Like him she enlisted followers who would obey without question, doing the work she directed with slavish devotion. Professor Mickey Moriarity and his wife Reba helped put up banners and posters while Simone Messerand was quickly enlisted in the effort to fold programs after she and Jacques arrived. Despite his degee from the Sorbonne, Petunia would have nothing to do with Jacques. "He stinks!" she judged forcefully and irrevocably. When Jacques accused her husband, Agamemnon, of flirting with Simone, Petunia became upset but discounted Messrand's accusations because of his uncouthness. Even for Petunia, there were limits to a love of internationalism. She insisted that Messerand apologize about his accusations or be reported to President Malmuth for malicious libel. She told him that she would proceed with a lawsuit if President Malmuth took no action. Even Messerand cowered before Petunia. He begged her pardon and assured her that she would hear nothing further of his accusations of Agamemnon.

Through FORTS members who taught in the Appalachian program, Petunia obtained a great deal more help. Notwithstanding Petunia's disdain for Appalachian arts, the faculty who taught in the Appalachian program helped with the Arts Festival on the theory that exposure to art of many kinds would stimulate appreciation for Appalachian arts even if they weren't represented at the Festival. Not that they didn't attempt to persuade Petunia to be more inclusive. Petunia answered them by telling them that exposure to the local arts was unnecessary. "These people see clogging and hear dulcimer music all the time. We need to show them other things."

"Don't you think they'll respond to the other cultures' arts better if you put these side by side with something familiar to them-validate the arts they're familiar with?" John Jaykyll asked.

"No, I don't think we need to validate their rustic arts," Petunia replied.

"She sounds like Malmuth, don't you think?" Sarah observed later.

"Unfortunately. Either that or I heard Malmuth's echo."

The inner circle of FORTS consisted of some fairly well to do women who prided themselves on being cosmopolitan—the social leaders of Pine Mountain. These women adored Jason Malmuth and invited him to dinner on a regular basis. Like him, they had used their education at prestigious schools of higher learning to little advantage other than to denigrate their mountain heritage. At the dinners they provided for the President, they and he delighted in casting themselves in a superior, sophisticated role as they hurled barbs at the local community and its customs. The more unsavory elements of the local populace were treated as the typical rather than the exception. The incest prevalent among the families in Jepson

Hollow, for example, was used to suggest that all unsophisticated, uneducated Appalachians engaged in this behavior.

"You know the old joke about mountain virgins," Jason offered his admirers after they told him of the habits of Jepson Hollow folk. "A mountain virgin is a girl of twelve or less who's fast enough to outrun her brothers and her grandpa."

After the laughter had died down, Rosy Stetson suggested that Jason was a bit off the mark. "I think you have the age wrong. I think ten or less is more accurate." Further laughter ensued.

"That's why they don't let the girls wear shoes. They're afraid it'll slow them down," Amy Vandiver added.

His circle of admirers listened with rapt attention as Malmuth complained about the rusticity of many of the faculty at Pine Mountain College and discussed his plans to bring a more sophisticated atmosphere to the campus. He praised Petunia Falta's efforts to open the community to international arts. "We need to offer our community something other than picking and singing and flatfoot. Garth Brooks, Merle Travis, and Loretta Lynn will never equal Beethoven or Mozart."

When Malmuth repeated this observation in public, John Jaykyll suggested to Roger Duvant that they consider having a joint Mozart-Merle Travis celebration. Roger laughed and suggested that it must be called the Travis-Mozart celebration. He inspired a student to write an editorial in the school newspaper proposing just such a school function.

To her credit, Petunia did not engage in the denigrating, snide wit of Malmuth and his inner circle, but she quite willingly enlisted the ladies of Malmuth's admiring throng to her projects as fund-raisers for arts activities that would bring the enlightenment of other cultures to the mountains. They were all members of FORTS. She shared with them and Jason Malmuth the notion that any so-called art native to Appalachia was rustic and thus unworthy of serious attention.

By far the most vocal supporters of President Malmuth among the faculty were Jacques Messerand and Ichabod Balboa. Messerand believed that anything not French was parochial and therefore unworthy of consideration. Balboa had a more practical reason for his vehement support of attacks on rustics. He hoped to win the President's gratitude and replace Jaykyll as chair of the English faculty. Drawn together at first by their support of Malmuth's anti-rusticity campaign, they found that they shared other interests, particularly an interest in the writings of the Marquis de Sade. Messerand was amazed to learn that Balboa not only had read *Justine* but had also studied *Juliette* and *One Hundred and Twenty Days of Sodom*. They engaged in spirited discussions about which of DeSade's works best illustrated the brilliance of his mind. Unlike the majority of DeSade's readers, they did not regard his ideas as at all warped. "A logical development of the Revolution," was a judgment that Messerand was fond of repeating.

They thought nothing wrong with DeSade's egocentric approach to the world and sexuality. It seemed to them that the Marquis was eminently correct in placing his own pleasures above the contentment of others. He was, after all, a French philosopher and should be taken seriously even though society had deemed it necessary to incarcerate him. They soon found that they shared another scholarly interest in the work of Pauline Reage, *The Story of O*. Balboa recommended it to Messerand as a bible to be used in his friend's relationship with Simone. The largest part of Balboa's contribution to their discussions was literary and theoretical, but Messerand from time to time introduced items based on actual experience. Jacques grew so fond of Ichabod (the Frenchman used the nickname Ichy) that he even invited him to his house and did not become jealous of his seeing Simone. In fact, Messerand sometimes included her in their discussions, asking her opinion on this or that sadistic pleasure. The two men spent long hours debating the most exquisite ways to inflict pain to stimulate sexual desire, and when they brought up this or that fine point, Jacques would often ask Simone to decide which of the two methods of torture, in her opinion, most stimulated sexual desire. Reluctant though she was to participate in their conversations, Jacques gave her no choice. He insisted on having her opinion.

When Messerand and Balboa discovered that John Jaykyll had also read widely in de Sade, they offered to include him in their discussions. They thought that they might perhaps organize a group devoted to the study of the man whom they considered the greatest of French philosophers. Thanking them, Jaykyll had declined when he discovered that they read de Sade with uncritical and undisguised relish. He did not reveal to them that he himself read the works of de Sade with disgust. They simply shrugged off his reluctance as mere bourgeois timidity.

President Malmuth was not unappreciative of the enthusiastic and vocal support that he received from Messerand and Balboa. He was fond of citing them as faculty who appreciated the need to improve the rustic image of the College. They lent scholarly respectability to his efforts, he felt. They in turn basked in the glow of his appreciation and became even more vocal in their support of Malmuth. He before long became determined to reward them somehow.

Attempted Murder and Mayhem

Failing Brakes

Later that week, Roger Duvant had a scare driving home from a collecting expedition. He had been up at Cracker's Nest collecting traditional tales from an elderly informant, Sardel Flannagan. It had been a very successful evening. Sardel had told him a number of new variants of well-known Jack tales. She also told of a dog haint or ghost. Sardel told it as truth. He had never heard any version of this one before.

    The evening began uneventfully. The long drive up to Cracker's Nest gave Duvant some breathtakingly beautiful views down into the valley from which he had driven. The sun was setting over the hills to the west, but there was enough light left to cast a rosy glow over the landscape. Here and there a migrating bullbat moved erratically through the sky. "Those nighthawks fly like they've had too much moonshine," Roger joked to himself. As he neared a point with a view down the ridge to the north, he saw a flight of five or six broad-winged hawks coming down to land in trees where they would spend the night. Late next morning after the hot columns of thermals began to rise they would resume their southward journey. "Have fun in South America, my friends," Roger thought as he pulled into Sardel Flannagan's driveway.

At the end of the drive sat a log cabin with smoke rising from the chimney. They had a fire to take away the coolness of the late summer evening. Behind the cabin were outbuildings. Set within a wire fence was a chicken house. In the yard were Plymouth Rocks and Rhode Island Reds. Several guineas accompanied the chickens to serve with their unearthly cackles to warn of marauding hawks, foxes, and weasels. A corncrib sat nearby next to a small barn. There was also an old but apparently quite serviceable johnny-house.

Sardel and her son Tom and her daughter-in-law Hattie were sitting on the porch enjoying the last glow of the sun. "Hello, there. Did you see the bullbats?"

"Sure did. One almost flew through the open door there. We was afeared it would, but it didn't go in. That's good 'cause a bird flying in the house is a sign of death. When the bullbats come by, it's about time to get ready for harvest. Gonna be a cold winter 'cordin' to the wooly worms."

"How can you tell from them?"

"Some folks think the number of rings on the wooly worms tells how many big snows there's to be."

They sat there for awhile on the porch and talked before going inside. Roger had brought his tape recorder from the car and, as agreed, taped all of the conversation. As usual, Sardel was at first a little self-conscious about being taped but forgot about the recorder as the evening wore on.

"Do you believe in haints, Roger."

"You mean ghosts. I guess I have an open mind."

"Do you believe in animal haints? Some people that believes in haints won't agree to animal haints because they don't want to admit animals has souls."

"I've not decided about that either."

"Well, I'll tell you a story that's true. Hit's about a dog haint. Back during the World War II, there was a fellow lived up at Persimmon Gap who enlisted in the army and left his hunting dog with his wife.

Now this dog of his'n was famous through this section because he had such a powerful voice. Dog's name was Bo. I'm goin tell you about Bo the way my old man, Tom's Pa, Kermit Flannagan, told it to me. He was over to Blackie to work in the mines, and on Saturday nights he would make his rounds of the honky-tonks. He was in one of them places one night carousin and carryin on doin whatever folks do in those places when somebody played a song on the jukebox. It was sung by Grandpa Jones, and he sung about this coonhound that had died while chasin a coon. When he got to the lines, "When the wind blows right on a moonlight night, you can still hear Towser bay," everybody got quiet. There was no sound in that room for a minute or two. When things came back to normal, Kermit asked the fellows sittin with him why that song had such an effect. They said that all the people there had heard ole Bo bay. Nacherly, Kermit asked them to tell him about Bo. Seems that Bo's owner was a young feller who got married just before the big war agin Tojo and Hitler started. He was about to be drafted and put in the army so he joined the marine corps. He left Bo with his wife at their cabin at Persimmon Gap. She kept Bo chained up so's he couldn't run off and chase coons. But atter awhile, that little wifey got tired of bein' alone and run off with some drummer passin' through. Didn't think about Bo-just left him chained to a tree. Bo howled a good bit during the next few weeks, but nobody paid no mind 'cause Bo liked to howl, and after two or three weeks nobody heard him for awhile. Then on the night of the next full moon, folks heard Bo givin' the mournfulest howl they ever did hear. A few weeks later a telegram came sayin' that Bo's owner had been killed in action. The feller who delivered it to the soldier's wife found her gone and Bo dead, chained to the tree. Looked like he'd been dead at least a couple of weeks. Kermit said the fellers tellin' the tale offered to take him up to the place the next full moon to hear Bo howl. So Kermit took 'em up on it next time there was a full moon. Two fellers and Kermit went up to Persimmon Gap, and they took him to the soldier's old home place. There was a notrespassin' sign there—said Stay out! Enter at Yore Own Risk. The moon was so bright they could see all around. There warn't nothin there to harm them that they could see. They went in anyways and waited. Sure enough, come midnight they heard a dog give a tremendous howl-seemed to be comin' from right under a big tree in back of the cabin. Kermit said he could feel the hairs on his neck rise. They heard the dog howl twice more-the howls three minutes apart. Now that's a true story."

"Can just anybody hear Bo howl?"

"Kermit said the fellers told him that he won't howl if a woman comes nigh. But I've heard say that ary man who hears Bo howl should look out—somebody's atter 'em."

Duvant stayed several more hours with Sardel and her family before making the drive back to Pine Mountain. The road up the mountain was steep and winding, but Duvant had traveled it and others like it many times. He had had no difficulty going up to Sardel's place. The return trip was more eventful. Coming down, he had his first hint of danger when he tapped his brake lightly approaching the first big curve. The brakes made a feeble response. Slowing, he began to drive very carefully. At the next curve, he pressed harder and found that he had practically no brakes left. That was the beginning of a very frightening ride. He managed to shift gears down to slow the car, but the vehicle continued to pick up speed all during the descent. He imagined that his howls of terror might well have outdone those of the coonhound Bo. At times Duvant thought of ramming the car into the mountainside, but he managed to keep the vehicle under control until he reached the valley, where he allowed it to roll to a stop at a pull off on the side of the road. When he had recovered from the wild ride, he restarted the car and drove slowly home, being careful not to do anything that would require the use of the brakes. With a sense of relief he left the car at a garage near the College and walked the rest of the way home.

Next day the mechanic at the garage called to tell him that someone had tampered with his brakes. "Looks like you've got somebody mad at you, Mr. Duvant." Roger asked if the problem could possibly be the result of ordinary wear and tear, but the mechanic assured him that this was not possible. "I think you oughta call the police on this one."

Roger rejected that idea, but Betty insisted that he call the sheriff's office. He refused on the grounds that Sheriff Mullgrab had an unsavory reputation of pushing marijuana and contracting murder for hire. "There may be a contract on me arranged by Mullgrab himself," Roger argued.

"What reason would Mullgrab have to kill you? And Malmuth hasn't been here long enough to arrange a contract on you even if Mullgrab does things like that." Declaring Roger's argument silly, Betty called the sheriff's office herself. Despite his squeamishness about enlisting official aid, Duvant did decide that he ought to confide in someone. Perhaps his being nearly run down by an automobile during his evening jog had not been an accident after all. Somebody was either trying to scare him or kill him. If the mechanic was right, the latter appeared the more probable. He knew the administration had an enemies list and that he was on it, but he found it difficult to believe that they would try to kill him. Perhaps it was the student who had tried to blackmail him a few years before. He attempted to brush off these possibilities. Still, he felt the need to discuss the attempted blackmail and his near-death experiences with somebody he could trust. He could talk about some of them with Betty, but not all. He decided that he needed to talk to John Jaykyll. Although John had been exhibiting some odd behavior lately, Roger felt that he could be trusted with secrets. Jay had always lent a willing ear and given him good advice in the past.

Jaykyll's Marriage

John Jaykyll had heard about and read about men who fall apart during what is popularly known as a mid-life crisis before Dr. Philwaggen mentioned that this might be Jaykyll's problem. It had begun to occur to John that he might well be undergoing something of this kind, but he shrugged off the possiblity as he thought that he had weathered the storms of mid-life without much difficulty. He had been mildly upset as he neared his fiftieth birthday, but he had moved through the next ten years of his life without notable incident.

On his next visit to Philip Philwaggen, the doctor encouraged John to discuss his marital relationship. Jaykyll began to explain that he had met Sarah after he had come to Pine Mountain College as an Associate Professor. She was a local girl who took several of his classes for entertainment and relaxation while she worked toward a degree in accounting. She loved to read. He had been happy to have such an avid reader in his class. Whenever he had had difficulty starting class discussion, he had been able to call upon Sarah to discuss the assignment and add some insights of her own to those of the critics the class had read.

Once she had completed his classes, Jaykyll had asked her for a date. Since John had been one of the more eligible bachelors available and she had long admired him, Sarah eagerly accepted. They had dated only a few months before they decided to marry. Their wedding had been the talk of Pine Mountain for several months. Jaykyll slipped into reverie as his thoughts drifted into the past...—

He and Sarah had led a life not unusual for young and middle-aged professors and their families, trying to make ends meet financially while raising children, building a house, and treading through the minefields of campus politics. Sarah took accounting work in to help keep their finances in the black. Though he had had at one time a great desire to do scholarly work and had shown some promise along these lines, his other interests and the administrative work that had been thrust upon him had overshadowed his bookish enterprises. Pangs of guilt beset him now and again, but he convinced himself that he really didn't want to fool with that damned thesis about the theme of death in the poems of that sometimes acclaimed American pioneer of poetry, Edward Taylor. Jaykyll often thought of himself as the bird of paradise in Taylor's poem immured in a wicker cage where it tweedled praise to God. He couldn't generate much enthusiasm to work further on his new article either. Transvestism in modern American literature did little to stimulate his curiosity anymore.

Semester melted into semester as Jaykyll taught his students about American literature and tragedy and comedy in contemporary drama. At a small school a professor must be versatile, he told himself whenever he longed to spend enough time with one subject so that he could develop his ideas for publication. He was convinced that tragedy could exist but viewed his own life as largely comic-or, in his darker moments-tragicomic. Despite the grayness that had surrounded him more and more since his fiftieth birthday, he was convinced that everything would turn out all right in the end. Though he often saw himself locked in struggle with an inept administration, he was certain of his lack of tragic stature. He had made Herculean efforts to see his adversaries as plotting, scheming, evil incarnations of the devil, but they had an annoying habit of proving to be only self-serving, shortsighted, ignorant, or stupid.

"Not the stuff from which tragedy is made," he often told himself, although his wife Sarah took every slight to her hero husband to her bosom as if it had been aimed at her. She was the only person whom she permitted to attack Jaykyll with impunity. Jaykyll had found living up to her image of him more and more difficult.

There was no denying it. Sarah lived too much through John, whom she guarded with a jealousy that the most loyal Praetorian guard would have barely matched. As long as Sarah had had the children to care for, her attention had been divided, and she could not lavish upon John her full admonitory zeal. There had been times, in fact, when she had come to bed tired and unwilling to accede to John's sexual demands, which were—she told him—inordinate. She was fond of pointing out to him that the husbands of her friends were lucky to get any sex at all.

"Why, those women detest sex," Sarah told him.

"Yes, but I didn't marry them; and if I had, I would have gotten rid of them soon enough."

Still, Sarah had been reasonably accommodating and never pleaded a headache for refusing John, if he were willing to do the necessary work himself.

After the children had left, she had become more responsive but also more possessive. The accusations that had bedeviled John for years became more frequent and more heated. She became sure that he was having an affair with Rose Ann Burns, the redheaded librarian at the College.

John felt very abused. He loved Sarah. He had been a completely faithful husband during their marriage except for the young blonde he had brought home for tea just after Sarah and he had married and the young author he had met a year later at the writer's conference that summer in Chapel Hill. The first had been entirely innocuous, although Sarah didn't believe that when she came home from work and found them deep in conversation on the couch in the living room. Sarah had never known about the young woman writer with whom he had engaged in heavy petting. Overcome by an attack of faithfulness, he had gone little further than kissing Blue and Blood Mountains, admiring the tender names that the woman had bestowed upon her rather ample breasts. Fortunately, John told himself, he was a confirmed buttocks man, not a juvenile breast aficionado.

From the beginning of their marriage, he had engaged in romantic daydreams, but he wanted a stable existence and felt that, in time, the marriage would develop into a fulfilling relationship. Over the years, whenever Sarah would accuse him of unfaithfulness, John would point out that academics are as a group the most faithful of husbands. Remaining unconvinced, Sarah more and more convicted him in her mind of an affair with Rose Ann Burns, the young librarian. Being a redhead herself, Sarah understood the peculiar fascination that redheads held for John.

"Well, if you professors are so faithful, what about George. And you can't deny that Adolpho cut a wide swath before he divorced Harriet and married that young co-ed. Don't forget that fool Bartley whose daughter was hot and heavy after Roger. Bartley divorced his wife and married a co-ed."

"According to the authorities, Academics who marry are the most faithful to their spouses-about 80% are completely faithful as I recall."

"I don't know where you get your statistics. I'd like to see that book."

Sarah took great pains to control John-always for his own good. When he offered friends a beer, she would say, "John, you can't have one now. It's the middle of the afternoon." Or she might make a cutting remark about his absentmindedness or his mechanical ineptitude in front of friends or the children. She had been determined to have her way, and John had retreated and allowed her do as she wanted without demurring because he had learned that otherwise he would suffer where he was most vulnerable, in bed.

As the years had passed, this threat had become less formidable as John's desires had become less pressing. By the time John had reached his late fifties, the need had become so much less pressing that he had become worried that he was losing his manhood. Not that his organs failed to function. This had happened once in awhile when he had been particularly depressed about the way his work was going. It was simply that he found his desire had diminished to the point that he wanted Sarah no more than once a week, or even less.

He had resorted to pornography to stimulate his flagging desire but felt foolish using these mechanical aids. "Why don't you just let me pose nude for you in some provocative poses," Sarah suggested.

His life had become less and less satisfying to him. He had neared and passed his fifty-eighth birthday in a malaise. It had become difficult for him to get out of bed in the morning. His life seemed dull beyond bearing. He longed for something new and different but could not exactly say what his problem was or what could be done to eliminate the dull ache in his chest and back.

Sarah diagnosed the problem as gall bladder trouble, put him on a diet, brought down his weight, and made him look ten years younger. With the loss of weight, his sexuality experienced a revival, but the general feeling of malaise did not disappear. He was not aware really that anything drastic was wrong, although a nagging sense of futility haunted him. He attributed his problems to the obtuseness of the College's administration and rued his limited participation in it.

The first real evidence that Jaykyll had had that anything more than gall bladder trouble was attacking him came when the back pains got the better of him again. Flat out on the sofa in great pain, he thought he could not make the trip to the convention in New Orleans. A desire to escape the late winter weather of the Kentucky mountains won out, however, and aching though he had been, he had forced himself aboard the plane at Atlanta to make the flight. Sarah drove him to the airport. Once aboard the plane, he for the first time drifted off into the grayness that preceded what were to become the experiences that he would term his "trances"—

The hurt hawk dragged its wing over the rocks of the high pasture. As it had soared over the dead carcass of a young steer, the crack of a high-powered rifle had shattered the stillness of the upper air and suddenly the bird's right wing was shattered. The bird quickly lost altitude and landed ungracefully in the open pasture at the top of the ridge. Drag-

ging its hurt wing, the hawk again and again tried without success to launch itself into the air again—

"Sir, sir, are you all right? Is there something wrong with your arm?"

Thrust back to consciousness, Jaykyll had assured the stewardess that he was all right.

No sooner had the plane left the ground and climbed above the cloud cover than John felt a sense of release. His pains began to disappear. By the time they reached New Orleans, the pains were gone.

He was lonesome in New Orleans when the conference was not in session, and scholarly debates and papers did little to allay the depression in which John found himself immersed. Nevertheless, the restaurants did provide excellent food, and Jaykyll regaled himself with fancy ices and seafood in the hotel and down in the quarter at Galliardo's, where the turning fans reminded him of the barbershops and ice cream parlors of his youth. The ceiling and walls were white, and the floor was covered with black and white tiles in symmetrical patterns. The tables and fans were also white. Everything gave the appearance of an eerie whiteness, and the fans provided a faint background noise into which the voices of the many customers blended. "Why the connection?" he wondered. "What do barber shops and ice cream have in common?" Not one to let a possibility of symbolism pass him by, John sought to create meaning out of the chance combination. "You get shorn of your hair in barber shops," he mused, "and ice cream is a sweetened version of mother's milk, or cow's milk turned to a sweetened trap to catch unwary suitors. Dalila probably used wine but ice cream would do, especially when it was covered with the green treat of creme de menthe. Eyeless in Gaza was Samson, sighing in New Orleans am I. Just another part of God's plan to heckle you, Jaykyll. Perhaps I am in the belly of the white whale. Call me Ishmael." After coming up with these doubtful rhymes and suspect symbolism, John felt better and consumed the ice cream in front of him.

The next indication that something grave was amiss with him had come to John when young Roger Duvant had been beset by the female student accusing him of sexual harassment to Dean Grudger. John had always laughed at the stories about lecherous professors, because his experience had led him to believe that the professors were more pursued by co-eds than vice versa. Shielded in his cloak of marital respectability, John had time and again managed to avoid the least entanglement since he and Sarah had married and he had become a tenured professor. Roger Duvant was less lucky. Rumors abounded about the handsome young professor....

Philwaggen brought Jaykyll back to the present with encouraging words. "I think you will make rapid progress if you continue to bring forth material as easily as you have thus far. It's too early for me to draw any firm conclusions, but I think you're making unusually good progress. I think we will need to explore your childhood to some extent." They arranged to meet again the following week.

Library Trouble

The horrified complaints of Roger Duvant and other members of the history and English faculty led John Jaykyll and Jonathan Large to make a foray to the library. This was not the first time that they had had trouble with the head librarian, Trillian Buchmeister. She had at one time been the head of a public library in a small town. She had a firm belief akin to religious faith that the books on library shelves needed breathing room.

"Books are living things, and living things need room to breathe," was Trillian's favorite phrase when dealing with faculty who questioned her management of the library. The Pine Mountain faculty were duly appreciative of the value of microfilm and microfiche, because microfilm and microfiche did not in Trillian's view require breathing space and therefore a huge amount could be packed away in filing cabinets without any danger.

Jaykyll and Large were exceedingly apprehensive as they approached the inner sanctum of the library, Trillian Buchmeister's office, or rather her lair as many faculty tended to view it. They had had the devil of a time getting journals replaced after Trillian had thrown them away. Whenever the subject of the head librarian came up, Jaykyll in particular became almost apoplectic. "Imagine," he would say to his listeners, "that woman threw away our copies of *PMLA*, the one journal all people teaching English must have. Just because she thought the books needed more breathing room. Some good did come of that, however, since we got a new library building with lots of room for breathing books."

Stolidly ensconced at her desk below a painting of Calvin Coolidge, Trillian Buckmeister greeted her visitors without warmth. Her clear desk hinted at efficiency or lack of activity, one could not be certain which. A tall, heavy-set woman, she wore pinz-nez glasses over her acquiline nose. Her head was generally held with such a haughty demeanor that she intimidated her subordinates without saying a word. Faculty were not her favorite people. They tried to fill up her library with so many books that none of them could breathe. Always suspicious that faculty visiting her meant trouble was brewing, she had rarely been wrong about this. A warrior who had missed her calling, Trillian Buckmeister waged unceasing warfare against faculty whom she particularly disliked. Pauline Hauptman, for example, had great difficulty avoiding book orders being lost. The situation had become so bad that Pauline now had Lavender Large sign all her book requests. Jonathan Large always tried to be diplomatic with Ms. Buchmeister. "Trillian, we have heard that you are removing books used for the Appalachian program from the shelves. Are you doing this and, if so, why?" Jonathan Large had agreed to begin because he understood that Jaykyll had great difficulty remaining calm when dealing with the woman he termed "the book ogre."

"Yes, I am removing those books. President Malmuth has requested that I see that all books that are intended specifically for that program be taken from the general collection. He doesn't want any books that contribute to a perception that this college wallows in rusticity out where everyone can see them."

"Are you planning to throw them away?" Jaykyll could hardly restrain himself enough to be civil. His efforts to fight off the grayness were Herculean.

For a moment, he lost touch—*A huge griffon appeared over a dessicated plain. It landed atop a promontory. It appeared to be devouring something. An animal perhaps, though it looked suspiciously like a book*—Nudged by Large, Jaykyll fought his way out of the grayness to hear Trillian's defense.

"No, by no means. I recall the hullabaloo that has been raised in the past about my attempts to prune the collection. I'm putting these books in a special room in the basement. They will be available only to faculty or, with special permission from faculty, to students taking courses in the Appalachian program."

Jaykyll and Large both breathed a sigh of relief. Jaykyll felt the grayness recede a bit. What had happened was deplorable, but the books would still be available to faculty and students enrolled in the Appalachian courses.

"That's not an ideal situation for learning," Jonathan observed.

"If it's not to your liking, I suggest that you take it up with President Malmuth. After all, I'm just a soldier following orders."

John thought to himself, "I'll bet you enjoy the hell out of doing Malmuth's dirty work." To Trillian, he merely reminded her that books were important to learning. "Books are sacred things, Trillian."

"Yes, Dr. Jaykyll, and this way they'll have more room to breathe."

On the way out, they happened to pass Rose Ann Burns. "You go ahead Jonathan. I want to speak to Rose Ann a minute-to enlist her in our cause." He had to admit that Sarah was at least correct in judging him susceptible to Rose Ann's charms. She reminded him of a younger Sarah.

Smiling at the young redhead, Jay asked how she was coping with the task of moving the "rustic" books. "Do you find the work exciting, Rose Ann? Are you certain the books are breathing properly? I want to make sure the books in the Appalachian collection are healthy."

"No, Jay, I find them dusty. Do you think your students ever read any of those books?"

"I must admit I sometimes have my doubts. But I place a number of them on reserve every semester and look to see who's checking them out. Some of them are being checked out, at any rate."

"Maybe so. But a lot of them aren't. Of course, I guess there isn't much of a demand for books on the history of coal mining and some of the other subjects you deal with. Only the history faculty have much interest in the census records from the early nineteenth century."

"I suppose people interested in genealogy would be. Books that aren't used very often can still be important. We faculty in the Appalachian program need a friend in the library, Rose Ann. I hope you'll look out for our books. We don't mind their breathing, but we want them to remain in the collection, accessible to students in the Appalachian program."

"I'll do my best, Jay. I have to be careful."

"May the force be with you and may all the books breathe deeply," looking back with this parting shot, Jaykyll saw that Rose Ann had indulged herself in a furtive snicker.

Malmuth and the Church

It was only a few days later that Jaykyll discovered with mixed amusement and chagrin that President Malmuth's anti-rusticity campaign had extended into the realm of religion. Pauline Hauptman brought him the news. "Jay, you're not going to believe this," she told him between laughing spells.

"What, Pauline? How can I find out if you keep laughing?"

After a few moments, Pauline gained control and passed on her news to Jay. "Malmuth thinks that Baptists are rustics. He's trying to close the Baptist Student Union. He doesn't believe anybody but Methodists and Episcopalians should preach the Gospel on the campus of Pine Mountain College. It's too droll for words. It's a wonder the man wants to permit Christianity of any kind on the campus. After all, Jesus was pretty rustic. Walked around in sandals and got himself in trouble with the law. Got stuck up on a cross. Had to turn water into wine. Couldn't afford the product of the finest French vineyards, you know. If Jake could just speak French or claim descent from English nobility Malmuth would like him better."

"Pauline, I don't know where the humor ends and the seriousness begins. Is he really after Jake Collier? What is it about our Baptist Student Union director that Malmuth finds annoying?"

"Almost everything, I suspect. He thinks Jake himself is rustic, and he has railed against Jake's baptizing practices. Wait until Jake tries to take another batch of the students down to the river for a baptism. We should make sure Malmuth gets to see it. Talk about something really rustic."

"An attitude like that won't win Jason Malmuth many friends in the local community. Jake's well thought of by everyone as far as I know. The man is practically a candidate for sainthood. He would be if he were Roman Catholic. He's always helping some poor souls in distress."

"Maybe it's just as well that Malmuth doesn't make many friends in the community. I don't think we want this man to garner much local support. He's dangerous." Jaykyll could feel the grayness closing in on him—*The cougar sprang upon the rabbit, striking it dead with one blow. The only sound was the scream of the rabbit as it died—*

"Jay, why are you cowering like that."

John retrieved himself with a joke, "Pretending the Lord is about to strike me dead for being rustic, Pauline. At any rate, in the coming struggle, God should be on our side. Even if our group contains a great many sinners, we're quite short on blasphemers."

"The campus ministries of the Methodists and Episcopalians have taken a stand for Jake. Much to Malmuth's disgust they pointed out to him that John the Baptist baptized Christ in a river. He might have used total immersion rather than sprinkling for all we know, they told Malmuth."

"I wonder what Malmuth thinks of Holy Rollers and snake handlers, Pauline? He probably thinks they're in league with the Devil to promote religious rusticity. The man must not realize that he is in the Bible Belt. It's a place where the Bible isn't read much, but people certainly do take their religion seriously. I hope the man doesn't do the College permanent harm. The religious community already tend to regard us as atheists or worse. He's just confirming their worst fears."

"Maybe we could form a group to serenade Malmuth at the mansion with *Onward Christian Soldiers*. Pauline laughed as she departed.

"No way, too rustic," Jay spoke to her departing form.

The fall-out from Malmuth's attack on Jake Collier reverberated through the community. As anyone could have told Jason Malmuth had he asked, the Pine Mountain area was not the best place to attack a dedicated and well-beloved servant of the Lord. President Malmuth became the subject of many fiery Sunday sermons about the sinfulness of those that attacked the Lord's anointed. Had Malmuth attacked some radical group like the snake handlers, the outrage might not have been quite so great. But he had had the temerity to attack a well-thought of and obviously sincere minister of a major religious group. Attacked not only a major religion, but the dominant religious sect in southeastern Kentucky. If Malmuth had set out to portray himself as a minion of the Devil, he could hardly have achieved greater success in making his name reviled among the servants of the Lord in the vicinity of Pine Mountain.

The local church leaders had always suspected that Pine Mountain College harbored many godless men. Now they were certain—godless men and women led by a henchman of the Devil. "O Lord, have pity on the poor students who labor in the vineyard of academe. Protect them from the ungodly among their professors and, most of all, from that godless man, Jason Malmuth," was a part of the Sunday prayer in every church from Big Lick to Frying Pan. There were high hopes among the saints that God would strike the sinner down. They thought it would be only a matter of time.

Explorations

Another Session

When Jaykyll next knocked on Dr. Philwaggen's door, again the psychiatrist asked him to take up where he had left off—with his concern for Roger Duvant. "I think you should be greatly encouraged, Jay. We're making splendid progress. And you have such an interesting case."

"More interesting for you than for me, perhaps. Well, I'm doing my best. I'll try to tell you about Roger. Even before I knew him well, I had heard a great deal about Roger from co-eds in my classes. They practically drooled when his name was mentioned. It was only when the problem with Grudger arose over the female student's false accusation of Roger that I demanded to know what real sexual activities might actually come to light. Not waiting for Grudger, I called Duvant in and told him, on the condition that what passed between us that day was confidential, that a student had accused him of sexual harassment. Duvant said that he needed to talk to me anyway. He had to talk to somebody he could trust about the attempts on his life.

"I was aghast to find out that somebody was trying to kill him. I wondered if it were connected somehow to the girl who was accusing him.

Jaykyll's mind drifted back to Roger's tale. "I don't believe that girl's accusation, Roger. I know you, and I have other information that convinces me of your innocence. However, you have something of a reputation on campus. What else in this line might surface if people begin probing? Whatever you tell me will not go beyond this office. I need to know the worst if I'm going to defend you."

Partly to Jaykyll's relief and—to an almost equal extent—his consternation, Roger thereupon confessed to Jaykyll in explicit and excruciating detail his liason with Melda Gilpin. First, Duvant thanked Jaykyll for the opportunity to completely unburden his chest and then began.

"John, you know Protestants don't have the luxury of confession, and I can't afford a psychiatrist on what Pine Mountain is paying me. I really appreciate the chance to get this off my chest. I need to talk to somebody besides Betty. She's probably the world's most understanding wife, but there are some details I just can't tell her. Not only do I have difficulties with the administration, but I believe somebody is trying to kill me. I've had two close calls in two weeks. The first time a car nearly ran me down when I was out jogging. I thought it was an accident, but two nights ago my brakes gave way when I was coming home from Cracker's Nest. I almost ran off the side of the mountain. The mechanic says somebody definitely tampered with my brakes. It may be the administration. I know I'm on Malmuth's enemies list. And Raucibelle Grudger had me in her office just two days ago. I suspect the administration of trying to frighten me into leaving Pine Mountain. I don't know. The only other possibility I can think of is the husband of a student. He tried to blackmail me a while back. I'll tell you about it.

My problem with this student began two years ago. She was a redhead and she approached me through a love letter containing the poetry of John Keats and Bob Dylan and a less than covert suggestion of her great desire for me and her desire to perform acts of love for me. "To hold your manhood in my lips" was one of the phrases she used. I confess I'm highly attracted to redheads. Perhaps you can understand, John. As I remember, that's a predeliction that you share."

Jaykyll nodded agreement as Roger continued.

"When Melda Gilpin had come to my office to talk about the letter, I assured her that anything between us was out of the question, as I was a man happily married. I had after all just celebrated my tenth wedding anniversary. I was as surprised as she was, and more shaken, when I reached out to her as she turned to say goodbye. Before I had time to think about what I was doing, I was holding her."

John was beginning to fear that Roger's case might prove more difficult for him to deal with than he had at first suspected. Just listening to this account began to push John into a grayness he found difficult to control—

High in the canopy of the jungle forest a red male monkey grabbed a bunch of fruit and then dropped it. A female monkey below him caught the fruit and looked up at her benefactor as she greedily ate. Seeing her satisfaction, the male tore away another branch of fruit and began tentatively to eat, smacking his lips greedily—

Roger had not fully understood the implications of Jaykyll's gestures.

"What's the matter, John?"

Called back to reality, Jaykyll, said, "Nothing, nothing, Roger—just anticipating the mile run I'll need to work off the dinner Sarah's cooking for me tonight. Go on, please."

Roger collected his thoughts and proceeded. "Somewhat shaken by the suddenness of my embrace, Melda flinched and groaned, then noted shakily, 'I thought you said that you are happily married.'"

"I am," I told her. "At least I think I am, but apparently I've got a lot of sympathy for you. Sit down and let's talk. You have a problem. Maybe we can help you by discussing it."

So they had sat down again and agreed that she would come in at nine o'clock for interviews on Tuesdays and Thursdays.

Though he had not fully realized it at the time, that had been the beginning of an affair for Roger, who had never before crossed the unofficial and indefinable but nevertheless real boundary that separates patient from doctor or student from professor.

At first their conversations dealt with Melda's problems with her husband and marriage, which was a strange relationship, barren, but necessary to please parents. A torrid courtship had preceded an all but sexless marriage as her husband had assumed the role of a child and had cast Melda as the Madonna-mother. In the resulting frustration of her sexuality, she had turned first to a female friend and now to Roger, whose class in literature had awakened her to both the reasons for her husband's actions and to the lack of fulfillment that she was experiencing.

In the beginning Roger was able to maintain a clinical attitude and give good counsel, although it soon became evident that Melda had not given up her desire for him. A male who had never succumbed to this kind of temptation before, Roger assured himself that all was under control and that he was merely helping a soul in torment. As the interviews continued, however, Roger had become more and more emotionally involved in the relationship, so that when Melda said again and again that there was no reason for him to avoid a closer relationship with her, he began to believe her.

"You won't be hurting anyone," she told me, "and you are obviously attracted to me as much as I am to you. We could at least hold hands. And it wouldn't compromise you much to kiss me once, would it?"

Jaykyll thought he could see where Roger's account was leading and it unnerved him. In the grayness, he saw himself drifting down a great river—

In the marsh formed in the lowlands where the river made a huge winding horseshoe within the jungle canopy, two cranes engaged in an ungainly courtship dance. The strange postures that these birds assumed would have seemed comical to an observer, had there been one anywhere in the huge rain forest that bordered the marsh. Jumping into the air and uttering loud squawks, the cranes danced their strange min-

uet. With long beaks capable of killing a man raised straight up in the air, they promenaded, now and again making loud noises by clacking their bills together enthusiastically—

"John, why are you jumping up and down like that?" A note of concern tinged Roger Duvant's voice. It brought Jaykyll back to reality again. He assured Roger that he was merely exercising to release tension.

The revelation continued. The more Roger had thought about the matter, the more he had agreed with Melda, and the electric thrill of her touch made the progression to kissing her easier. Melda's obsession had become Roger's, and soon the intellectual therapy of their conversations was heavily interladen with physical therapy. For the first time in his professional life, Roger had allowed his passions to spill over into his office environment. He felt guilty—even horrified—when he considered the implications of his actions, but had to admit that the illicit atmosphere lent extra zest to the sex. He loved Betty, but he could not rid himself of his desire for Melda.

Soon Melda persuaded him that they should meet away from school, so Roger arranged to meet her after her night class on Tuesday. She drove to a nearby lake, where they abandoned themselves in the dark to the warmth of each other for an hour. It was almost like high school again, Roger had thought. They did not achieve any fulfillment; they merely created stronger desires.

Melda persisted in persuading Roger to go with her to a motel for an afternoon of lovemaking. Finally, he agreed. Roger put up many objections, but Melda overcame each one. She told him to find a meeting or lecture that he would like to go to and tell Betty that he was going to that. Though not very conversant in how to manage these affairs, Roger had told Betty that he was going with Jack Barnett to Lexington to hear John Updike speak at the University of Kentucky.

Roger had next told Melda that he had no condoms and that he could not buy them locally without exciting suspicion, since Betty had already had an operation that made further pregnancy an impossibility for her. That was not the truth, but Roger told the lie in an effort to dissuade Melda. Since Melda and her husband were not bedding with each other and Melda had proclaimed her desire to remain childless, she certainly would not wish to risk a pregnancy either.

Roger's ploy proved unsuccessful. "I'll buy the condoms and other things we need," said Melda, "don't worry about a thing."

Not entirely reassured by her assumption of expertise, Roger nevertheless agreed to the rendezvous. They had met downtown and had driven in her car to Middlesboro, where Roger rented a room under an assumed name at the Highland Motel. Once inside the room they abandoned themselves to their bodies. Roger immediately began to massage her with his lips and tongue, thinking of young Don Juan ministering to Donna Julia in the amusing episode in Byron's Don Juan where young Juan is apprehended by Donna Julia's elderly husband. He was glad, he thought at the time, that at least he didn't have to worry about an avenging husband.

Jaykyll had again slipped into grayness and this time eased out of his chair onto the floor—

In a dead snag beside the river a tropical kingfisher waited for its prey. Immobile and watchful, the patient predator gazed at the water below, searching for a fish. After what must have been at least a quarter of an hour, the bird suddenly took wing and hovered in a spot above the middle of the river. Then it folded its wings and plunged straight down into the water, rising a moment later with a fish clutched in its beak—

"Jay…Jay…Professor Jaykyll. Why are you on your knees waving your arms? Do you want me to stop?"

Getting back into his chair somewhat disheveled, Jaykyll assured Duvant that he was merely exercising and all was well. He told Roger to proceed with his account, although he need not linger on the details quite so much.

Roger told Jay that he was nearing the end of his narrative.

Afterwards, the two lay down together for awhile and then took a shower before leaving. For Roger the room had assumed a drabness that had gone unnoticed before, and he was glad to leave it.

On the return drive, Melda had told him more of her family and of her husband. The sun was setting and dark was descending upon the mountains as they moved again into themselves. From what she told him, it became clear that her unhappy marriage had been preceded by an unhappy youth presided over by a tyrannical father.

Melda's sessions in Roger's office now grew beyond his ability to control them. At times the need to cool passions grew to the point that they went outside to walk, often going to the campus woods. The danger of this office activity did not make it less enjoyable for Roger and Melda. She grew eager to experience the scene she had described in her letter to him. She became insistent, and Roger finally gave in to her pleas. Later, he thought that he could sense that she felt somewhat strange about their having acted out the scene that she had imagined, but he dismissed his feeling.

He was quite unprepared for the telephone call that he received the next week. It was Melda's husband, abusive, accusatory, and threatening. Roger was of the kiss-and-do-not-tell school, so he certainly was not about to admit anything to this man. Unfortunately, Betty had heard enough of the conversation to arouse her suspicions.

It was worse than John had anticipated. Jaykyll felt the grayness coming toward him again—

The leopard awoke from his slumber and stretched. Shaking the sleep from its fur, the animal plodded to the entrance of its lair. Looking out over the brown grass of the nearby plain, the cat turned its muzzle toward the green ribbon that bordered the river to the east and sniffed the air. The odor of zebra and wildebeest and gazelle hung faintly in the air, and the leopard began to move dreamily toward the river, flushing the antelope before it—

With great effort, Jaykyll managed to cling to consciousness. So that Roger would not detect anything amiss, Jay pleaded a need to relieve his bladder and took a quick walk down the hall. When they resumed the interview, John asked Roger to finish his account as succinctly as possible. Roger agreed to try. He said that he had felt like a limp dishrag when he faced the suspicions of Betty. Not being able to lie to her, he told her the truth, which she accepted unhappily but easily, because it was what she had already suspected. She thought that every young co-ed must have set her cap for her handsome husband. Betty did not intend to vacate the playing field to some younger player. Roger promised her to put an immediate end to the affair. He felt relieved to have the matter out in the open. At their next meeting in his office he told Melda that they must end the relationship. To his surprise, Melda made no protest but asked him where he kept her letter. She said that she was worried someone else might find it. He opened the desk and showed it to her. He was startled when she asked him if it were safe there. It might not be, he thought, so that afternoon he took it home even though he ran the risk of Betty's finding it.

The next week John had a call from Melda, who accused him of bragging to others about their relationship in gross terms of "good piece of ass" and "a real hot f...." John protested that he didn't discuss sex with others and that he in any event didn't use that language. He didn't know which accusation to be more incensed about.

"Don't you have any trust in me at all? Do you think that I talk like the red necks you've been associating with?"

"Tommy told me. He knows a friend of yours. You told this friend and he told Tommy."

"But I haven't talked to anybody about us. Do you think I'm crazy? You must have told him yourself."

"Well, Tommy says he wants that letter."

"Then tell Tommy he'll have to come get it himself."

It was only later, after he had talked to Tommy and told him that he would have to come in person to get the letter that Roger began to comprehend what was going on. The truth had become clearer when

Melda came to visit him again and her husband knew of the visit the same day. Tommy began to make threats.

He made an appointment to meet Roger at his office. He missed it but made another and showed up, evidently hoping more for hush money than for physical satisfaction. He was visibly disappointed when Roger told him that his wife Betty already knew of his infidelity. The irate husband insisted upon having the letter, which he quoted enough for Roger to accept that Tommy knew its contents.

"What had prompted Roger to get into such a compromising situation?" Jaykyll wondered. The threat of blackmail was horrific enough to push John toward the grayness again.

Lifting itself from the carrion on which it had fed, the condor clumsily ran across the barren landscape of the upper mountain and launched itself into the air. Once airborne, the grace of the flying machine asserted itself and the bird rose without great effort into the clouds above the highest part of the mountain. Seemingly unable to maintain its place in the clean upper air, however, the bird soon returned to the carrion that it had recently deserted.

Fortunately, Jaykyll with great effort was again able to hang on to consciousness. But the effort caused him to perspire profusely, and he took out his handkerchief and wiped his forehead. "I hope you didn't give in to blackmail, Roger."

"Having made several copies of the letter, I agreed with seeming reluctance to go home and get the letter. Before giving it to Tommy, however, I cut it into small pieces in front of him, even though he expressed anger at this proceeding. I replied that this was in payment for Tommy's having turned something beautiful into something smutty, but I began to pity the man, who was willing, it seemed, to suffer any ignominy to keep his father-in-law's favor and thereby Melda's place in her father's will. I felt sorry for the pair of them. A few weeks later I felt sorry for myself because I had developed a urinary infection."

"You couldn't expect to get off scot-free. I appreciate your telling me this though it has seened as difficult for me to hear as it was for you to tell. No, that's unfair. I'm sure it was more difficult for you to tell me than for me to hear it, although I didn't find it easy. At least I won't be blind-sided if this should come up. Is there anything at all else I should know?"

"No, John, I don't think so. Not now. I've avoided other entanglements despite temptations. I suspect I may have a problem with Rauncibelle Grudger, but that involves the assessment of my classes. Surely I'm on safe ground there. If it isn't Tommy who is trying to kill me, then it must be somebody in the administration. I can't think of anybody else."

"Of course, I can't say what the future will bring, Roger, but you are certainly forewarned. I can't imagine either the husband you described or anybody in the administration trying to kill you even though it's obvious that Malmuth is trying to get rid of you. I do believe Malmuth is certifiably crazy, but he doesn't strike me as a murderer. And your jealous husband didn't even have the guts to pursue blackmail. He'd hardly be capable of murder. Keep thinking. There must be another possibility."

As Roger Duvant departed, Jaykyll slumped back in his chair, worn out from the exertion of maintaining his contact with reality....

Jay awakened to the voice of Dr. Philwaggen. "I believe we are making progress, Jay. Other than on the airplane, was it that time you were in Dean Grudger's office discussing Mr. Duvant that you first began to slip from reality recently? And then you had that problem with the young woman and more trances when Duvant discussed his affair with you?"

"Yes, that was the first time I remember its happening recently. It did happen once or twice before a long time ago, but not to this extent. It really has become troublesome."

"As you no doubt see upon reflection, part of this behavior is obviously associated with your need to avoid conflict. Your symptoms have been increasing because of the great tension you've been under since the new President arrived. You have had many conflicts thrust upon you recently. Perhaps we should explore your childhood experience. There must be something there to explain what is happening. We'll try to explore that at our next session."

Malmuth Summons Jaykyll

John approached the President's office with considerable misgiving. He did not know whether he could remain in control during what was certain to be a rather difficult confrontation. He was sure that Malmuth wanted to browbeat him into becoming an advocate, or at least a silent adversary, of the anti-rusticity campaign. He did not know what approach Malmuth would take, but he was certain that he would find it objectionable.

Sherri Widderbee Whetman greeted Jaykyll with a smiling good morning. Sherri and he had always gotten along well before she became Malmuth's secretary, and they had remained friendly even after it became apparent that Jay was not to be Malmuth's favorite faculty member. Malmuth had encouraged her to remain on as friendly terms as possible with all faculty so that he could assess their thoughts. He had particularly asked her to find out what she could about Jaykyll's attitude toward the anti-rusticity campaign. John was still unaware that an intimate relationship had developed between Sherri and Malmuth. As a result of his ignorance, Jaykyll had slipped and made jocular disparaging remarks about the campaign against rusticity—even going so far as to put a straw hat on his head and a corn-cob pipe in his mouth one morning when he dropped by to see Sherri. Affecting a country farmer's persona, Jaykyll told Sherri, "I heared you folks was alookin' for a prize bull, so I thought I'd bring old Elmer down." Sherri had laughed uproariously, so much that Malmuth came out of his office into hers. He had obviously been less receptive to the joke.

With a forced smile, he had feigned admiration for Jaykyll's outfit. "How becoming your hat is, Professor Jaykyll. So few people wear hats anymore."

Two days later Jay had been summoned to this early-morning meeting with President Malmuth and Provost Bottleby. When he arrived at her desk, Sherri ushered him into the inner sanctum, where Bottleby and Malmuth awaited with dour countenances.

Jaykyll attempted to muster a friendly demeanor. "Good morning President Malmuth, Provost Bottleby."

"Good morning, Professor Jaykyll. Please sit down." President Malmuth was attempting cordiality, also, Jay surmised.

"What did you wish to see me about?"

"We are wondering if you would help us with a problem concerning a faculty member in your department."

"Who would that be?" Jaykyll thought it wise to pretend ignorance, although he was sure they had Roger Duvant in mind.

"We believe that Roger Duvant should be replaced. He is one of the faculty most culpable in furthering the rustic image of the College."

"Roger has been here a number of years. He has proven to be an excellent teacher. He's well liked by his students despite his demanding a high quality of work, and he gets along well with almost all of his colleagues. Furthermore, he has made numerous contacts in the surrounding communities. He's greatly increased local support for the College."

"I understand that a student recently made a complaint against him for sexual harassment."

"Yes, but the charge was investigated and discovered to be completely unfounded."

"I also have heard that he upset Professor Messerand by flirting with Simone Messerand."

"Roger merely gave her a ride to the grocery store to buy groceries and back home. Messerand appears to be quite jealous. He had a similar altercation with a member of the maintenance staff, I've heard."

"Where there's much smoke there's bound to be some fire."

The inane use of the old adage set John's teeth on edge. Jaykyll struggled to maintain consciousness—*The moor was dark and gloomy. The rabbit fled for its life as a fox pursued it and a goshawk hovered above waiting an opportunity to pounce. The rabbit sought a burrow for safety—*

"Are you ill, Professor Jaykyll? Why are you slumping in your chair so?" Jeremy Bottleby appeared genuinely concerned.

"Probably worried I'll have a heart attack in Malmuth's office," John Jaykyll thought as he managed to straighten himself and assure Bottleby that nothing was wrong.

"Just a habit of mine. I do exercises while I'm sitting. It helps me to stay in shape."

"I think we must ask you to warn Professor Duvant that he is on notice that his social behavior will be a part of the evaluation of his tenure. Even the appearance of sexual harassment will not be tolerated at this college."

"Yes, of course, we all oppose sexual harassment." John tried to fight off the grayness that threatened again. *The rabbit sensed the fox was upon it and fled from its hiding place.* With some difficulty he rose.

"If that's all, President Malmuth, I'll be going. I have a class soon. I know you wouldn't want me to be late."

When Jaykyll had left, Malmuth turned to Bottleby. "That man's going to defend Duvant strongly. There's no doubt about that. He seemed to act rather strangely, though. What do you know about him? Has he exhibited any unusual behavior recently?"

"Grudger has told me that Jaykyll has been behaving oddly this year. He's undergoing psychiatric treatment and seems to be improving."

"Then we'll have to work fast. Maybe we can ship him off to a mental institution for treatment. That would rid us of him and remove a defender of Duvant at the same time. Call together a group of senior faculty. Persuade them to tell Jaykyll to get extended treatment. Tell them the College will pay the expenses of the treatment."

Malmuth then explained to Bottleby that he had other ideas about changing the image of the College. A very successful folk festival had been held on the campus for many years with the support of the College, which provided the place. The work of staff, faculty and students also aided in helping to make the Chalmer Botts Festival a successful effort in keeping alive mountain traditions. For Malmuth, it was a very public display of the very rusticity he so deplored. This year's festival had been funded and organized long before Malmuth had become the President of Pine Mountain College. However, he was determined to see that this festival never graced the campus again. He told Bottleby to withdraw all college funding and other support from the festival, which henceforth was to be banned from the campus.

"I can see the elimination of funding and other support as an excellent means of attacking Duvant. We can always defend those actions on the basis of needing more funds for other activities. But I'm less sanguine about an outright banning of the festival from the campus. Perhaps we shouldn't be too hasty. Maybe they'll be so angry about the withdrawal of support that they will leave on their own."

"Bottleby, I don't want this left to chance. No. It must be a clear ban."

With misgivings, Bottleby conveyed this message to Hiram Grudger, whom he instructed to inform Roger Duvant. Appalled, Grudger cautioned, "President Malmuth may be creating more trouble than he expects. I'd advise against an outright ban."

"I've already warned him that's a bad course, Hiram. He won't budge."

"Jeremy, have you ever considered that we may have climbed aboard a ship that's headed for disaster."

"Let's hope that's not the case."

When Duvant and Jaykyll heard the news, they were not surprised but were incensed. Jaykyll was especially angered, because he had worked for many years before Duvant arrived to get the festival on a sound footing. He had succeeded. Then Roger arrived at the College and took over management of the Festival. He had transformed it into one of the more popular events at the College and in the community. People came to it from all around. It drew large numbers of people who never otherwise came to the campus.

"We'll go on this year as planned, Roger, except we'll move the festival off the campus. Next year we'll just have to make other arrangements. We'll tell the local members of the festival committee that they'll have to take the leading role in the future."

Roger agreed, and at the next meeting of the festival committee they broke the news. Virgie Jones uttered a few lady-like curses but then announced her intention to form a local non-profit corporation to continue the festival. They would simply move the festival to the Jackson County Fairgrounds.

"I think that would be the best course of action, since the administration has become so hostile. Let's make an effort to really have a good show—meet Malmuth's challenge with flags flying, dulcimers playing, and feet dancing. Let's make this a Chalmer Botts festival to remember, one that'll stick in Malmuth's craw," Virgie advised, "I have connections that can make life difficult for Mr. Malmuth. He's gone too far."

The Festival

As he did every year, Jaykyll prayed for sunshine on festival day. This year he was rewarded with a pleasant sunny day. A frost had turned the world to reds and golds, and the temperatures were just cool enough to make it very enjoyable to be out of doors.

An outstanding array of singers had been assembled. Jean Ritchie had been enticed back down to Kentucky from her New York home. Pete Seeger was to be there also, and Jeanette Carter was coming over from Hiltons. The man that had begun the Dock Boggs Festival over in Virginia, Jack Wright, would be there to to play the mouth harp. Led by a former President of Pine Mountain College, The Caney River Boys were to play at least three sets. The Goose Creek Band and a number of lesser acoustic groups were to perform. Flatfoot dancing and clogging would be provided by the Sugarfoot Dancers from Black Mountain. If the weather held, the setting would do justice to the performers, because the trees, touched by the early frost, had put on a gorgeous array of yellows, reds, and purples to accompany the remaining still green leaves.

There were to be lots of local crafts and foods. The Mountain Mothers had prepared a traditional mountain meal of cornbread, beans, and greens with stack cake for desert and cherry birch lemonade to drink. Other groups were making sorghum molasses and apple butter to sell along with sourwood honey straight from the hive. For those who didn't want the traditional food, especially the youngsters, the fraternities and sororities were providing hotdogs, hamburgers, and soft drinks. Several dulcimer makers had arranged to have booths during the festival, as had basket and chair makers and toy makers. Despite the apparent readiness and beautiful weather, Jaykyll and Duvant were nervous. They were worried that moving the festival off campus might lower attendance. They wanted this festival to be the best there'd been, just so that people would bring it to Malmuth's attention.

Luckily the weather's turning fair the weekend of the festival enticed people to come out of their homes. Cool, comfortable weather with plenty of sunshine provided a beautiful day and a large turnout of people. Even a large contingent of college students attended-not just those involved in selling food and drinks. Many actually came to listen and look because they were reacting negatively to Malmuth's attacks on their heritage. Duvant and Jaykyll were happy to see that many of the students from their folklore and Appalachian literature classes were there-to obtain extra credit, no doubt, but still there. And a large percentage of the Pine Mountain College faculty attended also, although Rauncibelle Grudger was the only member of the administration whom Jaykyll could detect. He had no doubt that she would make a full report to her husband, Bottleby, and Malmuth.

Duvant couldn't resist asking Belle to dance when the opportunity arose for audience participation. To his surprise, she obliged with alacrity and cut a mean flatfoot.

"Belle, I didn't know you were so expert at flatfoot."

"I reckon I'm jest a mount'n girl has got above her raisin', Roger," Belle joked.

For a good ten minutes Roger and Belle whirled about the concrete pad on which the dancers performed. When the music shifted, they dropped out and stood talking for awhile.

"A mountain girl should support the Appalachian Studies program, Belle."

"You know the saying, 'Politics makes strange bedfellows.' At heart I'm a great supporter of the program, but it's not a notion I want to display publicly right now. It's not too popular in the administrative circles I travel. Let it be our secret."

Jaykyll enjoyed listening to the music. He was particularly fond of the old ballads, especially those that he knew dated back at least to the thirteenth and fourteenth centuries. In the 1890's Harvard Professor Francis Child had declared the ballad tradition dead after he had ransacked the libraries of the British Isles to compile his monument of scholarship, English and Scottish Ballads. Two decades later, the Englishman Cecil Sharp had discovered Jean Gentry singing the traditional ballads here in these Kentucky mountains over in Letcher County. He had rushed back north to declare the ballad tradition still alive. Jaykyll was happy to see that it was still a little bit alive even in the latter part of the twentieth century. Many of the performers at the Chalmer Botts Festival had a Child ballad or two in their repetoires. They were live bearers of the tradition, unaware of the age of the songs they were singing. They lumped a thirteenth-century ballad like *My Goodman* with a nineteenth-century American ballad such as *In the Pine* or a local ballad like *Jordie Mullins* or Dock Boggs' *The Wise County Jail*. For them, they were all "old songs." These old songs took their places along with current tunes by Bob Dylan or local songwriter Jethro Hylton, a local boy who attended Pine Mountain College and had made a successful career in Nashville.

The Caney River Boys' repetoire proved his point. They presented *O Death* and *My Goodman* (which they termed *My Little Wifey*), definitely Child ballads. But they rendered a version of *Sourwood Mountain*, *Wise County Jail*, *Butterbeans*, and *The Drunkard's Dream* as well as a couple of contemporary songs by Jethro Hylton. Jaykyll was amazed that former President Jim Smithy could still play and sing like a youngster. Whether they knew it or not, Smithy and the others were part of an ancient tradition. He was a rather heavy-set man with a face that suggested a fun-loving disposition. He had presided over Pine Mountain College before Malmuth's immediate predecessors. If Malmuth wanted to find rusticity at the College, he should look up Jim, thought Jaykyll, who couldn't help feeling a sense of nostalgia for the old days when faculty didn't have to defend an interest in mountain culture. "Back then," he thought, "we took it for granted. Now we have a fight on our hands if we acknowledge there are mountains around us."

Jaykyll was enjoying the event. He and Sarah had partaken of the mountain meal and had bought some honey and apple butter. Jay had even pulled her onto the dancing area for a couple of bouts of flatfooting. He then persuaded Betty Duvant to leave her ticket table to do some dancing with him after Sarah pleaded exhaustion.

"You really seem to be enjoying the festival, Jay."

"I want it to be a great success, Betty, and I want Malmuth to gnash his teeth when he hears about it. Roger certainly has done an excellent job with this year's festival."

"I'm glad you think so, Jay. That praise coming from you really means a lot to me. I've been so worried about Roger. Did he tell you that there have been attempts on his life?"

"Yes, we've discussed those. I don't think any of the suspects that Roger has come up with are the guilty parties. You need to keep your eyes open."

Later, after dark, as Roger and John were overseeing the clean-up, Belle surprised them by staying to help. She was still there with Roger when Jaykyll took his leave. They were almost finished. Roger told Jay to go ahead, that he would finish up. Belle said that she would stay. A bit taken aback, Jaykyll headed home. Sarah amd Betty had both come separately and had already taken their purchases of honey and apple butter home. It took Belle and Roger about twenty minutes more to complete the clean-up.

"You see, Roger, I'm not hostile to the Chalmer Botts Festival. I'm not even hostile to the Appalachian Studies program. Why don't you come up to my office for a little while. We'll play some music and have some tea and discuss what can be done to save the Appalachian Studies program. But this has to be our secret. President Malmuth mustn't think I'm disloyal to him."

Despite misgivings, Duvant agreed to go with Belle. He certainly could not afford to alienate her, and if she were telling him the truth, she would prove a valuable ally. "I guess I could come—just for a little while."

Duvant had walked from the faculty housing, so Belle drove them to her office in her new red Porsche. On the way, Belle told him that she had read his poetry. Duvant was again surprised.

"I thought it beautiful, Roger. I especially liked the love poem with the imagery from the Song of Solomon."

Roger thought to himself that this poem would naturally be her favorite, but still he was flattered. "Thanks for the compliment."

Belle's office, now familiar to Roger, seemed the same as it had the afternoon that they had talked of assessment, only this time Belle immediately pulled down a shade to keep the light from showing through the frosted window on her door. To Roger's consternation, she locked it behind her. "Make yourself comfortable on the couch while I heat some water for tea and put on some music. We'll keep the sound low."

Belle again surprised Duvant when the strains of Beethoven's Pastoral drifted through the room. "That's one of my favorite pieces of music. Do you have Mozart's Clarinet Concerto in A?"

"Funny you should ask. That's up next."

When the hot water was ready, Belle offered him a choice of Darjeeling or Earl Grey. Then she sat down on the couch beside him.

"Roger, I've been asked to provide a fake assessment report damning to your Appalachian program. I don't want to do that, but there is considerable pressure on me to do something to provide the administration with ammunition to get rid of you."

"I suspected that they were out to get me. Did you know that there have been attempts on my life? Is the administration behind those?"

Belle's face expressed her shock. "Roger, you must be joking!"

"No. I've had two close calls recently, and the second was definitely an attempt to kill me. Somebody tampered with my brakes."

"I know Malmuth is rotten, but I don't believe even he would go that far. Besides, he wants to torpedo your program, not just you. You certainly can use a few supporters who have the ear of the administration, but I think you'll have to look elsewhere for your potential murderer."

"I'm relieved to hear that Malmuth doesn't have a contract on me."

"I don't think he works that way. But let's see how I can be of help. We need to establish *a quid pro quo* relationship, Roger. I'm prepared to do all that I can to protect you if you help me."

"Just what can I do for you, Belle?"

"You gorgeous hunk of man. I've had my eyes on you ever since you came to Pine Mountain College. All I want from you is a little taste of you. I always have liked a taste of sweet things." Roger was less surprised by her demand than he had been by her taste in music and her dancing ability. He had halfway suspected that she wanted an intimate relationship with him. He was in a quandary.

"Belle, I'm a happily married man. I don't want to do anything to upset my marriage. I love Betty. What about you, you're married too. Adultery is a sin, you know. It is also grounds for divorce."

"Hiram Grudger's no problem. I give him everything that he desires, but I have a lot of desire left over. He knows it. I have made it clear to him that as long as I satisfy him he must not complain about what I do with others."

"Betty is an understanding woman, but I don't think she would appreciate my having an affair with another woman."

"Even to save your position here?"

"Even for that. If I agree to your terms, Belle, you must give me your solemn promise not to reveal our relationship to anyone. As you said earlier in another context, it must be our secret."

"Agreed. Now, let me undress for you." Belle began to do a striptease for Roger. As she removed each garment, she threw it on the couch beside him, brushing her lips across his as she tossed it. When she was completely disrobed, he could not help but admire her excellent figure. "Do you like what you see, Roger?" She spread her legs and demanded that he kneel before her and kiss her. "There was an empress of China who required that of all her subordinates. I think she had a wonderful idea."

Duvant did not wish to lose his position at Pine Mountain College, and the task before hims was not altogether distasteful. Reluctantly but with a sense of a man accepting the inevitable, Roger complied. "You taste like apples. I'm very fond of apples."

Belle then proceeded to undress her reluctant lover. As she removed each of his garments, she kissed him, running her tongue deep into his mouth. When he was completely naked, she sat on the couch and told him to stand in front of her. "I want to admire the gorgeous man I am about to please." Roger surrendered himself to Belle's caresses.

Later, Belle beamed with domesticity. "Now you can rest for a little while, honey. I'll fix us another cup of tea. Don't put those clothes back on. We're not finished yet."

When they had drunk their tea, Belle insisted on more attention to her needs. Roger did his best to oblige her. He certainly didn't wish her to be disappointed. He could not afford to have her hostile to him. Afterwards, as they relaxed on the couch and drank a third cup of tea, Belle sighed. "Roger, if only we weren't married to other people. I would be happy if every night I could experience what we have had tonight."

"Belle. It was a fantastic experience, but I for one can't give up my marriage."

"I don't expect you to do that, honey. I was just dreaming. I couldn't give up the position I have as Hiram's wife either. Let's just agree that we have sealed an alliance and that this won't be the last time that we enjoy this sublime sensuality. It will be our secret."

"I don't think I have a choice, Belle."

"Don't you worry about the administration. You had better find out who is trying to kill you, though. I would hate to lose you."

Childhood Memories

At his next session with Dr. Philwaggen, Jaykyll told him of the confrontation with President Malmuth and how he had managed to fight off the grayness and make his escape. Philwaggen looked pleased. He took this incident as evidence that his sessions with Jaykyll were bringing about some helpful results.

"Let's go back and explore your childhood, Jay. I believe the roots of your fear of confrontations must be hiding there. We need to find out where this fear of arguments began. Just lie back on the couch and think back to a time when you were six or seven.

Jay followed instructions and was soon back at a time when he was seven.... The day was sullen. They grey skies drizzled. The dreariness of the weather matched the dreariness of the funeral in the small boy's mind. The beautiful flowers that surrounded the corpse did nothing to to ease the pain in Johnny's mind. He did not fully understand death, but he had seen Aunt Hattie in the coffin and he knew that she would not play cards with him again. She had been his instructor in rummy and had played it with him patiently for hours. She also had taught him to play solitaire, but he had preferred to watch her play that game so that he could ask his question over and over again to hear her answer and laugh with her.

"What are you doing Aunt Hattie?"

"Killing time, John, just killing time."

The young boy doubled up with laughter.

"How can anybody kill time?"

"I don't know how. I just do it."

Aunt Hattie and his Grandmother Powers stood together in his mind. They had rounded Celtic faces with blue eyes under their long gray hair. Both had iron wills, although in any contest of will, no doubt Grandma Powers would have won. She was always ready to impel John to work in his mother's flower garden by emphasizing the need to do what duty demanded, but John had to balance this fierce Calvinistic sense of what must done with the delightful banana fritters that she made when rewards were in order. Around Grandma Powers his mother always seemed even more like a fluttery schoolgirl than she ordinarily did.

One day the whine of an airplane in trouble came to the young boy as he played the solitaire cards. Jumping up he kicked over the card table and knocked down the lead soldiers that he prized highly and arranged meticulously on their mock battlefield. Running down the steps and out of doors, he looked into the air in time to see a navy trainer spinning and losing altitude. He watched excitedly as the plane disappeared in the woods on the horizon and then a plume of smoke rose into the summer sky. Another aviator had failed the test of the rapid training program that was part of the war effort in 1942. A week later Johnny went with the other kids of the neighborhood to the site of the crash. It was hot and humid, but the expectance of seeing the crash site made the long trip seem more interminable than it otherwise would have been.

The crash was deep in the piney woods. To get to it the column of youthful ghouls had to leave the dirt road beside the soybean field and walk along the top of the huge black pipe line that had been laid down to take water from the swamp lake to the city. The heat of the pipe ate through the soles of John's tennis shoes and seared his feet, but he and the rest kept on until they were abreast of the airplane wreckage. Then they had to beat their way through the brush to the downed plane.

There had already been many people at the site so that there were paths that they could easily follow through the myrtle brush and blackberry briars. As they looked through the badly mangled wreckage, it became clear that the cleanup had been hasty. Those that had come to collect the bodies had not done their job very well. The black and green parts of partially charred fingers and toes sickened Johnny, although Don, their leader—in an effort to establish his superior age and assert his leadership—made a huge joke of them.

"Dog meat, roasted meat to take home for the dogs," he laughed as he plucked out the prize piece, a whole foot intact from the ankle down.

They found other small fragments of human flesh and bones, but it was the foot that remained etched in John's memory. It appeared regularly in the nightmares that disturbed him for several months. The image of the foot never left him. Years later it would still come back to remind him of that hot afternoon in the piney woods when death first became real and walked with him.

He had felt its hand grasp him firmly when he went with his parents to Aunt Hattie's funeral. The mist that rose from the warm ground under the drizzle gave the cemetery an eerie quality that reminded John of the setting of a Poe story or the A. Conan Doyle's hound of the Baskervilles that moved about upon an eerie moor. There were soon many people crowding about to dispel this grimly romantic view of the funeral, but John would not go under the tent to get out of the rain no matter how much his mother and father cajoled him to join them there. John felt miserable. He had been present at death before, but this death was far more disconcerting to him. He had been a favorite of his aunt, and she had always been willing to take time to entertain him. He especially liked to hear her tell of her trip to France after World War I. She went to see her sons, one in the hospital suffering from the effects of mustard gas and the other in a cemetery filled with row upon row of simple stone crosses marking the dead from the man-mangling battles of trench warfare. She showed him a post card with a picture of the cemetery. The plain white crosses had an elegant beauty that contrasted with the colorful vitality of post-war France. Aunt Hattie loved to talk of the trucks loaded with the long loaves of bread and the other sights of Paris, the Eiffel Tower and the tree-lined banks of the Seine.

The house on the river seemed immense to the small boy, and the space between the house and the marsh was huge, plenty of space for a small boy to play. On one side of the house and on the other side of the driveway his father had his large garden. Beyond the garage were the pigpens and the chicken house and the pens where the silver foxes had been kept. Living was relatively easy. John's father had had a job during the worst years of the depression and, though they were not well off, they ate well. There was always some food from the garden. Even in the winter spinach and collards grew well. Each fall there was a hog butchering after the weather got cold enough. John's mother insisted then on cooking chittlings, much to the dismay of John and his father. John couldn't help associating the sweet smell of the cooking chittlings with the smell of the hog pen, and he could barely keep from being sick at the table on days that chittlings were served. He couldn't eat souse or pickled pigs' feet either. It made him gag to think of where the feet had been. Forced to eat some of the sweet-smelling hog guts, Johnny had then rushed outdoors and thrown them up.

Not that John disliked hog flesh. He was not a vegetarian. John loved the ham, the bacon, the pork chops, and the pork roasts. Every week they had chicken once or twice. Johnny loved the fried chicken, but the Muscovy Ducks were his favorites. He loved the dark meat from the wide breasts of these birds, especially when this meat was complemented with the rich rolls made with duck eggs that his mother served on special occasions.

The chickens and ducks were also appealing away from the table. The colorful red of the Rhode Island Reds and the mottled pattern of the domineckers matched the white and blacks and greens of the Muscovy ducks. The somber plumage of the Muscovies was set against their red facial skin. Their hissings with raised head feathers and necks moving back and forth inspired awe in the young boy. In contrast the big yellow beaks of the white Peking ducks made them seem merely comical.

Occasionally they visited relatives in Tidewater, Virginia, who lived on a tidal river. The river was a cornucopia of crabmeat at certain times of the year, and at those times they ate crabmeat every day of the week until they could not any longer stand the smell of steaming crabs in the muggy summer heat. The heaps of blue shells turned bright red were gorgeous to the view, and the meat they contained was satisfying to the stomach. The real treat, though, were the soft crabs, those discovered just after a molt and fried instead of boiled. These were truly mouth-watering. Every week, too, the fish man came by with his old truck—the wooden bed piled high with fish on ice, all covered from the sun by a heavy tarpaulin. The flounder were good, but it was when the spot were running that the greatest delicacy was to be had. Fried spot tasted to John about as good as anything he ever ate, including the banana fritters his grandmother made out of overly ripe fruit.

His uncle Everett had expected to make a fortune raising silver foxes for the fur trade, but it turned out that southern Kentucky winters were not cold enough to produce fur of a high quality. The substantial five foot wire mesh that surrounded the pens gave testimony to the amount of money wasted on this fur-raising venture. John always wondered about the foxes, for he had been almost too young to remember them, even though he could remember many things from his childhood. Years later, he decided that his uncle must have been the man upon whom e. e. cummings modeled his uncle Silas in *nobody loses all of the time*. Though perhaps going broke with silver foxes was a more distinguished way of failing than going from vegetables to chickens to skunks to worms as Silas did. Many of his father's family lived with them in the large house when John was small, but by the time that he had grown old enough to remember well, there had been a great family battle and his mother had been left in sole control of the field. Nevertheless, the reverberations of this momentous struggle continued to swirl about the family and became part of the unseen and unwritten context in which all matters were decided. The young boy in the beginning knew only that he missed all the people who had given him attention, especially Auntie

Jane and the other the female cousins and aunts who showered affection upon him, the only male heir of the Jaykyll family.

Any time that the family visited, John could be sure that he would be the center of attention. Aunt Jane especially showered attention upon him. She was an overpowering woman, and her expressions of affection included hearty hugs that took the breath away as well as plenty of advice over any topic that happened to be broached. She swarmed into a house, which ceased its normal functioning when she arrived and organized its activity around her whim until she left. Aunt Jane regarded John's mother as a scatter-brained butterfly from the wilds of Tennessee who through no fault of her own had had the good fortune to decide to come to Kentucky.

"Dear Elizabeth," Aunt Jane would say, "Kentucky is the garden spot of this world and you should thank your stars that you ended up here rather than in some Tennessee swamp bottom."

"Jane," John's mother would reply, "there is better society in Jackson, Memphis, Knoxville, and Nashville than you could ever hope to find in this red-neck town. Why, you have to go to Louisville to find any refinement in Kentucky, I believe."

Aunt Jane loved to recite for John the nursery rhyme "Jack be nimble/Jack be quick/Jack jump over the candlestick."

"You'll be clever and quick like that Jack," she told him.

"Is that the same Jack that climbed the beanstalk and killed the giant?" he would ask her.

"I don't know for sure, but I'll bet he was. That Jack was pretty nimble, too."

Aunt Jane had used her inheritance to study art in France and John's love for drawing made her even more inclined to pet and pamper her nephew. "You may be a great artist someday Jack," she told him. "The Jaykylls are a talented family even though sometimes they have turned their talents in unbecoming directions. You must use your talents wisely. Remember the parable of the talents, Jack." She was the only person who called him Jack. When he asked why, she told him that it was a nickname for John and that she had once known a very handsome, talented young man named Jack. Perhaps her husband, his Uncle George, had loved John because of Jane's devotion to the young boy. Whatever the reason, he had spent long hours beside John's crib and playpen before he disappeared.

Some of John's earliest memories were of Uncle George beside his playpen, spending hours with the small boy. He had nothing better to do after the crash had wiped out George's automobile dealership in Tidewater Virginia. He and Aunt Jane had lived well-so well that there were no reserves for starting over. George was never the same after he lost his business. He came to live with the Jaykylls while Aunt Jane went out to work as a lady's companion. Johnny missed George when he failed to appear beside his playpen, and whenever he could get out, he went to look for his old playfellow. That winter one morning they found the young boy wandering through the snow looking for his vanished playmate. Nothing his mother or anyone could say could comfort him. He always remembered the gray day and the snow that he wandered in searching; the gray sky—especially when it hovered over snowy fields—always brought a sense of loss to John, even when he had learned to throw snowballs, build snow forts, and snowmen.

The grayness of this day of Aunt Hattie's funeral reminded him of that winter day when Uncle George had disappeared even though this funeral day was a spring day. Green grass was underfoot and the forsythia was in full bloom and the sweet gums and maples were bursting into bud. That cold day when George disappeared there had been snow on the ground and a strong wind from the water. They had found him wandering in the snow-covered fields far from the house calling, "George! Uncle George!"

"I do not like being left alone," John thought, "but I had rather be alone than get that close to death." It was a long time before he became a member of the death camp, before he could accept that all life must die. He remembered the day when Emmet Jaykyll came to visit. He was the shell of a man whose lungs would not allow him much exertion, but he had managed to survive the mustard gas and live on through another war. Like his brother killed in France, though, Emmet had died before Aunt Hattie. After Emmet had died, Thomas had told John solemnly one night at supper, "You're the last Jaykyll, son. It's up to you to carry on the family name." He had been particularly affected by Aunt Hattie's funeral. The smell of the damp, steaming earth was rank in John's nostrils as he had watched them lower Aunt Hattie's casket into the grave. "She spent so many hours killing time," the boy thought, "Now time has killed her." Long after, when he encountered the syllogism, "X is a man and all men must die, therefore X must die," John always substituted Aunt Hattie for X.

Another scene that always remained with him was that of a gray November day. John was playing by himself in the yard. Suddenly the sun burst forth from behind the clouds as an all-white gull sailed in from the river and over the boy's head. In the sunlight the gull turned blue and then pink as if it were a litmus paper bathed first in a sour and then a sweet sky. Hovering over the boy's head for what seemed a motionless minute in time, the gull sailed back to the river as the clouds closed again over the sun and turned the November world gray again....

Dr. Philwaggen called Jaykyll back to the present. "We're making good progress now. I believe your fear of confrontation stems from your childhood and is linked with your fear of death and deprivation of love. From what you have told me, I believe that you can help yourself fight off these trances by thinking of a white gull breaking through sun-pierced clouds. Think of the gull as uttering cries of triumph."

Learning Experiences

Sherri and Jason

Sherri Widderbe Whetman had been highly flattered when Jason Malmuth had selected her to be his secretary. It was, after all, a plum for a staff member to be the gatekeeper to the inner sanctum. Besides, she found Moomaw attractive. He was handsome and well-mannered-a distinctly different sort from her husband, Bill Whetman, from whom, she was happy to say, her divorce would soon be final. Bill Whetman and she had two children, boys, both of whom apparently were juvenile delinquents following their father's path to trouble. Whether or not they ended up rich like Bill, they were bound to be as unprofitable to the social order as he had been. Sherri did what she could to guide them into socially acceptable activities, but to little avail. Like their father, they were certainly males whom Jason Malmuth would label as rustics even though their money allowed them access to social circles to which the ordinary rustic could not reach. Like Bill, they could chew and spit tobacco with the most proficient of their acquaintances.

For Sherri, working with Jason was life in another world from that which she had been used to experiencing with Bill and her sons. She enjoyed her work, and she was not at all unhappy when Jason Malmuth asked her to work late and then to have dinner with him by candlelight at his home. His praise of her work satisfied her more than a margarita or a bourbon coke. Malmuth's wife was dead, and he was all alone in the large house that the College had provided for him. Sherri could not help fantasizing a little about being the second Mrs. Malmuth. She went out of her way to please Jason. It was only natural that he should ask Sherri to be his hostess at the numerous social functions that a college president was expected to conduct. Sherri showed herself to be an excellent hostess, marshalling the staff of the cafeteria service that Malmuth had brought to the College as if she had been catering social events for years. Her taste was impeccable, and she insisted that Malmuth provide good wines as part of these affairs. She knew former students who had influence to get these wines for the College at a reduced rate-even in some instances as an outright gift. Malmuth began to think of Sherri as indispensable. She became his unofficial hostess at College events both at the school and at the President's mansion. She arranged everything to Malmuth's satisfaction with no apparent effort. In short order he became very dependent on Sherri.

As his secretary, Sherri made the arrangements for all of Jason's social engagements. One of the more important of these were the semi-annual meetings of the College Board. Appointed by the Governor of Kentucky, the members of the Board had to give their approval for all major actions undertaken by the College. It was important, therefore, for Jason to develop further the favorable impression he had made upon these people at the time of his hiring. He viewed the board meeting in the late fall with some trepidation, but he was confident that Sherri would do everything possible to make these people receptive to his proposals. He was especially concerned that Senator Bert Woodville, the Chair of the Board, support him. He instructed Sherri to pay special attention to keeping the Senator happy.

Unfortunately for Jason Malmuth, Bert Woodville had local connections. He was Virgie Jones' first cousin once removed. In any matter concerning Pine Mountain College, Woodville would not act before he had discussed what his decision should be with Virgie. As a result of Malmuth's attack on the Chalmer Botts Festivlle, Woodville had received very unflattering comments about Malmuth from Virgie. He was therefore not disposed favorably toward Jason at the fall meeting of the Board. He kept his peace while Malmuth ran through his proposed budget and other perfunctory items on the agenda. However, when the item labeled College Image came up, Woodville was prepared. Malmuth presented his campaign against rusticity as an effort to give the College nationwide recognition as a first-rate liberal arts college. He termed it The Move to Olympus Campaign. He told the Board that he was exerting every effort to transform the College into an institution of higher learning whose sophistication would rival that of the Ivy League.

When Jason concluded his appeal for support of the Olympus Campaign, Bert Woodville first congratulated him on his energetic efforts to improve the quality of education at Pine Mountain College. "However, President Malmuth, I have some serious reservations about the details of your campaign. What I've been hearing leads me to believe that you may be going about achieving your goal through quite undesirable means. When we hired you, we made it clear that we wanted a first-rate liberal arts college, but we also tried to make clear to you the importance of this school to the region.

A number of us on the Board have considerable reservations about whether or not you show the proper concern for the local community. I was particularly upset when I heard that you had banned the Chalmer Botts Festival from the campus. That festival helped assure the community that the College had a proper respect for local arts and traditions. I think you should consider that it will do the College little good to have a positive national reputation if its local reputation is entirely negative."

Never one to openly confront his superiors, Jason Malmuth assured the Board that he would in the future be more careful to consider local attitudes in making his decisions. Bert Woodville was skeptical, but the attentions of Sherri Widderbee Whetman proved so charming that he said little more concerning the negative comments about Jason Malmuth that he had been receiving. Despite their misgivings, Woodville and the other Board members who had concerns about Malmuth's activities decided to give him more time before coming to any conclusions about the Olympus Campaign. The final reception for the Board at the President's mansion was a great success. To counter the rumblings about Malmuth's hostility to mountain traditions, Sherri engaged a local bluegrass band to play music for entertainment, and she saw to it that there was plenty of good food and drink available.

All in all, the reception proved a great success. Assessing the affair after saying goodbye to the final Board member, Malmuth told Sherri that he considered the affair a notable triumph. "You hit just the right note, I think," he told her. "It was worth listening to that rustic band to get the Board off my back. Thanks."

"You're quite welcome Jason. Now, isn't there something else I can do for you tonight? It's rather late. Could I sleep over?"

"I wouldn't want you to make the long drive home at this time of the morning."

After a month or two of their working together during the day and many evenings, it was hardly surprising that Sherri should find herself growing very attached to Jason Malmuth. It was not surprising either, when she found herself in Malmuth's bed that night at the end of the reception for the College Board of Rectors. She knew that she was more responsible for her being there than was Jason, who did not seem to her to be what anybody would call aggressive in his dealings with women.

Sherri had brought a nightgown with her just in case—a very short, very low cut, very beautiful pink gown to set off her dark hair and blue eyes. She was not surprised when Jason put on pajamas in the bathroom before coming to bed. She anticipated that she would have to be the aggressor if their relationship were to become intimate. She could imagine Malmuth, left to his own devices, spending all night without touching her.

Once he was in bed, Sherri snuggled up to him and ran her hands through his hair and under his pajama top. "Jason, do you like the perfume I have on. It's not too heavy, I hope. It should just give a faint hint of roses."

"Yes, you have a wonderful fragrance, Sherri."

"Why don't you kiss me, then, Jason? Maybe you would find me tasty as well as fragrant."

Sherri pulled him to her and kissed him. He decided that she was tasty and they spent a considerable time engaging in this taste test. Eventually Sherri felt Jason hard against her belly, and she grasped him in her two hands while they were kissing.

"I guess you're not Jewish, Jason," she observed. "Why don't we see if you can find a place to put that."

Before they went to sleep, Sherri asked Jason whether he had enjoyed their evening.

"Yes, indeed I have. I think we ought to spend more evenings like this."

"Jason, I can't think of anything that would please me more."

Senior Faculty Meet with Malmuth

The night with Sherri certainly put Malmuth in an excellent mood. The next day he exuded friendliness to almost all he met. He remained unmoved concerning his campaign to transform the image of Pine Mountain College and his gambit to commit John Jaykyll in order to achieve his goal. His first act of the day was to call Jeremy Bottleby to remind him of the proposed meeting of senior faculty. "Jeremy, I've come up with a name for our campaign against rusticity. It will be the name of our new capital campaign: The Move to Olympus Campaign."

"That's a great name, Jason. I've already arranged the proceedings for the meeting." He had asked Professors Rufus Webbot, Mickey Moriarity, Wilhelm Betrand, Adolpho Hoppersmith, Harlis Williams, and Mark Yeats to attend. Rauncibelle Grudger would also attend. Professor Williams would chair, as he was the most senior of the group.

"Are any of these people close to Jaykyll?"

"I'm afraid it would be difficult to find many senior faculty that are actually hostile to Jaykyll. Mrs. Grudger might be about the only one."

Bottleby had arranged for them to meet with Malmuth at 3:30 p.m. that afternoon. "I checked with Sherri to make sure you were free then. I hope that suits you."

"That will do quite well. Thanks."

The group that met in Sherri Whetman's office that afternoon was mystified. Think as they might, they could not decipher what common bond had led to their receiving their summons to meet with President Malmuth.

"Two of us, Mickey and me, are on the Athletic Committee," Mark Yeats observed, "but I can't imagine that being the cause since Wilhelm and Adolpho are here also. You two don't even know in what sports the school competes."

Even Rauncibelle Grudger was at a loss to explain their presence. The meeting had been arranged without the knowledge of Hiram, she was certain, for she wormed all secrets out of him during their sexual encounters. "Do you know why we're here, Sherri?"

"No, Belle, I haven't the faintest. I didn't have anything to do with making the arrangements."

At the appointed time, Sherri announced to Malmuth that they were all present for the meeting. Then she opened his office door and told them to go in.

Malmuth rose to greet them and asked that they sit down. After a few pleasantries, Malmuth broached the reason for their being there. "I asked Provost Grudger to assemble a group of senior faculty to discuss a very serious situation with one of our colleagues, John Jaykyll." The professors looked at one another in surprise and disbelief as Malmuth continued, "Professor Jaykyll has been exhibiting some rather bizarre behavior recently. It is my opinion that he is suffering a mental breakdown. He is under psychiatric care, that much is certain. It is my belief that Jaykyll should be institutionalized until his behavior returns to normal. The College would of course see that the cost of this treatment is taken care of without any expense of him. I am giving you the charge of meeting with him and speaking to him as concerned colleagues to convince him to undertake this course of action for his own good and the good of the College."

Provost Bottleby had informed Harlis Williams that he was to be chair of this committee. Now that he had heard the purpose of the committee, Williams was very reluctant to accept the charge. "President Malmuth, I have to tell you that you need to find another chair for this committee. John Jaykyll is as sane as you and I, and he is not a man to be trifled with. Perhaps Mrs. Grudger would find the chairing of this committee more acceptable than I do."

"No, Professor Williams, I must insist that you chair the committee. Provost Bottleby assures me that you are the right person for the chairmanship."

"I would sooner tangle with an angry nest of hornets than approach John Jaykyll with something like this," Adolpho Hoppersmith murmured. "He's a very mild-mannered fellow, but if he feels that he's being treated unjustly he can prove a formidable opponent. I think that you should reconsider, President Malmuth."

"No. I've decided that this must be done. Present it to Jaykyll as a sabbatical. I hear that he's always wanted one."

"I don't think Jaykyll will be fooled into thinking a sabbatical should be spent at an institution for the mentally diseased," said Wilhelm Bertrand. "If you want to send somebody to a mental hospital, you might consider Professor Messerand. I believe the man to be quite mad."

"Well, I find Professor Messerand has had the good sense to support my anti-rusticity campaign. I leave it up to you faculty as to how to present the sabbatical to Jaykyll."

Several days later, the committee met with Jaykyll. This time Sherri Whetman made the arrangements. She told him that he was to meet with a group of "senior" faculty at the President's request. The group met with John in a seminar room late in the afternoon when very few faculty or students were around. He noted immediately that none of those there could truly be termed "senior" faculty except for Professor Williams. Harlis Williams began the meeting by explaining Malmuth's wishes as tactfully as possible and then asking John if he would like a fully-paid sabbatical.

"You've always wanted time to write, John," Williams concluded.

"Yes, but I don't want to spend my sabbatical at a funny farm. I don't believe a mental institution would be conducive to creative thought, even though many great authors have been half-mad and even though Emily Dickenson said that much madness is divinest sense."

"How did you know what we were going to suggest?" Belle asked.

"My office is just above Malmuth's. He doesn't seem to realize it, but I hear half of what goes on down in his office. Let me tell you, much of it isn't very pretty. He wants to ship me off so that I won't be around to defend Roger Duvant. I have a counter proposal for you to take back to Malmuth. If he will join me for a year at a mental institution, I'll go. If not, he should prepare himself for a lawsuit for defamation of character." Jaykyll congratulated himself on his luck. "Forewarned is indeed forearmed," he thought. "I don't know how I could have avoided slipping into the grayness if this had been thrust on me without warning."

"But John, Malmuth says you're under psychiatric care." Harlis seemed to be genuinely concerned.

"Yes, Harlis. That's true. And my psychiatrist thinks that I'm making great progress. He thinks that I'm rapidly getting control of my problem."

"Well, that's what I'll report to Malmuth."

The upshot of the meeting was that President Malmuth had several extra layers of insulation and sound-proofing materials installed in the ceiling of his office and Jaykyll planned to see a lawyer about suing Malmuth for defamation of character—not the outcome that Malmuth had hoped to achieve.

Donnybrook at Student Life Council

Not content with waging his campaign against rusticity among the faculty of the college, Jason Malmuth took his campaign to the Student Life Council, a group whose duty it was to represent student views to the administration. The event that prompted his presence at the meeting of the Council was the arrest of Sampson Sturgis, a member of Delta Theta Chi. Malmuth harangued the student representatives for almost an hour about the uncouth language of the student body, the smoking of pot on campus, the unseemly panty raids and mooning of visitors. His major attack, however, was reserved for Delta Theta Chi, the campus fraternity with the most unsavory reputation. They were acting like animals, their house was a filthy pigsty, and they had made it their particular mission to organize panty raids and campus moonlit runs by naked students after drunken bouts at their fraternity. Now, one of their brothers, Sampson Sturgis had been arrested. Not just for smoking pot, mind you, but for growing it on campus. "Sheriff Mullgrab assures me that he has caught Mr. Sturgis admiring his ill-grown crop and that Sampson Sturgis will receive the full penalty of the law. I would like to know what the Student Life Council has to say about this matter."

Malmuth looked directly at Mark Hanna, the President of the Student Life Council. "What does the Council say about this, Mr. Hanna?"

"Well, first of all, Sampson is a very popular student. He's full of fun. I suspect that the reason Sheriff Mullgrab arrested him is that Mullgrab doesn't like anybody competing with his selling hash to high school and college students around here. You may not be aware, President Malmuth, that many of our students buy their pot at the county jail. The marijuana that the county police confiscate goes on sale soon after it's confiscated. Anybody who wants to make moonshine or grow pot to sell in Jackson County has to pay Mullgrab for the privilege. I imagine Sampson didn't pay promptly. That's why he's in jail. All Sampson has to do to get out of jail is find some good angel to pay Mullgrab enough money to drop the charges. Why, there are rumors that somebody in the sheriff's office or the sheriff himself is involved in murder for hire."

Laughter filled the room. Surprised by this response, Malmuth could not respond immediately. He was reluctant to believe that Sheriff Mullgrab was as venal as these students thought. If their assessment were true, however, he reflected that he might be able to use the sheriff's venality to his advantage. Perhaps for a price the sheriff could be brought into the anti-rusticity campaign.

While this discussion of his plight was occurring, Sampson Sturgis was resting more or less comfortably in the county jail. Samp was not a young man to be easily intimidated. He felt certain that he could get out of this scrape if he could raise enough money, but he wanted to stay around long enough to get the price down to a reasonable amount. From what he knew about how Sheriff Mullgrab operated, he believed that the more eager he seemed to get out, the higher the amount Mullgrab would demand. So Samp had his fraternity brothers bring him some of his textbooks, and he prepared for a week or two of living in the jail at county expense. To help pass the time when he tired of studying, which was frequent, he struck up a relationship with his jailer, Corduroy Carl Sims. Corduroy was a dark-haired, very chubby fellow with a large moustache. Had he put on a large sombrero, he might have been mistaken for a Mexican bandit on a Hollywood set. Corduroy had received his nickname on account of his always wearing corduroy pants, winter or summer. Apparently he owned no other pants but tan corduroy pants that matched the tan uniform mandated by Sheriff Mullgrab.

Sampson taught Corduroy to play gin rummy, and they spent many hours passing the time playing. Samp made it a point not to win any money from Corduroy. The wily student won enough hands to keep from mounting a large debt but lost just enough to make Corduroy believe he was a proficient card player. That put the jailer in a very good mood and loosened his lips. Samp found out what the going price was for getting out of trouble. He also discovered information that he hadn't sought. After their cozy relationship had matured, Corduroy hinted that, if Samp ever needed some person eliminated, he could have that done-for a price, of course. Samp expressed his gratitude to Corduroy for the information but insisted that he didn't have any enemies that he knew of just at that moment.

Two weeks after his incarceration, Sampson Sturgis emerged from the county jail refreshed from relaxation, regular meals, playing gin rummy, and studying. He had paid the minimum amount necessary to secure his release and to drop all charges. As part of the deal, however, Sampson had to agree to stop selling pot to high school students and to college students except for those in his fraternity. Mullgrab was very definite about the terms. "You keep messin' with me and your ass ain't gonna be around to graduate. Do I make myself clear?"

"Yes sir, Sheriff Mullgrab. I think I understand."

"Good. Then I think we'll get along."

"I sure hope so."

During his time in jail, Samp had been kept up to date about Malmuth's attacks on the rusticity of the students in general and that of Delta Theta Chi in particular. Once back on campus and once again in the bosom of Delta Theta Chi, Sampson was brought into discussions of how to handle Jason Malmuth. "He's out to get us, Samp," Set Mullinberg claimed.

"Don't you worry none, boys. If it comes to a situation that we can't handle, I know where a solution can be found. But I've been thinking about how to handle old Jason. He's a real twit. Ever did you shake his hand? Limp as a dishrag and clammy to boot. Let's start a rumor that he's homosexual. That ought to keep him too busy to bother us much."

"Do you know anything to back up the rumor?" Set asked

"Nah. But we can manufacture something."

"I don't know. It seems a pretty nasty thing to do."

"Do you have anything else to suggest?"

Set admitted he was fresh out of ideas, so they all agreed that Samp's ploy was the one to adopt.

Hike to White Rocks

Aware of the attraction that the fall leaf colors of the Appalachians held for many people, Nathaniel Boone decided to open to faculty and friends of the College participation in a mountain hike that he had planned as a field trip for his ecology class. He planned to hike up from the floor of the valley at Cumberland Gap National Park to the ridge of Cumberland Mountain at a place known as the White Rocks. There were a number of faculty and friends who decided to accept the offer. Almost all the Appalachian Studies faculty asked to come, and Rufus Webbot, and the Messerands also signed up. Virgie Jones also asked to go with Nathaniel and his eight students, one of whom was Sampson Sturgis.

The sun was shining in a cloudless sky the day of the hike. It was a beautiful day-a perfect day for a hike thought Betty Duvant as the group gathered. Both students and guests betrayed their high spirits. The College bus accommodated the entire group, which left the College on a Saturday at seven o'clock in the morning. Their drive took them over an hour. It was after eight when they began their climb. Since Nathaniel had warned them to bring drinks and a lunch, two out of three persons had daypacks on their backs. Fairly wide at the base of the mountain, the track up the mountain narrowed as the ascended. Their pace presented no difficult for even the least experienced hikers and those in less than adequate physical condition because Boone stopped frequently along the way to point our plants and animals. Many of the students and some of the other hikers took notes on Nathaniel's explanations of the life forms and their interrelationships. "The pyramid of life's complex web reveals itself to us," he explained. "The caterpillars eat the leaves of the shrubs and trees. They are grazers, like cattle, but some of these caterpillars will turn into the moths and butterflies that will sip the nectar of flowering plants and, in the process, pollinate the flowers of these and other plants and thus enable them to reproduce. Along the way, some of the caterpillars, butterflies, and moths will provide food for many species of birds and animals. Warblers and other small birds will eat the caterpillars and keep them in check. Flycatchers of various kinds and small mammals will dine on butterflies, and whip-poor-wills, nightjars, and bats will consume night-flying moths. These predators, in turn, provide food for hawks, owls, foxes, and wildcats."

When the hikers reached a place where gypsy moths had denuded the trees, Nathaniel pointed out that these alien creatures had been introduced into the American ecosystem by man. "Here in North America they had no natural predators to keep them in check, but nature is gradually adjusting. Blue jays are learning to eat them, for example. Nature abhors instability. It develops checks and balances to keep the natural world in equilibrium. If a species threatens the balance of nature, nature will react to restore stability. We human beings should try to remember that instead of thinking that we can do anything to our world that pleases us. That commercial on television that had an actress saying "Don't fool with Mother Nature" was not far off the mark. If we upset the balance of nature too much, nature will recoil upon us. Epidemic diseases are one obvious natural response to excessive population. Deer without predators to keep their populations in check destroy their habitat-literally eat themselves out of room and board and destroy the habitat for them and other wildlife. Their food sources disappear and the weakened deer are attacked by brainworm disease. People might consider the possibility that influenza and AIDS are nature's reply to excessive human population and tampering with the environment.

"You are beginning to sound like the Reverend Jerry Falwell, Professor," Samp Sturgis observed, punching the student beside him.

"I don't necessarily want to do that, Samp, but remember the margarine ad—'Don't fool with Mother Nature.'"

As they moved up the trail, Sampson Sturgis made sure to avoid Jacques Messerand, who walked behind Betty and Roger Duvant. Stalking along with a wild, disheveled look, Jacques attracted Samp's ridicule. Staying a safe distance behind his professor, Sampson imitated him quite well—to the considerable amusement of other students and some faculty. Messerand and Simone studiously kept their place behind Betty and Roger Duvant. Nathaniel had been surprised when Messerand had asked whether he and Simone could join the hike. They did not seem to him to be the outdoor type. Because of the group's slow pace, however, they were able to keep up with experienced hikers like the Duvants without much difficulty.

Looking across the draw to cliffs on the other side of the stream that had cut a gorge in the mountain, Boone spotted a turkey vulture's nest with two ungainly, rather ugly young chicks that were just beginning to replace their baby down with true feathers. The group crowded up to the edge of the chasm. "Be careful," Nathaniel cautioned. Betty and Roger were among the first to the edge. They were admiring the vulture chicks and commenting on their ungainly appearance when Roger yelled as he felt a sudden shove from behind that caused him to lose his footing and slip over the edge. He was about to plummet down seventy feet onto the rocks beside the stream. Betty screamed, but she grabbed Roger's backpack and Nathaniel grabbed Roger's arm as he began to disappear. With great effort, they stopped his fall and pulled him back up to the path.

Almost everybody crowded around to congratulate Roger on his narrow escape and Betty and Nathaniel for their quick reactions. "Folks," Nathaniel cautioned after the excitement had subsided, "We've got to be careful. If we go to the edge of the precipice again, don't shove if you're in the back. Wait and take your turn. There'll be plenty of time."

The hike continued uneventfully, but the high spirits in evidence at the beginning of the journey had become a bit subdued—not altogether a bad result as far as Boone was concerned. Maybe it would be easier to keep his students' attention now. He was able to point out some bird songs—wood thrushes, towhees, and titmice. Higher up the ridge, they heard a melodious, rolling flute-like call that reminded them of the wood thrushes but was obviously different. Boone identified it as a veery. "It's an indicator species. It tells us that we've reached an elevation high enough and therefore cool enough to sustain a northern hardwood forest. We're almost at the top of the ridge." The top itself was a disappointment to some of the hikers, because there was just a clearing in the forest with a few white rocks that didn't seem very impressive.

"Where are the white rocks?"

"Look back up here when you're back down. You can see the bare white rock on the side of the mountain from there.

Right now, you should enjoy the view of the ridges around us. They're spectacular. These ridges have resisted erosion because they're capped with very hard rock."

To Nathaniel Boone's relief, his hikers retraced their steps without any more accidents, and the bus trip back to Pine Mountain proceeded without incident. Back at the College's campus, the group expressed their thanks enthusiastically. It had been a very pleasant experience despite Roger's close call. "We really did have a great time," Betty Duvant told him. "Roger's had a lot of close calls lately. We know it wasn't your fault, Nathaniel. He should have been more careful."

"Well, to quote the noble bard, 'All's well that ends well,'" Roger joked.

"Just glad you're all right, Roger." Nathaniel Boone was exceedingly relieved to have all of his charges back both alive and well.

Before walking back to faculty row, Roger suggested to Betty that they linger behind the others so that they could talk without being overheard.

"That was a close call, Roger."

"Betty, I don't think it was an accident. Somebody pushed me deliberately. It was too forceful to be somebody jockeying for position to look at those vultures."

"If that's true, Roger, the person who has been trying to kill you was in our group."

"I hate to think so. Maybe I'm wrong."

Poetry in Arms

Since Roger Duvant's arrival at Pine Mountain College, he, John Jaykyll, and Katy Carlyle had sponsored poetry readings in informal settings. Both students and faculty were encouraged to participate by reading original works or works of others that they found particularly appealing. In addition to the prepared program, fifteen to thirty minutes was scheduled for impromptu readings. Duvant did not allow his current problems to alter his enthusiasm for these readings, although he did shift the main responsibility for organizing them to Katy.

The first reading of the semester was scheduled for the week after Roger's latest narrow escape. Several original student poems and prose pieces began the program. The quality was excellent. Then professor Large rendered a spirited reading of Tennyson's "Charge of the Light Brigade," announcing after his stirring reading that this was his favorite piece of poetry. Roger followed with a poem about the fragility of human life, a subject that had been much in his mind of late. After several more student readings, Jaykyll offered a piece of comical verse he had penned for the occasion entitled, "Here's to You, Sigmund Fraud." Katy and several other faculty members read poems also, but the hit of the evening came in the time allowed for impromptu readings. It was a piece of verse read by a student entitled *Ode to Malmuth*. All of the faculty were dumfounded when Sampson Sturgis rose and announced his sub-title, *The Rustic*.

"I find this hard to believe, Roger," John whispered to his colleague.

Though his meter limped in spots, Samp gave a very spirited reading: "I'm a subject for critique,/Not one of the elite./By lineage I am a cur./Uncouth, I drive Malmuth frantic/And he labels me a rustic/As rough as sandpaper./He says I must be thick/'Cause I say crik instead of creek/And my expletives are antique./I don't fit into his clique."

Loud and sustained applause greeted the conclusion of Samp's poetic effort. Later, as everyone sipped punch and ate cookies, Roger and John complimented the young poet. "With a little work, Samp, you could write good poetry. You should consider taking creative writing next semester."

Jaykyll concurred. "Lyric poetry is the vehicle for expressing deep emotion, and apparently you have some emotions to give vent to, Samp."

"I'll think about it, professors. Right now I'm just tryin' to get through French."

"Are you having difficulty with Monsieur Messerand?"

"He has it in for me because of those two weeks I spent in jail. He thinks that I cut his class deliberately. He refuses to believe that I spent the time in jail and that I studied while I was there."

"Maybe at our next session you'll favor us with an ode to Professor Messerand, Samp. He's a strange fellow. He's my next door neighbor, you know," Roger joked.

That was the end of the conversation, because Samp was dragged off by admiring female students.

"Some of our young ladies are quite enamored of Samp's poetic prowess," Jaykyll told Katy when she joined him and Duvant.

"Yes, John, I think that Samp is discovering the power of the pen. He appears to be more successful with the women as a budding poet than he ever was as the school's prime practical joker."

"The proverbial power of the pen," Roger chimed in.

"Seriously, though, we've seen tonight that President Malmuth is not very popular with the students. He seems to be running out of supporters very rapidly," John observed.

"The sooner, the better, as far as I'm concerned. Perhaps I can outlast him," Roger muttered. "The man has no interest in whether or not the students obtain a decent education. As long as they present what he considers a favorable image for public consumption, he could care less about how much they know about poetry or world events. He supports our teaching something he terms Standard English, but only because the lack of that seems to him to betray rusticity. If a person could speak a broad dialect and still be labeled sophisticated and socially acceptable in what he terms 'the best circles,' Jason Malmuth wouldn't give a rat's ass whether these kids used standard English grammar."

"Agreed. Malmuth is all show and little substance. I'm even surprised he cares about our students using drugs and visiting gambling dens," Katy added.

"That merely proves the point. The reason he became so angry with Sheriff Mullgrab was that Mullgrab's arrests got into the media. Unfavorable publicity. Nothing bothers Jason Malmuth more than unfavorable publicity. It ruins the image he's so eager to create."

Jay Relives the Past

Philwaggen Explores Again

With a sense of satisfaction, Jay reported to Philwaggen that he had survived the ordeal of meeting with so-called "senior" faculty. Phil congratulated Jay on his successful handling of the situation. "You're definitely making progress. It was an obvious ploy on Malmuth's part. But you handled it very satisfactorily."

"He certainly lacks subtlety. Of course, it helped me immensely that I had overheard what he was up to."

"Still, it is a hopeful sign that you were able to deal with conflict so well when you had advance notice. Let's continue to explore your childhood. Just relax and tell me more about the time when you were six or seven years old."

John thought back to his childhood and continued. "When we left the old house and its wonderful yard with huge oak trees overlooking the marsh, I felt that I had been displaced. I did not yet know death well, but the sense of loss made me feel sad. I remembered the Barn Owls that had lived in the garage and attacked anyone who entered. After my father Thomas Jaykyll had had his head severely lacerated by the birds, he decided that they must go. They had caused considerable difficulty, but I cried when I saw the bodies of the dead owls hanging outside the garage. I remembered too the nest of small, pink mice that my father had showed me just after he had turned them up with the plow. I had found their blind wriggling laughable, but I was sad when the cats claimed the mice as their prize.

"We lived for a time with friends, while our new house was being finished. I felt that my world had been disrupted and invaded by strangers whose hearty manners and good intentions did not soothe my sense of loss of that wonderful place on the river. John gradually slipped from his conscious mind and relived his early experiences....

The boy's sense of disruption was even greater when they finally moved to the new home. Conscious of the conflict that had arisen between his mother and his father, he blamed the house and its barren surroundings. His father had bought part of an old farm, and the house had been built on the front portion. There were no trees and shrubs around the house, and the summer sun beat down unmercifully upon the Cape Cod cottage. It was well built, but it was miles from the city. To hear John's mother, it was miles from any vestige of civilization. She could not drive the car, so she was stranded from her friends. Without bus or trolley service, she felt that she had been lifted from the abodes of civilized human beings and placed in a desert where the only human forms were uncouth savages. John's father was content that he at last had his own house and land, but his mother never forgave her husband for taking her into what she considered exile in a waste place.

As the years went by her bitterness increased. The coming of the war did nothing to ease her pain, and when his father sold their old 32 Chevrolet just before Pearl Harbor, her cup of hemlock brimmed over. It was exactly the wrong time to sell a car, no matter what its age. The car was sold just after Thanksgiving. After the war broke out a couple of weeks later, all automobile manufacturers suddenly turned to building machines for the military. They lived, then, throughout the war in this "desert" place without transportation and under a growing cloud of bitterness that increased with every begged ride and every social event in the city missed. John's father raised a large garden every year, and their chickens and ducks provided them with eggs and meat that other people were glad to pay well for when the Jaykylls had extras, but John's mother was not appeased.

When John's sister was fourteen, the bitterness overflowed. His mother grew morose when the troop convoys began to pass the house day and night. Often they stopped for fifteen minutes or so, and when they did, John and his sister, who was now thirteen and very pretty, went out to talk to the soldiers. Before long Margie was writing to three different servicemen, contributing to the war effort, much to her mother's dismay. To her mother's way of thinking, he boys at school were no better.

"I will not have you married to one of these country bumpkins, Marjory."

"But Mother, they're nice boys."

"Maybe they're clean and honest, but they're not for you. Look at Ingred. Her father and brothers are bootleggers. I don't want you marrying somebody like that or worse."

Mother began writing her mother and her sister Audrey in Athens, Tennessee. Audrey's husband had been killed a few years before in an automobile accident, and John's grandmother and Audrey had lived together in Athens until the war began. With the war effort came war bond drives, and a family friend in the government smoothed the way for Audrey to become the assistant for war bond sales in Washington, D. C. It was arranged, then, for Margie to go to live with her grandmother in Athens while her aunt went to Washington to answer to need of the nation. Father was opposed to the move, but Mother prevailed. Despite her southern gentility, she fought like a tigress so that her daughter could grow up in what she considered "society." Life became tense after Margie left. Mother moved into the room Margie had vacated. Although a truce reigned, the conflict between his parents was never far from the surface, and John often felt that he had wandererd by mistake on to the battlefield or had himself become a battleground. Over him the verbal exchanges issued back and forth. It was as if two opposing artillery battalions unleashed their salvos over his head.

There had always been a tension between his mother's family and his father's. Neither side felt that the proper mate had been selected. John learned later, after considerable questioning of his mother, that his father had been married previously and that her family had never accepted her marrying a divorced man. Father's family, on the other hand, felt that they were the social equals of any Tennessee family and that Mother had entrapped him while he was recovering from the heartbreak associated with his first marriage. In fact, they liked his first wife greatly and were unaware that Father had come home to find her in bed with another man. So it was not difficult for either parent to find a sympathetic ear within the family. Mother especially relied on her family to support her determined effort to see her daughter grow up in Tennessee society.

As the struggle continued, John was drawn into their belligerency, generally by his mother, who sought an ally in her war against his father. The loudness of their conflicts often exceeded the bounds of parlor warfare when his father's exasperation could not be contained. At these times Mother dissolved into tears. John had always been pampered and petted by Mother and all of his aunts and female cousins since he was the only male Jaykyll of his generation and the hope to carry on the family name. Now, however, Mother looked at him as a potential ally and, not consciously but in fact, began treating him as her lover. Father was not blind to what was happening, though he never admitted it, and therefore the normal friction between father and son was increased. When the artillery barrages grew too loud, John complained.

"I don't want to hear this high-tempered talk."

If that didn't work, the boy went to his room, shut himself in and read books. He devoured every novel in the high school library. He read all of James Fenimore Cooper's Leather-stocking tales, *The Scottish Chiefs*, *Kidnapped* and *David Balfour*. When he ran out of adventure tales, he moved on to books like *Jane Eyre* and *Wuthering Heights*. Or he would run outside and lose himself by walking or running over the farm in the summer and on weekends during school time. If he was in a particularly upset frame of mind after listening to the combat all day, not having the escape of school, John would torture the chickens and ducks by chasing them out of the shade into the hot sun. It was an odd sort of relief. For relief he also read about the war or went to some of the innumerable movies that were being made to whip up patriotic fervor against the enemy. John found the comic books about the war far more satisfying than the Captain Marvel or Superman comic books. In these the violence was too contained, too antiseptic. The comic books about the war, like the war movies, were more redolent of blood and uncontrolled violence. They came closer to satisfying John's need to feel some release from the war effort he had to make every day.

Elizabeth Jaykyll was a beautiful woman, even in her fifties. Vivacious and used to having the attention of men and the friendship of women, she found herself sinking into depression in these years of isolation in the country. She grew less and less vivacious and more and more inclined to sing the virtues of Tennessee and her family at great length. Once the love that she had felt for Thomas had soured, she found herself lashing out at him more and more, dissatisfied with their life and their lack of money. After the war she attempted to remedy the lack of money by running first a restaurant and then a soda fountain, but neither of these brought her much money despite the hours of hard labor they required. As it became more and more obvious that fate did not have much happiness left in store for her, she sank more deeply into depression.

As her antagonism to Thomas grew, she devoted her affections more and more to John. He became the fair-haired prince on whom all her hopes were set. He was an honor student and would attend college and do great things in the world. He would be a mover and shaker of men. Sometimes her love of John became so openly a wooing that the young boy found it embarrassing. Still, he did not avoid her when she moved through the house in nothing but her slip. If he were lying on the floor, he did not turn his head as she passed by. The images set in his mind.

John got his growth early and began to shave by the time he was thirteen. His interest in girls grew accordingly, but he had formed from his reading a great many romantic notions that did not help him in dealing with Marilene and Beatrice and Dolores but kept him out of trouble at least. It was not that girls were not interested in John but that he lacked the courage to turn their interest into any sort of relationship. Masturbation and fantasies aided by magazines became a large part of John's life. Some of the fantasies that came to him in dreams were so violent and disturbing that he felt a tremendous sense of guilt whenever he happened to recall them in his waking moments....

Philwaggen brought John back to consciousness. "Jay, we're making very rapid progress now. I'm certain I was correct in my prognosis. Your fear of losing love, your fear of death, and your fear of conflict are all linked. We'll continue from this point next time." Jaykyll left Philwaggen's office with a sense of optimism despite the fact that he was drenched as if he had been in a downpour. He was wet all over from the perspiration that had occurred during the session.

Poison

John Jaykyll and Roger Duvant were just sitting down to have lunch in the cafeteria when Wilhelm Bertrand and Jacques Messerand joined them. "May we sit with you, John?" Bertand asked.

"Of course, Wilhelm."

Jaykyll knew of the trouble between Duvant and Messerand, so he assumed that they owed the pleasure of the Frenchman's company to the fact that the majority of tables had been taken by students. John and Bertrand had taught together at another college and had been together at Pine Mountain College for many years. They had many old stories to tell. "Have I ever told you about Little Hitler?" he asked Roger and Messerand.

"No, John, you haven't. Was he the Pine Mountain version of the Fuhrer?" Roger joked.

"Well, he had a moustache and he looked a little like Charlie Chaplin's little dictator. He was the town drunk. He spent most of his time in the Pine Mountain jail sleeping off his binges. But he was a master handyman. He could fix anything. He could do plumbing and electrical work. He could do drywall. He could do roofing. Little Hitler could do just about any maintenance job you could imagine. Back in those days the College had even less money than it has now, if you can imagine that. But President Smithy had considerable political clout. Whenever we had any really challenging jobs, Jim would go down to the jail and get Little Hitler out to do our work. He worked cheap, and when he was done, Jim would give him some bourbon and take him back to the jail. It was an arrangement that worked well. I suppose President Malmuth would consider an arrangement like that the epitome of rusticity."

"I would like to have Little Hitler do my maintenance work," Messerand growled. "The young man that they have sent to work at my house has as you say 'made a pass' at Simone. I had to chase him off."

"Well, Little Hitler is long dead from cirrhosis of the liver. I'm afraid he won't be much help."

Roger agreed. "Perhaps you misunderstood the young man's intentions, Professor Messerand." Then he excused himself to go back for dessert. While he was away, Jaykyll regaled Bertrand and Messerand with a story about the day a tornado tore through the area near the College. It demolished the housing near the College but left the school unscathed. "God must love Pine Mountain College's rusticity, even if President Malmuth doesn't."

Roger returned with his cherry cobbler and sat down to enjoy it. After a bite or two he drank from his drink. He had drunk about a third of it before leaving the table to get his cobbler. Now the lemonade tasted strangely different. More bitter perhaps. "There's something wrong with this drink. Did anyone put something in it while I was gone?" Recent events had caused Duvant to become very suspicious, and Jay understood fully why Roger was concerned about his drink. None of them admitted to having seen anything suspicious, so Duvant sampled his lemonade again, then examined the glass carefully. "There's definitely something wrong with this drink. Look at this residue on the bottom of the glass. This lemonade was presweetened. I didn't add sugar or any other sweetener to it. Somebody put something in this drink while I was away from the table. Didn't anyone here see who put this in my drink?" Both Bertrand and Messerand claimed that they had seen nobody near their table.

"I suppose we were too busy talking, Roger. I'll tell you what. Let's have somebody in chemistry analyze what's in the drink." Roger agreed that was a good idea, but said he was feeling a little nauseated. Fighting off the grayness, Jaykyll said that he would take the drink to Daniel Crockett and see what he could find out. "You go to the infirmary, Roger." Only when he reached the science building did he allow the grayness to envelop him—*The jungle was closing about him. The lushness of the vegetation bore down on him oppressively. The tendrils of the vines seemed to be grasping for his throat. Before him in the trees were small reddish brown monkeys who chattered away as if they were laughing at him as they hurled fruit at him. He raised his arms to ward off the impending blows—*

"Jay, I'm not going to hit you. Why are you holding your arms up that way?"

"Oh, it's you Dan." Jaykyll peered anxiously at Daniel Crockett. "I thought someone had thrown something at me trying to break this glass."

"Nobody here but me, and I'm not about to break your glass. What's in it?"

"It's supposed to be lemonade, but there's reason to believe that somebody might have slipped in some poison. Could you get Farley Tyler or some other chemist to check it?" The chemical analysis of the material at the bottom of the lemonade glass indicated that it was rat poison. Daniel Crockett relayed this information to Jay, who asked if Dan were sure about this conclusion. "As sure as I am that my ancestor Davy Crockett killed a bar or two, John. No doubt about it at all. Of course, it would have taken longer to find out if you hadn't suggested that it might be poison."

Jaykyll telephoned the infirmary to let the nurse know what had poisoned Roger. "How is the patient?"

"He's doing quite well. Now that we know what caused the problem it shouldn't be too difficult to take care of it. But I'm sending him on to Pine Mountain Hospital just as a safety precaution."

Thinking back over the incident, Jaykyll's suspicion lit upon Jacques Messerand. He had had the opportunity to slip the poison in Roger's drink. Jay and Wilhelm had been too engrossed in their conversation to pay any attention to what Messerand had been doing. He was a logical suspect, since he had already had an altercation with Roger. Could he be the person behind the other attempts on Roger's life? He would have been able to observe Roger's movements since they lived close by one another on faculty row. It was difficult to believe that a college professor at Malmuth's unduly rustic college would be plotting the murder of one of his colleagues, yet Jay could not help being suspicious of Messerand. Still, there was absolutely no proof. Surely even a faculty member as demented as Jacques Messerand would not attempt to kill a colleague.

A Little Learning

One morning shortly after the poisoning incident, Jay had a visit from a very despondent student advisee, Alfred Molymo. Alfred was noted for his athletic accomplishments as well as his difficulties in dealing with literary endeavors. His more classically oriented student buddies had nicknamed him Ajax, because of what they perceived to be his slowness of wit. Ajax had avoided Jaykyll's classes with Jaykyll's unacknowledged aid, for he had judged Ajax to have a vocabulary insufficent to allow him success in one of Jay's classes.

"Professor Jaykyll, I need help bad."

"What's the problem, Ajax?" Jaykyll thought highly of the boy despite his lack of scholarly attainments and he used his student nickname.

"Everybody thinks I'm dumb. Last night President Malmuth used me as an example of what's wrong with Pine Mountain students. He said I don't know no words. And my grammar's bad. At least that's what the fellows translated for me. He said my language is atrocious."

"You're not stupid, Ajax. You just haven't used the brain the Lord gave you very strenuously. If you exercised your brain as much as you do your body, you'd soon become a well versed (that means well-prepared) young man. You should begin by increasing your vocabulary, by learning words. People judge others' intelligence to some extent by their vocabularies."

"Can I do it fast?"

"Well, the best way to build vocabulary is by reading and looking up every word in the dictionary, but there are short cuts. They would help in your situation."

"Would you help me, Professor?"

"If you promise to work hard."

"I do. Let's start today."

Jaykyll pulled off his shelf a textbook dealing with Latin and Greek prefixes, suffixes, and roots. Handing it to Alfred, he told him to begin at the beginning and study a chapter a day. "Come in once a week during my office hours, Ajax. I'll quiz you to see how you're getting along. Remember, to use a sports metaphor, the ball is in your court. You must do the work. You should not just look at the book. You should practice by introducing the words you learn into your everyday speech."

Alfred Molymo took the book from Jaykyll as if it were the Holy Grail. "I'll work hard, Professor Jaykyll. You'll see."

After Alfred had left, Jaykyll had a private laugh. Unknowingly, Malmuth was contributing to student learning.

At his next meeting with Philwaggen, Jay told him about Ajax's desire to become a more educated person. "I believe that the boy is serious about doing something to confound Malmuth. I hope that I can, too. I'm not so sure that I can pull it off." Then he told Philwaggen of the attack he had had while delivering the poisoned drink for analysis.

"I feel that I'm not sufficiently in control of myself to give Roger the help that he needs. This was the third attack on his life."

"You are too hard on yourself. I think we are making splendid progress, Jay. You'll be fully ready to help your friend in no time. Take my word for it. Most patients do not progress this rapidly even if hypnosis is used. Now let's proceed with your childhood experiences. What about school?"

"I broke out of my shell late in elementary school, and in high school I attempted to conquer my tendency to stay on the sidelines. After early problems, I became a top student, but I learned in high school not to excel too much. I wanted to be a regular guy. I contented myself with having the best academic record of any boy in his class, seemingly without effort and largely because I read everything I could get my hands on. I became a student leader in high school and found it easy to date. I learned a great deal about kissing and petting but did not, as his friends phrased it, convince any girl to go all the way. Whenever the opportunity arose, I managed to bungle the moment and anger the girl. Perhaps it was the bookish romanticism on which my knowledge of woman was based or perhaps the violent images from my dreams seized my mind and hindered me. Women in the abstract were very appealing to me, but when I began to feel strong emotions for one of them my mind grew confused and I thought myself torn in many different directions by conflicting emotions that I could not control....

Jaykyll slipped into reverie. It was not until his first year of college that friends took him, half-drunk, to a local whorehouse, to accomplish, in the exquisite language of his peers, getting him laid. The moments that John spent with the tall, thin, un-buxom blonde who introduced him to the sex act were not the most memorable of his life. Next morning, trying to recover from the hangover, he could hardly recall what had happened to him, but he no longer felt women to be quite as mysterious as they had once seemed.

It was the fall after this that that John met Ellie and had his first affair. Ellie was a buxom, tall blonde from West Virginia. She sat beside him in his comparative religion class at the University of Kentucky. Here they learned together of the Great Mother and other elements of the fertility religions of the ancient world. She was also in his biology lab section, and it was not long before they became lab partners. Ellie had been home-coming queen at her high school and was quite certain of her desirability to men even though she did not dress well since her family had recently lost all of their belongings when their house burned down. Her father was finishing graduate school, so they had little money available to replace their losses. Ellie was obviously bright and she had an earthy sense of humor. Despite John's naive romanticism, he found himself attracted to Ellie, who smiled demurely and hid her interest in John behind large glasses though she quite evidently reciprocated his interest.

Not wanting to appear unknowlegeable in Ellie's eyes, John began making trips to the library to read up on sexual matters. He read all that he could find about sex, even delving into Havelock Ellis, Kraft Ebbing and other works that were somewhat off the beaten track. John began to see that there was far more to be learned about human sexuality than he had suspected from heavy petting, looking at pornographic comics and girlie magazines, or visiting a prostitute in a half-drunken stupor. The dreams that had haunted him and caused him to feel guilty now seemed less troublesome. They were, after all, fairly tame by comparison with what his researches had turned up.

One day as they worked over the dogfish shark that they shared, Ellie asked, "I think that cutting into this shark is really sexy, John, don't you?"

"I hadn't thought much about this shark except as something to do for a grade."

"Do you have any girlfriends, John?"

"Sure, but nobody special. Do you have any boyfriends?"

"Nobody special."

"What about Mike. I see you two walking to class together a lot."

"Oh, Mike is a friend, that's all. We don't date."

"What's your idea of something to do for a date?"

"Well, going to a movie is good for a start."

"Then would you like to go see *The Lavender Hill Mob* tomorrow night?"

"I live way out in the country."

"I don't have a car, Ellie."

"I can arrange to stay with my cousin and we can walk."

As they walked to the movie, Ellie told him a little about her life in West Virginia. She had been a majorette and very popular, she told him.

"I was the homecoming queen."

"I can see why. You're pretty enough—all that blonde hair and a body that makes me drool."

At the movie they laughed so loudly that they worried about making a spectacle of themselves even though loud comments and noises were the order of the day in the theater at the Students' Haven, the shopping area near the University grounds. They held hands and Ellie put their hands on his pants leg, inside his. He was soon breathing heavily and placed his other arm around her, letting his hand fall to her breast.

After they left the movies, they stopped for drinks and then walked slowly across the campus. Ellie claimed that she could get high by drinking aspirins in coca-cola, and this combination did seem to put her in a very good mood and cause her to be extraordinarily responsive. John didn't feel the need of anything to drink when he was with Ellie. The shadows of the trees and large shrubs put much of the lawns and walks in darkness, and the harvest moon provided a romantic light that bathed many unlighted areas in an eerie twilight. Near a statue of a faun pursuing a nymph, they stopped and John pulled Ellie into the shadows and kissed her. Her lips met his eagerly, and they were soon lost in tactile delights.

When John touched Ellie's breasts underneath her blouse, she quivered and ran one of her hands through his hair and pulled his head to her lips with the other. Kissing his ear lobe, she laughed when she noticed his body trembling and felt inside his thigh, squeezing him. The walk to Ellie's relatives' house took a long time.

John and Ellie went to the movies again and to other events on campus. Ellie was more than happy to help him put into experiment some of the theoretical information about sex that he had acquired. She obviously had had more experience than he, but his researches in the library had at least provided him with a depth of theoretical knowledge that impressed her. John felt easy with Ellie, whose intelligent earthiness caused him delight although it did not square with his notions of the romantic. She was definitely not the pedestaled Emma Delgado of his high school daydreams, and she could make him laugh. Ellie treated sex as a natural bodily function. She enjoyed it almost as much as roast beef, she said.

The lack of an automobile encouraged the originality of their experiments. The invention of the motor car, it occurred to John, had done more than anything else to free his generation of parental supervision. The wheels of freedom were denied Ellie and John, however, so that they, for lack a motorized room and bed, were forced into ingenuity to satisfy their desire for each other. They were ingenious and brazen in the places that they chose, but the risks they took added zest to their lovemaking. The study carrels in the most remote library stacks became a favorite spot for them.

John gave himself only half enthusiastically to the sensuous pleasures of the relationship. Despite his desperate need to be loved, he was haunted by the same feelings of guilt that had followed his liason with the woman to whom he had lost his virginity. He could not help feeling dissatisfied. He sensed the sexual passions that he and Ellie aroused in each other were not the love that he wanted, yet he could not resist her unabashed desire for him. He was embarrassed to have her show this too much in the classroom or walking across the campus. His romantic notions of what love should be gained from Victorian novels had not prepared him for something like this. His clinical readings about sexuality in Havelock Ellis and other authors did nothing to allay these feelings even though they enabled him to suggest to Ellie that he was far more experienced sexually than he was.

After a month had passed, Ellie told John that she had arranged to babysit for her cousin and that he could come sit with her and they would study together.

"Be sure to bring some protection. I don't want to have to see a man about a horse"....

Philwaggen's voice brought Jaykyll back to the present. "Good, good, Jay." Called back to reality, Jaykyll was amazed to see Philwaggen's excitement. He appeared ecstatic. "We're really exploring items that bear upon your current problem, I think. It's difficult to believe you're making such rapid progress. That's all for today. We'll take up there next time. Keep thinking about that white gull when your attacks come. See you next week."

Students Beware

Jacques Messerand had proved to be a taskmaster to his students. He assigned plenty of homework and time in the language laboratory. It was difficult to survive his classes without learning French, but his methods did not engender popularity. Though some of his students enjoyed his antics in class, the few triflers that bore the brunt of his sarcasm cursed his presence and vowed vengeance. Among these non-students pretending to be seeking an education was Sampson Sturgis, better known as Samp to both his friends and his few enemies. Messerand developed an especially great dislike for Sturgis when he skipped class for two weeks straight. The Frenchman was unbelieving when Sampson explained that he had been in jail but had tried to keep up with his studies.

Somewhat misnamed, Samp was not the strongman that his name implied. He was a slender, fair-haired young man of medium height. He came from a hollow along the slope of Black Mountain. An otherwise rather unremarkable young man, he was renowned among the student body for his practical jokes or rusties, as Samp termed them. Most of these involved fooling faculty members into believing him to be a more responsible student than he actually was, but there was a puerile, sadistic quality to some of his schemes. He was thought to be the person who had caught all the stray cats and dogs that could be found on or near the campus, tied tin cans to their tails, filled the cans with small rocks, and released the animals along faculty row and among the dormitories at two o'clock in the morning during the week of mid-term examinations. Almost all of the panty raids on campus could be traced to Samp's instigation. He was also often the instigator of water balloon fights in the dormitories, but his cruel streak came to bear in spreading false rumors about the sexual habits of young women students who had refused to date him. Samp was determined to repay Messerand for what Samp regarded as the cruel and unusual punishment of having Samp read aloud at the beginning of every class and then pointing out to the class the flaws in his French pronunciation and grammar. While Samp was debating just how to even his score with Messerand, he learned of Messerand's raging jealousy of Simone from Joe Walker.

"I feel sorry for you, Samp. That guy chased me from his house with a pistol just because I was talking to his wife."

"He's really jealous of her?"

"I'll say. I consider that I was lucky to escape with my life."

Left alone while Jacques taught or worked in the library, Simone Messerand had volunteered her services to Wilhelm Bertrand when he posted a notice asking for French tutors and workers in the Language Laboratory. She would be glad to help, she told him. She would be glad to work in the lab and do tutoring as well. Bertrand told her that he couldn't offer her much money, but Simone said that any amount would be welcome since Jacques kept her on such a tight budget.

Once Samp had decided on his means of tormenting Messerand, his behavior changed insofar as his French course was concerned. He became studious. He had rarely darkened the doors of the French laboratory before this, but now he became a regular attendee. Besides studying and attending French lab regularly, he asked for special tutoring from Simone Messerand. It was obvious that he needed much help, so Simone scheduled him for three one-hour sessions each week. Much more attuned to the ministrations of the buxom Simone than those of her overbearing husband, Samp applied himself diligently at these sessions. In a month, Samp had mastered a good deal of first-year French and his accent had remarkably improved. In fact, he had made so much progress that Messerand no longer called upon him. Samp had not forgotten his earlier humiliations, however. His plan for revenge was still proceeding. Gaining academic respectability in French had simply been the first step in the plan. Mysteriously, messages on Messerand's blackboard began greeting the overbearing Frenchman when he walked into class: "Cherchez la femme," "Voulez-vous couchez avec moi se soir," and "Sacre bleu, soixante-neuf" appeared. Samp or some other student that he had enlisted always demanded that Messerand translate for them. Messerand usually turned the tables, assigning the phrase to some unlucky student to research and translate the next class period.

This black board attack was a mere diversionary tactic. Samp's main line of attack was through Simone. After her tutoring sessions, he bought her coffee in the cafeteria, he brought her apples and flowers, and otherwise endeared himself to her. On a more sinister note, however, he was slipping amatory notes in her books and other papers. These suggested a rendevous, lauded the sweetness of Simone's kisses, proclaimed the beauty of her breasts, and touted the delicate rosy color of the *fleur-de-lis* on her inner thigh (Samp had happened to see that one day when Simone's dress slipped up very high and revealed it and the fact that she wore no undergarment). Besides these notes, Samp surreptitiously dropped a couple of purported love letters to Simone among the papers on Messerand's desk.

After Messerand discovered these, he became livid and searched Simone's belongings. When he found some of the notes that Samp had placed in Simone's books and papers, he became convinced more than ever that she had a lover.

"You have a paramour. Who is this man?"

"Jacques, dear, I have no lover. What has brought this to your mind?"

Messerand showed her the love letters and the notes that he had discovered. "How do you explain these? Is it the work of that Joe Walker or is it that professor, Roger Duvant?" He struck her across the face, knocking her down.

Simone was almost speechless. She could not understand what was happening to her. Through her tears, she proclaimed her innocence. "I haven't seen these before now. I don't have any idea who is writing them."

At their next tutoring session, Samp observed Simone's bruises. Now it was time for the next step in his revenge. That night he took his guitar to the faculty house where the Messerands lived. He was pleased to see that the windows and doors were open. Standing in the backyard behind a large tree, Samp began to play his guitar and sing love songs. In a disguised voice, he loudly dedicated these to Simone. It was not long before Messerand appeared, pistol in hand.

"Who is there? I'll teach you a lesson you philandering yokel." Messerand fired his pistol toward the sound of the guitar. It grazed the oak behind which Samp stood but did him no harm. Laughing, he yelled in his disguised voice, "You shouldn't stand in the way of young love, old man." In a fury, Messerand ran into his backyard brandishing his pistol, "Tu muerde, you'll wish you had never heard of Jacques Messerand." Laughing, Samp slipped away, yelling back, "Sacre bleu, soixante-neuf." A bullet whizzed by him but did him no damage. Samp considered that he had exacted a modicum of revenge. When Simone appeared in lab the next day with many more bruises, Samp decided that he had obtained sufficient revenge. He had become fond of Simone and didn't want to cause her more suffering.

Everyone on faculty row had heard the shots, and a number of them came out of their houses to investigate the noise. They found Jacques Messerand running up and down the street waving his pistol and yelling, "Where are you, swine? Show yourself so that I can teach you the lesson you deserve."

"What is wrong, Jacques?" Adopho Hoppersmith was bemused by what he was seeing. "Have you any idea of what a spectacle you are making? Put away that gun and go home."

"Never has man had so much provocation, Adolpho." Seeing Roger Duvant standing among the onlookers, Messerand shouted, "There he is. There's the philanderer. Duvant." Messerand started to raise his pistol and aim it at Roger, but Adolpho and Mark Yeats grabbed him and took his pistol away.

"I've been in my house watching television with Betty. You can go ask her if you like. I have no idea what you are talking about."

"Do you play the guitar?"

"A little. What's that got to do with anything?"

"Somebody with a guitar was in back of my house serenading Simone with guitar music and love songs."

"Maybe it's a love-struck student. It certainly wasn't me. I've been in front of the television set grading papers all evening."

"I'll turn this pistol over to campus security tonight, Jacques. You can pick it up tomorrow after you've calmed down. It strains credulity to believe that Roger would be serenading Simone without his wife's knowledge." Adolpho waited until he was out of earshot before he began laughing. He enjoyed telling the campus security officer on duty about the incident. He even exaggerated a bit for comic effect.

"Sure does beat all. That Messerand's got a screw loose. You suppose he's the one that's been after Professor Duvant. He's had three attempts on his life this fall."

"I don't know. He sure would've tried to shoot Roger tonight if Mark Yeats and I hadn't stopped him."

Comedy Not Divine

Jaykyll again voiced his concern to Philwaggen that he was not making progress quickly enough in view of Roger's close calls and the undoubted hostility of the administration.

"On the contrary, Jay, I think we are making rapid progress. Don't worry. I'm encouraged that your trances are growing less frequent. Tell me what happened during your date with Ellie. According to my notes, that's where we left off."

"That night, I arrived at eight o'clock, books under my arm and the condoms in my pocket"....

Jaykyll slipped back into the past. Ellie smiled warmly as she let him in. She had made hot tea. They sat down at the table opposite each other to study, but only a few minutes had passed when John felt Ellie's foot touch his chair between his legs. Soon her toes were at his crotch rousing him with caresses. They moved their chairs together and John unbuttoned Ellie's blouse and massaged her breasts.

"Kiss me, Jay."

Books fell to the floor as he put his arms around her and kissed her, running his tongue deep in her mouth. They read no further in those books that night. Later, when John recalled the evening, he thought of the passage in Dante's *Comedia* where Paola and Francesca are overcome with desire while reading a particularly erotic passage. He and Ellie had not even needed an erotic passage to read.

When John first entered Ellie, he felt that he had crossed a great boundary in his life. For the first time he partially understood what the pleasure was that impelled so many people to destruction. The excitement of a sense of union with another being almost overwhelmed him with waves of emotion. He almost lost his sense of being somehow aside from the act he was performing. After a time, he felt that he was in love with Ellie and thought of her pleasure as well as his own.

As they lay together on the bed later, Ellie told him that she had never experienced anything quite like that before. She loved him. What about getting married?

Alarms began to ring in John's mind. He had no means of supporting a wife, and he did not wish to forego his education. Although they continued to make love for another hour, it was as if his mind were an observer taking note of the functions in which his body engaged.

In the days that followed, despite his attempts to suppress his desire for Ellie, thoughts of her began to thrust all others from his mind. The desires he was unable to control were dealt with by circumstance, because Ellie's relatives had become suspicious of what had happened the night that he and she babysat. Ellie would not let him avoid her, but their meetings were reduced to encounters after class in the library. He began to take a certain amount of sadistic pleasure in finding small ways to humiliate her. He would pretend not to want her in order to make her beg him for attention. Whenever she steered the conversation to the topic of marriage, he offered some examples of the unpleasantness created by that institution.

Gradually they drifted apart. Ellie found it easy to find other dates who did possess transportation, and she taunted Jay with them whenever they happened to meet after class. It was not pleasant for Jay to hear her tales, true or concocted, about her dates. He was forced to believe that much of it was true, as Ellie evidently had been in some rough sex and had hickies and other bruises to show him. John began to avoid her whenever possible. It was too painful for him to be with her even though he wished to see and talk to her....

Jaykyll found himself perspiring profusely when Philwaggen brought him back to the present. "I think we've made some positive breakthroughs today, Jay. As I suspected, your present attacks result from your wish to avoid conflict. I have come to believe that you must have had some of these trance-like attacks earlier in your life. Think back. Try to remember."

Having developed great faith in Philwaggen, Jay tried to oblige. Jaykyll thought back to the time when he was a young professor, a time before his marriage to Sarah. He remembered Karen Cleaver. "Yes, something similar happened a long time ago, but it didn't interfere with my professional career in any way, and I didn't completely lose consciousness very often."

"It is obviously important, Jay. We'll try to deal with it at our next session."

The Winter of Discontent

Malmuth Winter

When the leaves fall from the trees leaving them to stand like barren sentinels upon the hills and mountain slopes, the mountains seem to close in upon those living beneath them and in their hollows. It is a time when even minor emotional insecurities express themselves in bizarre ways. This winter, to be long remembered at Pine Mountain College as the Malmuth winter, proved to be a particularly unpleasant time for Betty and Roger Duvant. "Sardel's wooly worms were right," Roger thought when the Thanksgiving holiday brought with it a sixteen-inch snowstorm and motorists trying to reach home for the holiday stranded all around the region.

The wooly worm prediction continued to prove itself with two more large snows in December, two in January, and one in February. These were followed by one in mid-March and one in early April. The thirty-inch snow during the Christmas holiday was the deepest, but it did not cause the College community great difficulty because of its timing. The fall semester had ended, the students had gone home for the holiday, and a peace had settled upon the campus. Or at least it seemed peaceful to the casual observer. Underneath that seemingly benign, snow-covered exterior, danger lurked for Roger Duvant. For the Duvant family, the Christmas holiday held little peace while they were in Pine Mountain. They spent several weeks visiting family but returned to find that Roger's would-be killer had not forsaken his murderous schemes in recognition of the season. Roger first realized that he should not let his guard down one morning when the thermometer registered well below freezing. As was Roger's habit, he rushed out his doorway before breakfast for his morning sprint to the newspaper box. He was unpleasantly surprised when his feet flew out from under him as he set them on his stoop.

He tumbled head over heels down the steps and slid down a walk covered with ice. Another trip to the emergency room at the hospital ensued. This time Roger had a cut scalp, a broken arm, and fractured ribs. After taking her husband to the hospital and bringing him home with bound ribs, his arm in a sling, and bandages around his head, Betty walked up and down faculty row to examine the other walks and stoops. None was ice-covered. Few showed any signs of ice at all. Only theirs had a thick coating of ice. Betty's suspicions were confirmed. Whoever was seeking Roger's harm had not taken a break during the holiday season, though his efforts appeared to have become less deadly. "In honor of the Christmas message, no doubt," Betty thought. She shared her findings, some eggnog, and macabre humor with the invalid.

When Roger had recovered from his mishap and could move about without wincing, the ground was again covered with a thick blanket of snow. The world appeared pristine, pure, with its white blanket. His sons Tim and Johnny begged Roger to help them build a snowman and a snow fort. He helped as much as he was able. They were having great fun—the snow man completed and the snow fort half built—when Roger made a very unwelcome discovery. A large spring trap met his hands as he was gathering more snow to finish the fort. Luckily for Roger, he had touched only the lower part of the trap. Carefully he uncovered it. Large enough to trap animals as large as a wildcat or even a bear, the naked trap looked deadly. He had had another narrow escape. While the boys finished the fort using tested snow, Roger spent the rest of the afternoon going through their yard with a broom handle in hand, pushing it down into the snow every few inches to determine whether there were more traps lurking under the snow. He paid particular attention to any areas where the snow appeared disturbed. He congratulated himself when he found two other traps hidden under the snow. He felt like an army sapper clearing mines in a war zone.

The Duvants tried very hard to avoid developing a siege mentality. Roger in particular wondered where and when the next strike would come, but he was determined to keep living normally. When the snow had melted in January, Roger proposed that the family take a hike in Cumberland Gap National Park on the weekend and then have a picnic lunch. Betty made turkey sandwiches and fixed a thermos of hot chocolate. To the satisfaction of Tim and Eric, she added a batch of her Christmas cookies to the picnic basket. Dressed warmly, the four of them clambered into the car for the thirty-mile drive to the trailhead. The sun was shining, casting a bright glow on the landscape wet from the melting snow. The temperature was in the thirties the air was crisp against their faces when they began to hike. There were still large patches of snow here and there in shady places beside the trail and pools of water in the trail's low spots. They decided to hike a lower loop trail that would bring them back to the car after a three-mile hike over fairly level terrain except for two fairly steep hills. They had not hiked far before the boys ran ahead. Roger called for them to stay within earshot, but he and Betty weren't upset to have the noise moving ahead of them. They stopped to examine some tracks that Roger identified as those of raccoon. They heard ravens croaking as they circled overhead, and blue jays called from the trees around them but just beyond their view. About a mile and a half down the trail, they stopped again when Betty spotted some tracks in a patch of snow next to the path. As Roger bent over to look at them, an arrow whizzed past Betty and over Roger's head. It lodged in a poplar ten yards beyond them.

"Run, Betty!" Roger ordered.

They ran up the trail to where they heard the boys. Reaching Tim and Eric, each of them grabbed a boy by the hand and pulled him up the trail.

Roger gave another order. "Run, boys!"

They ran until they were completely out of breath. Slowing down and stopping to rest, they stood and looked all around. Nobody. The woods appeared empty except for the calls of a feeding flock of birds—chickadees, titmice, nuthatches, kinglets, and woodpeckers. Having recovered their breaths from the run, they began walking again-fast, getting back to the car uppermost in their minds. They covered the remaining mile in less than twenty minutes. Looking around where their car was parked, Roger found another set of tire tracks leading to and from a parking place where another vehicle had recently been parked. Had somebody followed them? That question dominated Betty's and Roger's minds on their trip home, although Betty and Roger kept the conversation on other topics to avoid frightening the boys more. They ate the picnic lunch Betty had packed after they returned home and the boys were settled in front of the television set watching *The Wizard of Oz*.

When Betty and Roger compared thoughts that night, Betty asked him about the tire tracks that he had found near their car. "Somebody arrived after we did and left before us. Do you think somebody followed us there?"

"I can't think of any other explanation. Not many cars go there this time of year."

"Then the bowman must be the person that's been trying to hurt you."

"I think so. Whoever it is must be getting very frustrated."

"By the way, Roger, what were those animal tracks we were looking at?"

"It looked like a bobcat was chasing a rabbit, but the rabbit got away."

That night they lay awake a long time before going to sleep in one another's arms.

Suspected Unethical Behavior

On a small campus like that of Pine Mountain College rumors develop rapidly and careen across the college community and into the larger world at full gallop. The rumor that President Malmuth was homosexual began to circulate soon after he had denied further funding for the Chalmer Botts Festival. Naturally enough Malmuth suspected that somebody connected with the Festival had concocted this unethical lie about him. Jaykyll and Duvant did not know who was to blame. They did know that Malmuth had blamed them, because he called them into his office. His brows were knitted and his voice shook.

"Which one of you is responsible for the rumor?"

"What rumor? I can think of several dozen going around campus and none of them involve you." Jaykyll was taken aback, but managed to fend off the grayness.

"You know what I mean. The scurrilous rumor that I am a homosexual."

"I hadn't heard that one, President Malmuth. Surely everyone here on campus knows that you are a widower."

"The rumor didn't start until after the Chalmer Botts Festival. It is just a coincidence, I suppose."

"It certainly is. Roger and I were too ecstatic about the success of this year's festival to start any rumors like that."

"All right. You deny it and I have no proof. Just keep in mind that I'm watching the two of you."

On their way by Sherri Whetman's desk, Jay bent over and whispered to her that the President had accused them of spreading a rumor accusing him of homosexuality. Sherri laughed. "I can assure you that rumor is false, Dr. Jaykyll." After they left the President's office, Roger asked Jay whether he had heard any rumors about Malmuth.

"Not that one, but I have heard one about his mishandling college funds. According to that rumor, he's using college funds for personal expenses. That seems a lot more serious to me. Maybe we should try to find out if there is any truth to that rumor. The rumor has it that both Bottleby and Malmuth are stealing money from the College. Do you know any way to check that, Roger?"

"Maybe. I know a young lady in the business office who might give us some information."

The need to combat Jason Malmuth had become clear to many more faculty than Jay and Roger. Lavender Large had decided to take drastic action. There was great secrecy about the meeting that she called. Lavender did not trust her message over the telephone. She delivered it by word of mouth out-of-doors with no other person around. Lavender was taking no chances. There was to be a meeting of the teachers involved in the Appalachian Studies program that weekend at the Large house on Saturday night at nine o'clock. It was extremely important to have 100% attendance. After John Jaykyll had agreed to come, Lavender told him that everyone would be there.

"They're all coming, Jay. I saved you for last because I knew we could count on you. See if you can get a ride with someone. We want as few cars as possible."

"I'm touched by your faith in me, Lavender. I'll see whether Nathaniel will give me a lift."

When everyone had arrived, Lavender served drinks. Then she announced that she and Jonathan had been thinking for sometime how to combat President Malmuth's campaign against rusticity. "We finally concluded that ultimately the most effective counter measure would be the removal of both Malmuth and Bottleby. To achieve that outcome, we believe that we need to form a secret group to coordinate our efforts to protect the Appalachian Studies program. Saving the program would be our immediate goal. Removing J.M. and J.B.

would be our ultimate objective. To that purpose we propose the formation of a secret society: RAU, Rustics Anonymous United."

"Hear! Hear! A marvelous idea, Lavender." Pauline Hauptman's enthusiasm was evident. "Through RAU we will create a row for Malmuth."

Jaykyll suggested that this could best be accomplished by enlisting the help of the Chalbotfest Committee, the community group that had been organized to continue the Chalmer Botts Festival after Malmuth withdrew the College's support.

"I think that many of the Chablotfest Committee and others who actively support the Festival might well be willing to participate in an effort to discredit Malmuth. I think we should contact Virgie Jones. She's president of Chalbotfest now, and I know she detests Malmuth. We should also enlist the members of the Pore Folks Frolic. That includes a great many of our graduates who have worked tirelessly for the College."

All agreed that Jaykyll's suggestion had merit. Lavender Large said that she saw Virgie when they both worked as volunteers at the Pine Mountain Hospital. She could talk to her there and enlist her help. Virgie's daughter Carole was on the Board of the Pore Folks Frolic, so she thought they could count on Virgie to tell Carole to enlist the support of the Frolic. They agreed that their first effort would be a peaceful public demonstration against Malmuth.

When Lavender told Virgie that she needed help in dealing with Malmuth, Virgie responded enthusiastically, "Honey, I'll be glad to help embarrass that bastard. And I think the Committee will vote to have a demonstration against him. I think we could probably round up a couple of hundred people. Where do you want us to demonstrate?"

RAU had already agreed on a demonstration route, so Lavender had only to tell Virgie what they had decided. The demonstration should start downtown in front of the courthouse and then march out to the College, where they would hang and burn a dummy representing Malmuth. The police needed to be alerted to the planned route, and a dummy Malmuth would have to be brought to the gathering spot at the College by somebody to coincide with the arrival of the marchers. Virgie was ecstatic. "Won't Malmuth be furious? Why don't we label the dummy Mercenary Malmuth, and the pile of wood we use for the fire to burn it could be labeled Rustic Faggots for the Faggot." Lavender told Virgie that she thought her idea a stroke of genius and that she should make sure that a reporter and photographer from the local paper were present.

"Get somebody from a TV station nearby or even one over at Lexington, too, if you can," Lavender told Virgie. "It would really be good to see the Malmuth effigy burn on the evening news."

The day of the demonstration came two weeks later. All was in readiness. The combined efforts of Chalbotfest and RAU produced a crowd of close to 300.

First, there were several fiery speeches condemning the elitist attitude of President Malmuth to get the crowd in the mood for action. Then they marched the mile down Main Street and out Arthur Drive to the College. When they arrived in front of the administration building, the effigy entitled MALMUTH THE MERCENARY had arrived, together with a tall post from which to hang it. When they had erected the post and strung up the effigy, they built a pile of brush beneath it. In front of the pile, they put up the sign reading RUSTIC FAGGOTS FOR THE FAGGOT. As another speaker harangued the group, cameras clicked and camcorders whirred. Soon throngs of students joined the rally. Their evident anti-Malmuth enthusiasm played well for the cameras.

Jaykyll spotted Alfred Molymo among the student demonstrators. "Hello, Ajax, are you enjoying the rally?"

Using the fruits of his months of labor, Ajax replied, "Indubitably, Professor Jaykyll, I find it difficult to recollect when I have enjoyed a castigation more than this. Unquestionably its blaze will provide highly symbolic message for our leader."

"Have you spoken to President Malmuth recently, Ajax?"

"I done...did what you told me, Professor. I went to see Malmuth. Assuredly I have. A few days ago I marched into his office and proclaimed my intention to go to graduate school in philosophy upon my graduation. I think it accurate to say that our leader was struck dumb. He finally found his voice and offered his congratulations on the improvement in my language skills."

"Did he say anything else?"

"He congratulated me on escaping the syndrome of the hollow. He said that he hoped I would never regress, never go back. Professor Jaykyll, I didn't like the sound of that. I don't want to give up my family."

"Just because Jason Malmuth turned his back on his family doesn't mean that you have to do it. Malmuth's a mountain boy who truly got above his raising, as the saying goes. You don't have to give up your ma and pa just because you've learned a little standard grammar and acquired an excellent vocabulary. It's up to you."

"I'm glad to hear that. Malmuth made me think that I shouldn't go back home."

"What you've learned will open doors for you, but it doesn't have to close any unless you choose to close them."

"I don't want to close any doors."

"I'm glad to hear that. Your success has been a real gift to me, Alfred. If I had any doubts about the worth of teaching, you've erased them. Nobody, not even President Malmuth, considers you to be stupid anymore, Ajax. Isn't the power of words amazing?"

"Truly wonderful. My classmates look on me with awe. I'm a living testimony to the power of words. They've made me secretary of my fraternity. Thanks for your help. You'll be in my thoughts constantly."

Finally, the great moment arrived. Virgie Jones was given the honor of torching the faggots. Smiling into the cameras, Virgie loudly proclaimed, "In lighting these faggots, I strike a blow for the

Chalmer Botts Festival and all mountain folk who are unashamed of their rusticity. May this fire be the pyre of the evil forces arrayed against mountain tradition." Loud cheers went up as the brush caught fire. Even louder cheers resounded when the effigy caught fire. It was nearly completely burned when the sound of fire engines was heard in the distance. Apparently Malmuth had called the fire department. To loud cheering, Virgie Jones dismissed the crowd. "It's time to leave. We can sleep better tonight knowing we have struck a blow against the tyrant." The demonstrators later found out that Malmuth had called the sheriff's office as well as the fire department. Sheriff Mullgrab had refused to interfere, however. Not only had he been informed by Virgie of what was to happen and asked to stay away, he was also privately incensed about Malmuth's interference with the college students who had been frequenting the sheriff's gambling establishment.

Watching from a window in the Administration Building, Malmuth and Bottleby were less ebullient. "This bodes ill for your anti-rusticity campaign, Jason."

"I will not be frightened from my course by a mob of yokels."

"Perhaps a bit of caution might be in order, however."

They were even less sanguine when they watched the proceedings on the evening news and read about it in the local and Lexington newspapers. The furor did not die down quickly but instead increased for a number of days. Sherri Whetman was kept busy answering irate calls from board members, donors, legislators, and many others who were not pleased by the negative publicity for the College.

Over cocktails, Jay and Sarah Jaykyll savored the moments as they relived them watching the evening news.

"It looks like our campaign is well under way, Sarah. I never thought we could garner so much public support. I suppose I underestimated the anger that Malmuth has generated."

Malmuth Winter Ends

The end of Malmuth winter came in late March, soon after the rally against Malmuth. The clouds disappeared and warm termperatures signaled gardeners that it was time to be about their spring plowing and the planting of early crops such as peas and potatoes. A gray haze could be seen hovering about some yards on the first warm afternoons as the more old-fashioned gardeners burned off the dead material from last year's crop. Where more contemporary methods had been employed, the green cover or leaf mulch was being plowed under the drying earth while the green buds were bursting forth from the birches and red buds from the maples.

Students at Pine Mountain College could be observed taking advantage of the warm spring sun all over the campus. The grassy areas adjoining the dormitories were speckled with blankets adorned with sunbathers. The women sun worshippers outnumbered the men, but groups of males in shorts and no t-shirts made their way through these islands of blankets. Ogling the scantily clad young women and offering their comments to their comrades-often in voices loud enough to be heard by the objects of their study-the young men offered their judgments. Those judged in turn were delighted that their charms were not unappreciated or chagrined if the comments overheard suggested a negative appraisal.

More athletically inclined students engaged in tossing frisbies, throwing baseballs, or playing tag football. Here and there, mixed groups of male and female students gathered about ice-filled tubs from which they pulled cans and bottles from time to time. Some of these looked suspiciously like beer containers, but the campus police had sense enough to avert their eyes and allow these rites of spring to proceed unfettered.

Forgotten were the dark, chillingly damp winter days when clouds continually hovered over the hilltop on which the campus stood. Those bleak days when the bare hardwood trees rose gaunt and gray on the hillsides had passed once again, and the redbud, sarvis, and dogwood blooms festooned the greening hills. The need for physical activity had drawn almost every student into the out of doors. Faculty row was not immune to the delights of spring. In front of almost every house there were faculty families sunning themselves or cavorting about over the lawns. At several houses, erected barbecue grills offered promise of festivities to come.

Even the current inhabitant of the President's mansion caught spring fever. To counteract the negative publicity stemming from the demonstration against him, Malmuth decided the time was appropriate for a large party to honor friends of the College and to woo prospective donors. He asked Sherri to get together a list of all of the board members, the federal and state legislators from the surrounding area, those who had made large donations to the College, and local people of wealth who might be persuaded to donate. "We'll have a big bash unless the weather turns cold. You never know here in the early spring, I've been told."

"That will be a large list, Jason. What if they all come?"

"We'll have this party outside and in and hope for good weather. We'll provide a large tent just in case the weather is bad."

Malmuth's luck held. The day of his great entertainment was as beautiful as the day of the Chalmer Botts Festival. Somewhere close to a hundred people showed up. The food catered by Malmuth's new food service proved delicious, and the Friends of Pine Mountain provided beer, wine, and hard liquor in satisfactory amounts. Sherri saw to it that everyone had plenty to eat and drink. While Jason Malmuth greeted his guests at the door, she buzzed about, seeing to it that everyone met the proper people and that they got to see the videotape about Pine Mountain College that had been set up to play in the den. "Pine Mountain has a wonderful story to tell," she assured them. We don't want you to miss it." To make sure they didn't, she had a second bar and video set up in the den.

Among the guests were the very large and very wealthy Ernest Becker, who had made his fortune in coal mining, and his daughter Melissa, who had recently graduated from Sweetbriar College in Virginia. She was a tall, willowy young woman whose blonde hair fell down to her shoulders. She might well have appeared on the cover of Vogue or McCall's or, better yet, been one of the girls to adorn the swimsuit issue of Sports Illustrated, thought Malmuth as he greeted her father and peered past his huge bulk to look at his beautiful companion.

"President Malmuth, let me introduce my daughter, Melissa Becker. She's come to work for me since graduating from Sweetbriar. She's beautiful and brainy."

"I'm very happy to meet you, Miss Becker. Had I known that you would be attending this gathering, I should certainly have had this group together sooner."

"Thank you, President Malmuth. It certainly is a gorgeous day for your party."

"More gorgeous because you're here, Miss Becker. Please call me Jason."

"Of course, if you will call me Missy."

"I'll be delighted. Mr. Becker, you and Missy go on in and make yourselves at home. I'll join you once I've greeted all my guests."

As they went in to the house and began putting food on their plates, Melissa chided her father. "To think I almost didn't come. Daddy, you didn't tell me that President Malmuth is handsome. Is he married?"

"I'm told he's a widower."

"Then your oversight was very reprehensible. I'm going to spend some time with that man this evening."

"Don't be too exclusive. I see another eligible young man over there. Not many faculty to be seen, so I guess Daniel Crockett's here because his old man has given so much money to the College. He's good-looking, and I can tell already that he has looked at you with more than a casual interest. I think he's coming our way."

"Hello, Mr. Becker. Good to see you. I'm sorry my father couldn't be here. He talks about you and the old days all the time."

Offering his hand, Becker gave Crockett a hearty greeting, "Good to see you again Daniel. I want you to meet somebody special to me. This here's my daughter Melissa. Melissa, say hello to Daniel Crockett."

"I'm truly pleased to meet you, Miss Becker," Daniel said as he took her extended hand. "I can hardly believe I'm seeing such beauty at a college function."

"Thank you, Mr. Crockett. If you two will excuse me, I need to powder my nose." Asking Sherri the way to the ladies' room, Melissa headed off. She wanted to look in a mirror and see whether or not her war paint needed any adjustment before she encountered Jason Malmuth again. Not entirely happy about being left with the older Becker, Daniel followed her with his eyes.

"You certainly have a beautiful daughter, Mr. Crockett."

"Call me Ernest, son. Your pa and me go back too far for formalities. Yes, she's a beautiful girl and she's bright. But she's mighty headstrong. If I tell her something's white, she'll swear it's black. I can see you're mighty attracted to her. That's fine. You're just the sort of man I'd like to see her interested in. But I couldn't do you any good, I'm afraid. You'd sure have my blessing if you dated her. Right now, though, she seems to have her eye on Jason Malmuth."

"Rumor has it he's involved with his secretary, Sherri Widderbe Whetman. She's that vivacious woman who's in charge of things here. She's pretty and she's nice. She's divorcing her husband. Everybody thinks she has her cap set for Malmuth."

"I'm glad to hear that, Dan. Maybe you have a chance, then. I guess there's no truth to the rumor that Malmuth's gay, is there?"

"Not that I'm aware of."

Leaving Dan to load his plate, Becker went in to the den to get a drink and watch the videotape. Seeing several of his coal-mining buddies standing in front of the television screen, he struck up a conversation with them. "That view of Pine Mountain College is a little different from the one we saw the other week on the evening news, don't you think?"

"Sure is. I was really worried about that. It didn't look good at all!" Senator Bert Woodville exclaimed. "I don't like what I've been hearing from some of my constituents. Seems Malmuth doesn't like the idea of mountain traditions being a part of Pine Mountain College."

"Wasn't he born in the mountains in Virginia?" Becker asked.

"That's what I've heard. I'm afraid we're dealing with a mountain boy that's got above his raising."

"Well, we'll have to do something about that," Rob Taylor asserted. Rob was a fellow surface miner and Bert Woodville's cousin, so Ernest Becker heeded what he said. "I think that some of us should go together and give a big wad of money to the Appalachian Studies program they have here. My cousin Virgie Jones is the lady you saw on television putting the torch to the fire that burned Malmuth in effigy. She says that Malmuth is doing everything he can to destroy the program. He has what he calls an anti-rusticity campaign underway. We could build a building to house the program and endow a chair to run it. Virgie says Malmuth is trying to get rid of the fellow who's running it now. She thinks he's a fine fellow. Knows his stuff. We could insist that the College appoint him as its first director of the newly funded program."

"How much money do you think it'd take, Rob?" Becker wanted to know.

"I reckon you and me wouldn't come up to snuff with Malmuth. I'm about as rustic as they come."

"In your case and mine, Ernest, I believe we're permitted our rusticity. I think rusticity becomes more endearing to Mr. Malmuth if it's accompanied by several million dollars. I think we could get everything I've mentioned done for no more than ten million dollars. You and I could give a couple of million each on the condition that others matched it two for one. What'd'you say Ernest? After all, it's just money."

"Could we name the building the Melissa Becker Center? That would make a great present."

"Sure thing. I'd like the Chair of Appalachian Studies to be the Rob Taylor Chair. Everybody who donates at least a million could have a room in the Center named for him."

All of Ernest Becker's cronies thought that Rob Taylor had hit upon a first-rate way to counteract the bad publicity Malmuth had created. It would also put Malmuth on notice that the people of importance in the region were not willing to have their Appalachian heritage trashed.

"Say," Ernest Becker added, "I saw young David Crockett's son Daniel a while ago. He's here in place of his father. He teaches in that Applachian program. He could be our liason with the College. We could set up a foundation, name it the Davy Crockett Foundation for Appalachian Studies. Daniel's pa ought to be good for two or three million or more."

"Great idea, Ernie. You talk to young Crockett."

Unaware of the forces that he had brought together to conspire against his anti-rusticity campaign, Jason Malmuth was basking in the attention of Missy Becker, who had indeed begun a campaign to capture him. She had cornered him at the outdoor bar and they were convivially comparing notes over gin and tonics. Missy had discovered that, though Malmuth was a Harvard man, he had taken graduate degrees at the University of Virginia.

"I've spent quite a bit of time on the grounds at Charlottesville, Jason."

"I imagine you were in great demand for dance weekends. The UVa undergrads adore Sweetbriar girls, I was told. Unfortunately, I was a graduate student with my nose to the academic grindstone."

"What field did you do your graduate work in?"

"Social science. I did my master's in psychology, but I switched to sociology for my doctorate."

"I was just a little old history major at Sweetbriar. I always did like to read biography. I suppose that's why I chose history. I imagine a life for everyone I meet."

"What kind of life do you imagine for me?"

"It's too early to tell, but I think you've had some unhappiness. Also I think you like to have your own way about things."

The two of them were so engrossed with each other that they did not notice Sherri Widderbe Whetman glaring at them. Daniel Crockett was also nearby observing them, and he took notice of the angry glances that Sherri was giving the couple. Daniel moved over to Sherri, "Misery loves company, Sherri. At least that's the adage. So I've come over to commiserate with you. It looks like you have a bit of competition for Jason Malmuth's attention."

"Hi Daniel. If I could, I'd tear him away from her so that you could have a chance. I've been watching you panting and drooling over Missy."

"Yes. She's a fox. She really turns me on. But he's a fool to forget about you, Sherri. You're as good-looking as she is. Maybe better. But you know how some of us men react to blondes."

"I never figured that out. Do you think I ought to dye my hair?"

"No. You've got gorgeous hair. Don't ruin it. The way Missy has captivated him, I doubt that he would notice. Besides her looks, Missy is heir to all that money. You won't be able to compete with that even if you do get a generous settlement from your husband. My reading of Jason is that money might captivate him far more than beauty."

"I hate to say it, but I think you're right. Whenever he's mentioned other women, he's always talked about how much money they have, or are likely to have. He's usually not very interested in poor girls, no matter how good-looking. If it comes to a contest between my settlement and Ernest Becker's fortune, I guess we know which will win out."

"I hate to say it, but I don't think there's much doubt."

"He'll rue the day, though. I'm not going to stand by and let him have her without retaliating somehow. I've invested too much in that man. God help me, Dan, I love the bastard. I have to laugh every time someone brings up that rumor about his being gay. Right now I wish he were."

"We don't have much control over that, Sherri. I think I've fallen for Missy at first sight, but it's likely to bring me nothing but heartache. I wish my pa hadn't asked me to take his place tonight."

"Let's keep our fingers crossed. I'll root for you if you'll root for me. We either both win or we both picked a lemon in the garden of love." Sherri grinned wryly at Dan as she moved away to see that everything else was going according to her orders.

Lovers' Revels

Exploring Karen Cleaver

Philwaggen was again eager to begin their next session. He didn't waste any time when he and Jaykyll met again. "John, we need to go back to the time that we talked about at the last meeting, the time that you experienced similar symptoms. Even though you say you maintained consciousness through most of these, they were probably foreshadowings of what you are experiencing today."

"I'll try. It was a long time ago when I was a young professor. I had been dating another woman, a colleague in the art department, at the time that I became enamored of Karen Cleaver. Though we had not become intimate, Jane Sims and I had been dating for some time. The college where we taught had a rule against romances among faculty members. Jane was very possessive...."

John recalled the first time he dated Karen Cleaver. When she learned of Jaykyll's going to a movie with Karen, Jane became frantic. The recriminations of the days that followed Jane's learning of his first date with Karen often shook Jaykyll to the core of his being, but a subtle shift had occurred in his dream world where he led an animal existence. His old fantasy continued, but it was now complemented by another. John found himself becoming a figure similar to the Mr. Hyde of Stevenson's story. John did not require strange chemicals, nor did his Mr. Hyde betray the murderousness that beset his fictional namesake. Unlike the old Jaykyll, however, the new man was a man of action. He made decisions quickly and was not bothered by doubts about consequences. Exuding an air of confidence, he knew what he wanted and acted with celerity and without remorse.

It was Jaykyll's new alter ego who met Karen when she came to his office the next day. Pulling her to him he quickly kissed her despite her gasp.

"Don't do that here."

"Why? Nobody saw. Didn't you like it?"

"Yes. That's not the point. We have to be careful. I have to lecture in a few minutes. I'm waiting for my class to start."

"I know. I know. Get to work and behave yourself."

Having Karen near him during the day was comforting to Jaykyll, and when he could, he called her in the evening.

She was a buxom young instructor who had only that fall arrived on campus. Although the administration at their college had mandated no romantic relationships among faculty members, John could not quell his desire for Karen.

"I have to see you again, Karen."

"My uncle has a cabin in the mountains. We can meet there if you can get away one afternoon."

"Okay. Let's meet Thursday."

Karen told Jaykyll how to reach the camp and promised him a picnic lunch. The sun was shining in the crisp air of late September. The leaves were already changing from green to reds and yellows. The goldenrods were waving their golden banners in the breeze just strong enough to move the boughs of the smaller trees. Jaykyll drank in the beauty unconsciously, for he could think little of anything else that day other than meeting Karen. As he drove along the mountain road to meet her, the yellows of the goldenrod and the blues of the asters along the roadside merged in his mind with Karen's hair and eyes. For him she was rapidly becoming a force of nature which he could not resist. Just to be near her had become very important to him. When he reached the camp, she was already there and came out to meet him with a smile that did more to brighten John's world than could the rays of the sun that managed to make their way into the dark hollow.

They embraced with a fervor that, for Jay, betrayed a touch of desperation about it.

"I already love you, Blue-eyes. I've missed being with you."

"How are things with Jane?"

"Not too good, but I'm getting by. I think I can handle Jane better now than I could before."

The cabin was cool and bare except for a couple chairs and a pallet in one room. Karen took Jay to the kitchen and made tomato sandwiches for them, although he slowed the process by kissing her frequently.

The heat of the autumn sun seeped into the cool cabin, casting a faint golden glow over them. Even though it was late September, maturing squash and tomatoes planted near the cabin had been left untouched by frost. Today's coolness suffused with a warm glow reminded Jaykyll of late October afternoons in western Kentucky before first frost when he and his father had dug bushels of sweet potatoes. It had to be done before frost because if frost deadened the sweet potato vines, the roots would be damaged also.

Jaykyll had brought tapes and a tape player. As they listened to music from the sixteenth and seventeenth centuries, they slowly undressed one another, playing the music of their bodies in harmony with the sound of flute, recorder, and violin. Jay had been studying the mythology of the ancient Middle East, and he could not help thinking that he and Karen were incarnations of ancient gods and goddessess. The pallet that Karen had prepared for them in this setting surrounded by garden and forest was even more truly the couch of Inanna and Dumuzi than had been earlier ritual beds in ancient Sumeria that he had read about. The goddess of love had come to him from over the centuries, Jay imagined, transforming her dark golden hair from the drying corn husks and stalks waiting in the fall fields for harvest. He ran his hands through her hair and over her body as though he were the wind rippling through the tassels of the corn and the swelling ears.

It was as though this was an afternoon that he had desired all his life. The quick movements of the birds in the trees, small passerines in their frenzy of evening feeding before they leapt off into the night to journey southward for hundreds of miles, echoed Jaykyll's quick pulse—large dynamo echoing the smaller ones. There was no sense of detachment in his lovemaking. He was hardly consciously aware of what he was doing, lost in a sea of sensuous delights as he and Karen moved their lips over one another.

"There's one small problem—if it is a problem."

Breaking from ancient seas, Jay struggled to consciousness. Groggily he answered, "What's that Blue-eyes?"

"I'm having my period."

"What difference does that make. I love you. I love everything about you."

Karen laughed. "Somehow I didn't think it would be a problem. Are you sure, though?"

In answer, Jakyll began to kiss her passionately as he slipped back into the ancient seas from which he had unwillingly surfaced. Lush tropical plants enveloped him as he imagined his mouth sucking in the succulent red flesh of a ripened love apple, a tomato heated by the golden red sun. He had entered once again the gardens of the queen of love. The shepherd king, cerebral man, had forsaken the arid life of the hills and entered into the fertile world of flowing springs and rivers. "I come to my garden, my sister, my bride, I gather my myrrh with my spice, I eat my honeycomb with my honey, I drink my wine with my milk." Karen answered her lover with soft moans as she ran her fingers through his hair. "How sweet is your love, my sister, my bride! How much better is your love than wine, and the fragrance of your oils than any spice!" Karen pulled Jaykyll to her. Her hips moved wildly, making it difficult for him to continue kissing her as her springs began to flow more abundantly and she groaned ectstatically. With great delight she sits in his shadow, and his fruit is sweet to her taste. Her king feeds among the lilies. He caresses her rounded thighs that are like jewels, her breasts that are like two fawns, her neck that is like an ivory tower, her hair flowing like a golden robe that holds him captive. Again emerging from the primordial oceans, Jaykyll slipped on the necessary protective device both of them regretted having to use and entered Karen; as their faces and bodies melded again, he lost all sense of being separate from her. They became one being. We see by this it was not sex. That greater soul which from love flows defects of loneliness controls. We then, who are this new soul, must pay the debt we owe the agents who created us. So must pure lovers' souls descend to senses, to arms and legs and eyes, through which the soul may reach and apprehend, else a great Prince in prison lies. How beautiful are your sandaled feet oh Prince's daughter, how full of delights. When the final mind-shattering explosion came to them both together, they lay intertwined and oblivious to time and their surroundings as they floated on ancient oceans in a ship made of sandalwood covered with beaten gold, moved forward without any seeming motion by a magenta sail of silk. About them happy dolphins cavorted for their entertainment, breaking the water in effortless, gigantic leaps that made no sound to disturb their dream-like ease.

When they returned from their dream voyage, they talked and teased and laughed together with a freedom that was new to John. Friendship without emotional reservations came upon him with such force that he felt newly born, puppyish. Finally, the reality of his situation intruded upon them. He did not want to part with Karen, but he had to get back to campus for a late evening class.

Jaykyll's drive home was through land that had been strip-mined and reclaimed a few years before. There was lush grass on much of the land, which showed none of the high walls or cliffs that were common for land that had been mined under the old laws. The grass of the man-created prairie contrasted vividly with the leaf colors of the trees on the mountainsides that had not been mined. Jay wondered if he could survive change in his life as well as the land could heal the scars of change.

He was too full of happiness and delight in the golds and reds of the autumn leaves shining in the early evening sun to become depressed, but a sense of foreboding began to grow in him as he approached his apartment. Everything was quiet outside, so he shrugged off these feelings and went inside. The half-empty fifth of gin on the table caught his eye first. Then he saw Jane lying on the sofa. When he tried to rouse her, she wailed softly and turned from him. Jaykyll should have felt guilt, he thought, but he could not, though fear for her gripped him. It was not like her to lose control. He had always counted on her being in control of herself. After all, she had been in control of him. He feared for her death, yet he could not help thinking how much simpler her death would make his life. For a brief moment he wanted her dead. These thoughts caused him to feel considerable guilt.

"Jane, wake up." He shook her until her eyes opened. Then he made her stand up and walk around while he heated a pot of coffee. When he had got her to drinking that and she had gone to relieve herself of liquid a couple of times, Jay made another pot and drank it with her.

"Where were you?" Jane snarled when she finally recovered enough to deal with the situation.

"Jane, you're not my keeper." Jaykyll felt some guilt in saying this, but his new, assertive self demanded to be heard—*The animal heard the dogs baying somewhere close behind him. Panting from fatigue, the panther summoned energy from its reserves and moved away from the sounds of its pursuers. It was less fearful now that it had been earlier*—As this dreamscape opened to Jay, he kept control and decided that he had better take Jane home. He walked her to the vehicle, loaded her in, and took her to her apartment. There he opened the door and dropped her into a chair as he dropped wearily into another—*Exhaustion from the chase had drained some of its instinctive fear and replaced it with a desire to be free of pursuit. When the lead dog of the pack, far ahead of the remainder of the dogs, sounded close behind the cat, the panther turned and waited for them. As they blundered upon their quarry, the cat reached out a forepaw and swiped at them, throwing the one aside with a large slash along its belly and knocking the other down with a crushed skull.* Regaining his control, Jay took Jane's key from her purse and opened the door to her apartment. He knew where the bedroom was though he had never been in it, so he walked her there and placed her on the bed. Taking off her shoes, he told her, as pleasantly as he could, "Jane, I'll talk to you tomorrow." He covered her with a blanket, walked out into the dusky dark, got in his car, and began the drive back to his apartment....

Called back to the present by Philwaggen, Jaykyll once again found himself sweating profusely. This time his head hurt dreadfully. Philwaggen gave him a glass of water and an aspirin.

"Jay, we are definitely making progress. These current trances of yours appear to me to be derived from a defense mechanism that you developed very early in life. The symptoms are more acute and dangerous today because you are, I regret to say it, somewhat older and even less able to deal with emotional conflict than you were in your younger days. There's no doubt about it, though. If we can uncover enough of your earlier episodes, we can conquer your present difficulties."

"I'm glad to hear that, though I doubt that President Malmuth will be equally happy to learn that I'm on the way to recovery."

Duvant Asks Belle: Finances

Though Roger did not dread Belle's summons now as he had in the past, he still approached Belle's Bottom with some nervousness. It was late in the afternoon, and few people were around when he reached Belle's door. Peering in, he saw Belle sitting on the sofa examining papers. Roger had to admit that she was a good-looking woman, thin but well-shaped. Her dark hair and eyes adorned a face that could have served as a model for Delacroix. Her legs were long and shapely. It was difficult for him to believe that such an extraordinarily beautiful woman was the wife of Hiram Grudger.

"Hello, Belle."

"Hi, Roger. Sit down here on the couch. I'm just going over some assessment reports."

Roger sat beside her. While he waited for her to finish, he couldn't help noticing her cleavage below her low-cut blouse. Belle caught a hint of his gaze out of the corner of her eye and laughed to herself. She closed the folder containing the reports. "What are you looking at, Roger? I can't let you see these assessment reports. They're confidential."

"I wasn't looking at them, Belle."

"No. Then what?"

"You. I was just observing what a fine figure you have." Roger wanted to put Belle in a good mood. He wanted some information.

"I'll believe you because I like compliments." Belle rose, closed her office door and locked it.

"Belle, do you know anything about the finances of the College? Could someone in the administration be misusing funds? I've heard rumors that people are spending the College's funds for personal expenses."

"No. I have heard some rumors, but I don't know any more than that. If anybody has sticky hands, they haven't told Hiram. If they had, I'd know. There are times when he can't keep anything from me."

"Who might be involved, then?"

"I suppose somebody in the business office would have to know. The people who could misuse money easiest would be the Provost and the President. There aren't so many people scrutinizing their expenditures, and both of them have funds they can use for unbudgeted purposes."

"Can you find out something?"

"Maybe. Let's go over these assessment reports for the Appalachian program. They look very good, Roger. I've been wondering how I can give Bottleby what he wants without endangering you. It occurred to me that I could give him a falsified version but submit a true version to the state council. That way, he'll think he has what he wants, but the official record will show the accurate figures. That way you and I will both be safe. Look here, if I erase some parts of these numbers, take off a zero here and there and take out a few glowing sentences in the written portion of the report, I can make your program appear less popular than it is. And if Bottleby and Malmuth ever catch on, I can just say that something went wrong when their copies were being made."

"Belle, you are a conjuror. I can't object. It sounds like a way to make them think they're winning without endangering you or me. It'll certainly take some of the immediate pressure off me and the program. I need the time to figure out what to do."

"Roger, you gorgeous man, I think I can be of great help to you. If you'll indulge me a little, I promise to find out all that I can about what Bottleby and Malmuth are spending money on. Now let's have tea."

Belle got up and put on some hot water for tea. While they waited for the water to boil, Belle sat on Roger's lap and kissed him.

"I've been thinking about you ever since our last meeting. I'll bet you haven't given me a thought."

"*Au contraire*, Belle, I've been torn between pangs of guilt and pangs of desire. If I felt I had a choice, I'm afraid the guilt would win out."

"I don't know whether to be angry or to be flattered. You make me sound like a real *femme fatale*.

"Yes, but I'm hoping you're an angel in disguise."

As she fixed their tea, Belle laughed. "I'll try to be your angel, Roger, but you have to accept that I'm a very horny angel despite being very good."

While they drank their tea, Belle snuggled close to Roger and kissed his ear, running her tongue into it, and running her fingers through his hair. "Roger, rub my back," she ordered as she undid her bra. He obliged, putting his arm under her blouse and running his hands over her back, massaging her with with wide circular movements. "That feels so good. Being a double agent in the administration is stressful. It tightens the muscles."

"Perhaps I should have adopted a career as a masseur instead of opting to become a professor."

"Yes, you have a definite talent for it. Roger, do you know Sardel Flannagan?"

"I sure do. I've collected from her. She's a wonderful informant. Why do you ask? Do you know Sardel?"

Belle laughed. "I've known Sardel ever since I was a kid. I bought a love potion from her some time back. You've been drinking some of it in your tea during our meetings. I drove up to her place again the other day to get this." Belle held up a large medallion with a raised metal figure of a woman hanging from a chain. "This is a good luck amulet. It's supposed to ward off evil. I think that you need it with a killer after you. Here, let me place it around your neck. Kneel down." The amulet safely bestowed around Roger's neck, she pulled him toward her and kissed him. "Roger, you do have such a wonderful touch. We can't let some demented jackass kill you."

RAU Work

Late one evening Betty Duvant answered the telephone. A woman asked to speak with Roger. She said that she had something important to tell him-something that he had asked her to find out. Roger made an appointment to meet Sophie Mulleteer that night at the Hardee's in Pine Mountain. "I'll bring Betty along, if that's all right. That way we won't arouse any suspicions. We'll just be some acquaintances that happened to meet over coffee." Sophie agreed.

Sophie was already there drinking coffee when Betty and Roger appeared. Buying decaf, they sat down across the booth from Sophie. "Roger, you know you asked me to check the unbudgeted accounts of Bottleby and Malmuth. I did, and from what I could see they're using those accounts to buy a lot of things that are personal items, not materials connected with their jobs."

"That's what we suspected, Sophie. If there are any items about which there can be no doubt, we need to have copies of those."

"I'll do the best I can, but I have to be careful."

"Please be. We don't want to get you into trouble, and we certainly don't want to alert Bottleby and Malmuth that we're looking into their accounts."

At the next meeting of RAU, Roger presented what information he had obtained from his informant in the business office. "Our informant wishes to remain anonymous for now but has promised to try to obtain copies of any forms that definitely indicate a use of College funds for personal expenses. We also need to find any corroboration of this from other sources."

"Great work, Roger. I think Roger deserves a round of applause." Jonathan Large's suggestion led to furious hand clapping and cheers.

As the cheers died, Daniel Crockett spoke up. "I have some good news. Help is on the way. There will soon be an announcement about a huge donation to the College. Malmuth has been told that there are some people thinking of making this large donation. What he doesn't know is that it will be tied to development of the Appalachian program that he's been trying to kill. Right now all of this is top secret, but I thought that it wouldn't hurt to speak in general terms. We've experienced so much lately to be gloomy about that I thought that something positive would be in order. So just hang in there and work to get rid of Malmuth and Bottleby. We'll make certain that Pine Mountain College has something more than image to offer its students. We will prevail."

"Daniel, you're like a waterbearer offering water to parched lips in the desert. We needed to hear something hopeful. Thanks." His spirits lifted, Roger smiled at Dan.

"I'm glad to have made you happy with good news. It's certainly a positive development, but I wish we could get rid of Malmuth soon-before he has time to worm his way further into Missy Becker's affections."

"She's a beautiful young girl. Beautiful and rich. I can see why you and Malmuth are interested in her."

"I think he's much more interested in her money than her beauty. That's just an added attraction."

Messerand Unmasks Samp

Grading papers that contained answers to an essay question, Messerand encountered handwriting that seemed strangely familiar to him. It was a good paper. He looked to see which student had written it. It was Sampson's. "Strange," thought Messerand, "he usually prints. The progress that this student has made is quite remarkable." Messerand went to get the "love" letters that he had found on his desk. When he compared the handwriting of these with the handwriting of the essay on the test paper of Sampson, they seemed very similar. What differences there were could be explained by the haste with which the test was composed compared to what must have been the comparative leisure possessed by the writer of the letters. Messerand resolved to ask Sampson to come to his house to go over the paper. He would say that it was an excellent effort, but there were a few points that should be cleared up so that he would not make the same mistakes again.

Sampson Sturgis proved too skeptical to accept Messerand's invitation. He had not been dubbed Samp the Scamp by other faculty for no reason. Of course, some nicknamed him Samp the Ramp because of his bad breath during ramp season. Samp thought the bulbs of the wild onion *Allium tricoccum* particularly delicious and could not resist them, a taste that caused others to shy away from him after he had been on a ramp-gathering and ramp-eating foray. Foiled in his first effort to lure Samp to his house, the Frenchman decided on another ruse. He would use Simone's tutoring as bait. He ordered Simone to write a note arranging to have Sampson's next tutoring session at their home. The day of Samps' next tutoring session, the Frenchman left the note instructing Samp to meet Simone at her home on the door of her office at the tutoring center. To prevent Simone from warning his proposed victim, he tied his wife to a chair and tied the chair to the kitchen table. Then he gagged her. He planned to remove the gag at the appropriate time and force Simone (with his pistol at her head) to call to Samp that the door was open and to come in.

Following the instructions left for him, Sampson arrived at the Messerand house a few minutes after the appointed time and knocked on the door. As she was instructed, Simone called to him that the door was unlocked and for him to come in. Messerand quickly replaced the gag and moved toward the door. When Samp stepped into the room, he found Messerand's pistol in his face. "You wrote those love letters to my wife. You two have been carrying on an affair during your tutoring sessions."

Now Samp regretted his cleverness. It had backfired on him. He thought quickly. His best course would be to tell the truth-part of it, anyway. "Professor Messerand, no. I haven't been having an affair with your wife. You must be mistaken about the letters you mention. My handwriting is very ordinary. Lots of people write like me. But I think you ought to know that several people in the tutoring center know I came here. Besides that, some friends are expecting me to meet them back at our dorm in an hour."

Messerand paused to consider Samp's defense. While thinking it over, he tied the student to a chair beside Simone and gagged him. If Samp were telling the truth and he carried out his plan, he would be suspected immediately. Perhaps he should have Simone do the shooting. That would be risky, though. She might turn the pistol on herself or even upon him. He could force them to the bedroom and force them to have sex and then shoot them in the act. That would give him the defense of a vindicated jealous husband. He dismissed that idea after some thought. He'd lose Simone, and an American jury might not think his action justified. Perhaps he should consider a punishment less drastic than murder. A whipping might partially suffice. But besides the whipping, Messerand would make this lover of Simone suffer further. He would have sex with Simone before his eyes. He would torment him with a sexuality that he could not have any more, then he would abuse him. Yes, that seemed to Messerand to have the appropriate symbolic justness. "That will be my revenge. I will torture him with varieties of the beast with two backs. Even if he's not guilty of the letters, he is guilty of something with Simone."

No sooner decided than put into action. Messerand delivered his decision as if he were a judge pronouncing sentence. "You are both guilty. Therefore both must be punished. Since your guilty acts have created the beast with two backs, you will be punished accordingly." Messerand went to get the whip he used regularly on Simone, leaving the two captives to look at each other in horror. Returning with the whip in hand, Messerand released Simone and told her to undress.

"Do you mean undress here, Jacques?"

"Oui. Undress in front of this pig."

Simone slowly did as he ordered. Then he told her to untie Samp's legs and remove his lower garments, then retie him. Once Simone had completed all her assigned tasks, he ordered her to prepare Samp. As she followed his orders, Messerand began laying on her back and buttocks with his whip. After a few minutes, he asked her whether her lover was erect. She answered that he was, and Messerand pulled her away and began lashing Sampson's nakedness. Though Simone had endured her lashing in stoic silence, Samp did not. He howled in pain through the gag in his mouth. Despite the gag, his howls could have been heard throughout the house had there been anyone else there to hear them. Messerand could hardly contain his glee. "Fornicator, how does the whip feel? You have dealt me some blows by using my wife and now you must receive some blows from me." When the Frenchman tired of lashing Samp, he turned his attention back to his wife. Forcing Simone to bend over the table and present her backside to Samp, he whipped her until her buttocks glowed, then engaged her. Turning his head to leer at Samp, Messerand entered Simone. "Is this how you accomplished the deed, my young fornicator?" he asked as he turned his attention fully to Simone. By now Samp had become distraught. He rarely found himself in a state of terror, but he now found himself in exactly that state.

For some time he had been trying to free himself. He had succeeded in untying his hands first and, when Messerand was preoccupied with Simone, he untied his legs that Simone had retied loosely, threw off his bonds and ran for the door. By this time Messerand had become too engrossed to notice immediately. Samp made it through the front door. The maintenance crew that was arriving to do some work at the Duvant's house looked on in amazement as Samp, without his pants and with blood running down his legs, rushed out of the Messerand house, across the grass, and over to the Duvant's door. He knocked on their door with what was apparently his last energy. He was crumpled writhing on the stoop when Betty Duvant opened the door.

"Roger," she called to her husband, "I believe Samp Sturgis is lying half-naked at our doorstep." Roger rushed to her side and together they pulled Samp in the house just as Jacques Messerand peered out of his door looking for the student.

With amazed glances at each other, the college service crew pulled up their truck in front of the Duvant's house as they watched the strange scene unfolding in front of them. Joe Walker and his companion had been sent to repair plumbing at the Duvants. They saw Messerand appear at his door, whip in hand, in time to observe as Betty and Roger pull a half-naked and bleeding Sampson Sturgis into their house.

"You never know what to expect at Messerand's place," Joe Walker told his companion. "If his classes are anything like his home life, I don't want any part of them."

Malmuth and Melissa: Louisville

Enthralled, Missy had listened to Jason talk about plays he had seen and museums that he had visited in New York. She was eager to go with him and have him act as her guide in the Big Apple. She thought that it might also give her an opportunity to take a bite out of the same apple that Eve had sampled. But Jason pleaded work. Why not go to some place closer where they could drive for a long weekend? She agreed to save New York for the future. When he asked her to accompany him to Louisville for a long weekend, she accepted without a moment's hesitation.

Early Friday afternoon, Missy pulled into the parking lot next to the administration building in her sporty red two-door Mercedes. Shortly thereafter Malmuth appeared with an overnight bag, which he placed in the trunk. Then he got into the car on the passenger's side. Missy and Jason roared off while a very unhappy Sherri Whetman looked out through a window in Malmuth's office overlooking the parking lot. Sherri had made reservations for him in Louisville, and she suspected who was accompanying him. On 25E through Flat Lick and over to Corbin, Missy put the car through its paces on curvy roads at speeds five or ten miles above the posted limit. Past signs saying, "Honk, if you love Jesus" and "Slow down, the next life you save may be your own" she sped, passing slow-moving coal trucks creeping up hills and otherwise showing her mettle as a candidate for the race car circuit. Missy joked about the trucks displaying "Better coal than cold" and "We dig coal" signs. "They scatter it all over the highways, too," she joked. At Corbin they moved onto I-75 and headed north at 80 miles an hour. "How do you like the way this car handles, Jason?"

As he wiped his forehead, Malmuth agreed that Missy had a beautiful machine. "You drive well. I'm impressed. Beauty, brains, and driving ability."

"It was a graduation present from Daddy. You should see my aerobic form."

For the rest of the trip, Malmuth navigated. At Lexington they left I-75 and headed west on I-64. At Louisville they turned onto I-264 and headed toward Churchill Downs and the motel where Sherri had reserved a suite. When they had checked in to the Ashton Inn and found their way to their room, Missy hung up her clothes and investigated their lodgings. There were separate bedrooms, a large central room, and a room with a jacuzzi. Missy suggested to Jason that they put the jacuzzi to use immediately.

"That was a long drive. I need to relax before we eat."

Jason agreed that was a good idea. He changed into his bathing trunks and went in to prepare the tub. He set the machine on medium, stepped in, and sat down facing the door. He had a full view of Missy when she opened the door and entered. She had a marvelous figure, he noted, and he could see almost all of it. Missy's pink two-piece bathing outfit consisted of a scanty bra and an almost imperceptible thong bikini that did not completely conceal her blonde pubic hair.

"How's the water," she asked.

"Fine. I set the tub on medium. You can raise the temperature if you want."

Missy dipped her toes in to test the water. "No, it's just right." She sat down beside Jason and took his hand in hers. "Those jets feel great. I feel my muscles loosening already." She wound her right leg around Jason's left and wiggled her toes against his right leg. "Can you feel that?"

Jason agreed that he could. "You have beautiful legs, Missy. But your entire figure deserves that adjective."

"Do you like my bathing suit."

"Yes, it certainly doesn't hide your beautiful body."

"I think we should admire the human body. At college I took several art classes. One in the representation of human anatomy—my professor thought I had a flair for portraying the human figure. She thought I could make a living with my art. Why don't you model for me, Jason? I'd like to draw you sometime. Right now I'd just like to see your body. Why don't you take off those trunks. I'll take off my suit so that you won't be embarrassed bare ass." She laughed at her pun as she slipped off her bikini and threw the pieces over the lip of the Jacuzzi. Still laughing, she pulled Jason up and, despite some weak protests, pulled down his trunks to his ankles. "Now, Jason, put your trunks beside my outfit and let me look at you."

He followed her suggestion and stood self-consciously facing her. Malmuth worked out regularly and watched his weight. His lean, well-proportioned body did not betray signs of middle-aged spread. "You have the body of a young man. I definitely want you to pose for me, Jason. Don't forget."

"I don't think I could," he muttered as they sat down in the tub again.

"I feel much freer without the covering. The swirling waters can reach delightful places now, don't you think?" She had been observing him closely as she said this. "You're a rarity, Jason. You haven't been circumcised. All the models we drew in class were."

"I was born at home, Missy. My parents never bothered."

"Well, it certainly provides me with a new experience"

"I'm very confused right now, Missy. I think we'd better get dressed for dinner."

Still laughing, Melissa stood up and began toweling. After a few moments to recover his equilibrium, Malmuth stood and joined her in drying off. They went to dinner at a small Italian restaurant a few blocks from their suite. The clerk at the desk had recommended it. Over Alfredo fetticine and veal marsala, they talked about the race. That would be tomorrow, the first Saturday in May. Their rooms were fairly close to Churchill Downs. They could sleep late, have the continental breakfast, shower, dress, and still have time to visit the Kentucky Derby Museum adjacent to Gate One of the race-track.

They could see the exhibits, take the 30-minute guided walking tour of Churchill Downs and still have time to eat lunch before the races began.

"I'm really looking forward to the ambiance of the races, Jason. I don't care about any one particular horse. I don't even know the horses' names. They all look beautiful to me."

"To me also. I suppose we should bet a little, but there's no law that says we must. We can just watch them run if that's what you want."

"Let's. I don't want my experience of the race to be clouded by a bet. The next time I come to the Derby maybe…not tomorrow."

That night they watched a program about the Derby on television. Malmuth broke out a bottle of gin and some bottles of tonic water. They sipped several gin-and-tonics while they watched the Derby program. Melissa sat on the sofa, Malmuth in an arm chair. After he had given her a third drink, Missy tired of waiting and decided to take a direct, more aggressive approach. "Sit beside me, Jason. I won't bite."

Malmuth dutifully sat down on the sofa with her. "Does your father have business interests other than mining?" he asked.

"He does now. He started with strip-mining coal at a good time and did well. Daddy was smart. He diversified. Now he owns oil wells, motels—I don't know everything he owns. He has a lot of stocks, bonds, and real estate. Why do you ask?"

"He and some friends of his have discussed donating a large sum—millions—to the College."

"What friends?"

"David Crockett, Rob Taylor, and some others."

"They're good for many millions. I wouldn't do anything to rile them, though. Nobody can tell them what to do. They know what they want. So do I."

Turning to him and placing her free hand on his thigh, Missy told Jason to kiss her. He put down his drink, took her in his arms, and then kissed her gingerly. She pried his lips apart and thrust her tongue deep into his mouth. "You do like me, don't you, Jason?" she asked as she drew back after a long minute.

"Of course I do, Missy. I'm just not a very expressive person."

They kissed some more before going to their separate bedrooms. Missy thought to herself that, should she ever be in charge of reserving rooms on future trips, she would make certain there was only one bedroom and one bed. She wondered if the rumors that she had heard about Jason Malmuth's homosexuality were true.

The next day the excitement of the crowds and the races caused Missy to forget Jason's cool behavior the night before. Missy enjoyed seeing the history of racing in the museum. Names like War Admiral and Nashua meant a little more to her now. She still had very little interest in any of the individual horses racing that day. Too busy taking in the crowd, the many beautiful horses, and the rest of the scene, Missy could not be bothered to pay attention to any one horse. She cheered the winners of every race leading up to the Derby as well as the winner of the Derby itself. By the time they reached a restaurant for dinner, she had become ravenous. She ate a thick steak while Jason contented himself with chicken marsala. "You certainly developed an appetite today," he commented.

"It was an exciting day. I believe I could eat a horse if they served it."

Back at their suite, they settled down in front of the television set to watch Saturday Night Live and sip gin-and-tonics again. Tonight Jason sat beside Missy on the sofa without coaxing. After their second gin-and-tonics, Jason asked, "Have you ever thought about marrying, Missy?"

Surprised, Missy paused before answering. "Every girl has thought about marrying. I haven't yet thought about marrying anybody in particular."

"If I asked you to marry me, would you think about my proposal?"

"I don't like to deal in hypotheticals."

"Will you marry me, Melissa?"

"I'll think about it."

Jason drew her to him and kissed her. Then they went to their separate beds. This night Missy had a great deal to think about. Jason had yet to display any great passion or even much affection—really had not even made much of a pass at her, had been far too gentlemanly to suit her. Yet he had asked her to marry him.

Next day they did some sightseeing after a late brunch. Jason catered to Missy's interest in history. They visited Cave Hill Cemetery and Arboretum and the Locust Grove Historic Home, a restored 1790 Georgian mansion that became the retirement home of Revolutionary War hero George Rogers Clark. Missy drove the return trip with her usual speed, but it was dark when she dropped Malmuth off at his mansion on the Pine Moutain College campus. "Be careful driving home," he told her before giving her a good-bye kiss on the cheek. "I'll call you tomorrow."

Ambush

Though he was not absolutely certain that Sampson had written the love letters, Messerand was absolutely sure that Duvant had interfered with his revenge on Sampson. Together with his certitude that Duvant had played the cuckoo in his nest, Messerand could not refrain from simmering hatred of his colleague and neighbor. All of Messerand's suspicions were groundless, but by this time the Frenchman's jealousy had grown to such proportions that he had completely forsaken reasonable action where Simone and Duvant were involved.

Simone's life had become a living hell. She often visited Betty Duvant to talk about her troubles. A compassionate woman, Betty could only shake her head in sympathy when Simone told her of Messerand's treatment of her. She told the young girl that she knew of no other husband who treated his wife in this fashion. "If you had the money, you might divorce him. If you knew somebody living away from here, you could flee him. Since you have neither of these options, I guess I can only tell you to come here if things become too frightening."

Betty told Roger that she didn't know how Simone could live with the man. "Not only is he cruel, he is perverted. In bed and out. If you required of me what he demands of her, I would divorce you."

Despite the seriousness of the matter, Roger could not help laughing a little. "Betty, what on earth could he be asking of her? I thought that you and I had pretty well covered the possibilities for achieving sexual pleasure."

"Not by a long shot. You're not mean enough nor crazy enough to do the things he does. You haven't demanded intercourse over the john. And even that's not half of what he demands. The man has an anal fixation. He's gross as well as being a jealous maniac. He requires her to lick his feet before they go to bed just to symbolize that he commands the household. And not a day goes by, she says, that he doesn't accuse her of infidelity with any number of men, you included. Then there's that pistol. He often holds that pistol of his to her head while she provides him with oral sex. He jokes that there's a pistol to her head while she gives head to his pistol. Another case of his demented symbolic behavior. He ties her arms to the bedposts and beats her butt with a whip before having sex with her. He calls it warming the oven. It's a wonder Simone isn't completely crazy. I'm certain she's headed for a nervous breakdown. What worries me even more, Simone says that he is constantly threatening to kill you. I'll bet he's the one who's made all those attempts on your life."

"I'll try to be careful. You're right. He probably is the one."

Roger waved good-bye and set out on an evening jog. He tried to stay alert and not daydream just in case Messerand lurked somewhere. He fingered the medallion Belle had given him. "I sure hope this thing works," he muttered to nobody in particular. The dark was beginning to erase the last rays of the sun.

As he passed by the trees at the picnic ground, he heard the report of a rifle as a bullet whizzed by his head and hit a tree that he had just passed. As he dropped down, another bullet passed overhead. "Messerand, I'm on to your game," he yelled as loudly as he could. "You'd better quit now before I have you hauled in for attempted murder." Even if he were wrong, it could do no harm, Duvant thought. If he were right, he might throw enough of a scare into the Frenchman so that he wouldn't try again. He waited until a car passed. He didn't hear any more shots and he thought he heard somebody running away. It was probably his imagination, but he also thought he heard a dog howl. "I wonder if that was old Bo? If it was, I guess I'm not free of my would-be killer yet." Shrugging off the thought, he got up and finished his jog. When Betty asked him how his jog had gone, he told her about the shots, about what he had yelled, and about thinking he heard a man running off.

"Don't you think we ought to call the police about this, Roger?"

"No, we really don't have any evidence except the threats he's made."

"I hope we don't have to wait until he makes good on them to call the police. I'm tired of this, Roger. If you won't call Sheriff Mullgrub, I will." As Roger made no move to pick up the telephone, Betty proceeded to carry out her threat. She talked directly to Mullgrub, detailing the chain of events that had led up to the latest attempt on Roger's life. Mullgrub assured her that he would look into the matter.

After hanging up the telephone, Mullgrub turned to Corduroy Carl Sims, who had been making a report to him when Betty's call came. "There's something funny going on out at that college, Cordurory. Somebody's trying to kill Professor Duvant. His wife suspects that crazy French professor, but I'd bet Malmuth has something to do with it. The way I hear it, he's trying to get rid of Duvant. Jason Malmuth's meddled in my affairs more than I like. I'd be a happy man if I could pin an attempted murder rap on him. See what you can find out about what's going on out there. You have any college boys in jail right now?"

"No. Not now."

"Next time you do, pump them for information. I'll advise the men to make sure you get some college boys soon."

"All right, Sheriff. I'll do my best."

Malmuth Attacks faculty

As the time for the regular monthly meeting of the faculty drew near, Malmuth told Jeremy Bottleby to instruct Hiram Grudger to allot fifteen minutes on his agenda for a message to be delivered by the President. Bottleby informed Grudger that he had best expect to have a long faculty meeting. "President Malmuth wants the first fifteen minutes on your agenda," the Provost told an apprehensive Dean.

Rumors were swirling about the campus of Pine Mountain College. One of these rumors indicated that there were donors who proposed to give a large sum of money to the College on the condition that Malmuth step down. Another rumor had it that there was to be a holiday in place of founder's day and that it would be Malmuth Day. A third rumor held that Roger Duvant had been fired. Of course, there was still the rumor about Malmuth's sexuality—only now the rumor had been embroidered to indicate that the President and the Provost had been caught in a compromising situation in a motel in Middlesboro. Grudger suspected that Malmuth would address some of these rumors, and he did not look forward to the meeting. He told his wife that he anticipated a difficult meeting. She tried to assure him that all would be well, but he would not give up the notion that something dreadful was going to occur. In fact, he was so distraught that he refused Rauncibelle's offer to play a sex game the night before the meeting. She took his temperature. "Hiram, you must be coming down with something. I'll fix you some chicken soup."

The afternoon of the meeting the weather itself proved ominous. After weeks of beautiful weather, a storm hit just before the meeting started. Many of the faculty looked half-drowned when they arrived at the auditorium. After Grudger introduced the President, there was a little perfunctory applause.

Malmuth scowled at his audience before beginning to berate them in a surly, accusatory tone. "Ladies and gentlemen of the faculty. I have been President of Pine Mountain College for only a few months, but these have certainly been eventful months. I cannot say that all of my experiences here have been pleasant. I have made Herculean efforts to change the image of this college, but there are those among you who have fought we at every turn. I think that our efforts to change our rustic image have been thwarted far too often by a group hostile to me.

"The actions of many of our students contribute to the atmosphere of rusticity that I have tried to expunge from this campus. Not only is their language an affront to standard English usage, their growing of marijuana on campus, their predilection for panty raids, and their running naked over the campus all contribute to an atmosphere of rusticity. Now some of them have had the misfortune to be arrested for drunk and disorderly conduct in town. They were returning from a bout of gambling in a gambling den several miles on the other side of town. Sheriff Mullgrab has informed me that they will be held for trial unless some means (he hinted that the means would be monetary) can be found to persuade him to drop charges against them.

"That would be bad enough, but malicious rumors have been spread about me. Personal attacks that damage a person's reputation should not be a part of campus politics, but there have been vicious personal attacks on me. These attacks have not only sought to hurt me but have included Provost Bottleby as well. It is my belief that these attacks are largely the work of faculty involved in the Appalachian Studies program. I do not need to name names. You know who these people are. My sources of information suggest that they are responsible for the burning of me in effigy and then spreading the incident through the media.

"I want you to know that I will not consider these matters lightly. Evidence will be assembled and the guilty parties will be punished. It may take some time, but you can be sure that the guilty parties will suffer. Despite backbiters, we shall change the image of this school from that of a haven for rustics and rustic endeavors to one of sophistication and truly collegiate enterprises. Our Move to Olympus campaign is gaining support from prominent donors.

"In an effort to improve our image, I have had attractive signs put up identifying every building on campus, I have enlisted the services of a top-flight food service, and I have seen to it that our admission standards have improved. I would have improved them more except for the obstinacy of the Admissions Committee, which accused me of acting too precipitously."

Listening attentively though unhappily, Roger Duvant thought, "Yes, you thought that you could raise entrance requirements to the point that we would have no local students. You thought you could strike a blow against rusticity and the Appalachian program that way. You refuse to believe that there are other criteria than SAT scores."

Malmuth continued by announcing changes that he was orchestrating in the administration effective immediately. John Jaykyll would be replaced as head of the English Department. Ichabod Balboa would replace him. Roger Duvant no longer would supervise the Appalachian program. Young Julie Cabot would take on those responsibilities. In addition, Dr. Jaykyll no longer would head the Admissions Committee. Adolpho Hoppersmith would be the new chair.

After Malmuth's diatribe ceased, he was greeted with whistles from all directons—so many that he could not focus on any particular one. Dean Grudger stepped to the podium to intervene and calm the gathering. "I'm sure that we all will take note of the President's words and treat them with the serious attention that they deserve. Thank you for your comments, President Malmuth." Grudger did not want to run the risk of a donnybrook. He closed the meeting. "That's all we have time for today. We'll meet again in a few weeks. Meeting adjourned."

Afterwards, alone in his office, Hiram Grudger congratulated himself on his successful damage control. It could have been worse. Malmuth had expressed his wish to replace Wilhelm Bertrand as head of the language faculty. He had wanted to put that madman Jacques Messerand in charge of the department. It had required all of Grudger's powers of persuasion to convince Malmuth that it would be unwise to advance a foreign national to an administrative position. He had had to promise that he would find some other way to reward Messerand for his enthusiastic support of the anti-rusticity campaign.

"Perhaps we could give him the Outstanding Faculty award at graduation," he had suggested.

"Yes, that might be a fitting reward. Please see that is done." Though Grudger thought that this would make a mockery of the award considering Messerand's unpopularity with the students and his fellow faculty members, he sighed a great sigh of relief when Malmuth agreed with his suggestion.

Malmuth Plays Golf

As part of his efforts to curry favor with prospective donors to the College's Move to Olympus Capital Campaign, Jason Malmuth invited a number of wealthy golfers from eastern Kentucky to the Pine Mountain Resort for a weekend of golf and conviviality. The country club served much of southeastern Kentucky. It was a Mecca for monied people. Set above the town of Pine Mountain on a wide plateau, the colonial architecture of the clubhouse seemed very much in harmony with the wooded mountainsides that formed its backdrop. Not only its architecture but the entire ambiance of the clubhouse suggested that the entire operation had been transported from somewhere in the plantation south. The only feature working at odds with this colonial atmosphere seemed to be the white staff supervised by an African-American manager, Jim Nevis. He had received his degree in hotel management from a prestigious northern university. Nobody cared to inquire which—that it was a northern university told all they wished to know. Recognizing his handicap, Jim Nevis kept a low profile and saw to it that his chief of public relations, Carol Ann Breathitt, handled any matters that required interaction with the guests. Nevis thanked Providence that there was a black community in Middlesboro and that he did not have to reside in Pine Mountain, where there was no black community.

Notwithstanding his racial heritage and his "handicap" of having been educated at a northern university, Jim Nevis saw to it that the Pine Mountain Resort exuded an atmosphere of southern gentility and hospitality. Jason Malmuth had found Nevis a man in tune with his ideas. There was no rusticity at the Pine Mountain Resort that Malmuth could detect. Even the most menial help betrayed few traces of mountain dialect, and they were always eager to serve.

Jim Nevis himself played golf. No doubt as much for his own delight as for that of the guests, he saw to it that the resort course pleased both professionals and rank amateurs. For the amateurs, the holes were given par within easy reach of golfers who had advanced only a little beyond the average duffer. For the professionals, the course demanded a high degree of skill. The greens and fairways were kept in top condition, as were the trees and shrubs lining each fairway. Jim Nevis acted as his own golf professional, a plum that contributed greatly to his willingness to remain at Pine Mountain Resort when other enterprises sort to lure him away. During the interview process for the presidency, Malmuth had been introduced to Nevis and had played a few holes with him. This experience had contributed heavily to his decision to come to Pine Mountain, for Malmuth's interest in golfing could best be described as passionate, although some people termed it obsessive. He considered golf the game for the sophisticated person.

It seemed only natural, then, for Malmuth to use golfing weekends at Pine Mountain Resort as a means of raising funds for the College. Some time after the party at his house, he arranged a golfing weekend with David Crockett, Ernest Becker, Bert Woodville, and Rob Taylor. As they had left his get-together at the President's mansion, Becker, Taylor, and Woodville had indicated to him that they and David Crockett anticipated making a very large donation to the College, but they did not tell him what strings they were planning to attach to this donation. Malmuth had evidently fallen so far under Melissa Becker's spell that he merely thanked them and did not inquire about what they wished to provide the school. Preoccupied with arranging a trip to Louisville with Missy, he did not think much about their offer until the next morning. As usual, he left the arrangements for the golfing weekend to Sherri, although he told her specifically to include Melissa Becker in the invitation. "She's a golfer, too," he offered as explanation. Fuming to herself, Sherri had carried out his orders. "First that trip to Louisville," she thought. "I made all the arrangements and then he took her. Now this. That bastard plans to dump me for her. He'll rue it if he does."

The weekend weather cooperated with the golfers, although Malmuth spent almost all of his time in a twosome with Missy, while his other guests played in a foursome. The foursome took note of the arrangements.

"I think President Malmuth has his eye on Melissa, don't you, Ernest?" Rob Taylor joked. "I think he's willing to make an exception for us rustic fellows in some instances. I think he wants you for a father-in-law."

"Women have strange tastes these days. He's certainly not my first choice for a son-in-law. But don't you fellows come on too strong. If that girl knows I don't like him, she's sure to set her cap for him."

"I don't want to upset you, Ernest, but the way she's acting," Senator Bert Woodville observed, "I'd say the cap has already been set."

"I hoped she'd fall for your son Daniel, Davy. I'm afraid I should have kept my mouth shut."

When they perceived Malmuth moving his golf ball in a highly irregular manner on a particularly difficult hole, Ernest Becker displayed an even more doleful countenance than he had hitherto evidenced. "Damn. He cheats at golf.

Now I could stand his high-falutin' attitude about us good ole mountain boys, but I truly detest a man who'll cheat at golf, especially when there's no competition afoot."

"I'm afraid Missy didn't see him, Ernest. She wouldn't believe us if we told her. You should've brought a camcorder." David Crockett hid his disappointment. He too had hoped that Missy and Daniel would get together.

That night, over a dinner of prime rib, Malmuth pressed the men for a commitment to the College's foundation. He had support from Melissa, who told her father that he needed to contribute to the future of the region by supporting higher education. The men finally agreed that they would give ten million dollars to the College, but there would be conditions.

"We aren't prepared to reveal our plans just yet, President Malmuth. But you have our guarantee that we will donate that amount of money to Pine Mountain College for educational purposes." They assured him that they would make their wishes clear before the end of the spring semester. At present, their lawyers were drawing up the terms of the bequest.

Malmuth left that night feeling that he had achieved a notable success. Next day he again spent his time golfing with Missy and left his guests to play their foursome.

Not playing with him suited them well, but Ernest Becker and David Crockett could not help grousing about how the "damned prig" appeared to be hustling Melissa.

Karen Again

"Let's not waste any time today, Jay. I want you to go back immediately to the evening that you left Jane." Philwaggen seemed even more anxious than Jay to continue. Jay no longer had any doubts he was making progress as he thought back to his days with Jane.

"I went home and slept soundly. The next morning I taught my morning classes, then went by Jane's office. I told her that I had to break off our relationship because it had become dangerous for her and completely stifling for me. Her only answer was to heave a large sociology text at me. I retreated and walked across campus to Karen's office. We had lunch at the college cafeteria and agreed to meet again after our afternoon classes. We were too eager to see each other again to worry about the campus rules"....

John mind slipped back to that glorious afternoon. The drive to Jaykyll's apartment did not take long. Once in the bedroom, they undressed rapidly and came together to kiss. Pushing Karen upon the antique bed that had belonged to his grandfather, John ran his hands over her incessantly. He kissed every part of her body, abandoning himself to the passion he felt. The detachment he had often felt in love making did not exist with Karen. He was completely lost in a desire to become one with her—

A female otter moved in the warm waters of the lake followed by a male. Their playful swimming established a bond of movement, a love duet whose essence was their obliviousness to the surrounding jungle. Their cries and grunts told of the delight they took in surrendering themselves to their dance. The exhilaration of their desire expressed itself in gymnastic gyrations as they attempted to approach each other from every possible direction, touching one body to the other in every position possible. A delicate water ballet performed by artists raised to the highest pitch of art, the love duet existed only for them. Around them the jungle was silent—

"I've never felt this way about anyone before, Karen."

"I know. I love you, too."

Entering her, he felt a strange release of self—

The sun shone brightly in the morning sky. High up on the mountain, the cat found a warm pool fed by underground springs. Moving from the chill of the early morning mountain air, slowly the large animal moved into the waters, fearful but unable to resist the urge to immerse itself in the warmth. As the waters spread around the beast, its growling subsided to the purr of a house cat on its owner's lap—

Karen's voice broke his reverie. "It's wonderful to be here with you."

"I feel as if I have been reborn, as if I had been trapped in a cold, dark gray prison and have been released to a sunny beach. I'm swimming out into the warm waters."

Their voyage on uncharted seas lasted for over an hour. Jaykyll wished that he could hold this moment forever. He felt that he could last all day and night if it would please Karen. She soon became aware that her lover was not easily spent and encouraged him with words that were at the same time sensual and tender. Jaykyll began to believe that he was loved. They reached their climax together and collapsed in one another's arms. He felt that he had known Karen more intimately than anyone else had known her or would. For a long time they lay locked together in an oceanic world. Finally, Karen roused herself. Kissing Jay in the ear, she whispered, "I want you again, Jay."

He found himself in *terra incognito*—

High above the open plains of the upper mountain the great hawk soared. Had their been any eyes below to witness the flight, they would have thought the eagle inebriated of the air. The bird caught a thermal and soared up, then did loops down to another current, then up on another thermal to repeat the process. Oblivious to time and place, he performed his acrobatics to the watchful eyes of the female soaring calmly in the blue sky above him—

Afterwards, Jaykyll held Karen in his arms tenderly, kissing her again and again. When they could no longer summon the energy to kiss, he turned off the lamp. Karen snuggled against him under his arm. John felt closer to her at this moment than he had ever felt to anyone before.

"I feel that we have a special bond between us, Karen."

"Wherever I am, I'll always be there for you."

For a long time they talked, telling each other the most intimate secrets of their existence. Jaykyll soon felt that Karen knew more about him than anyone else and sensed that she had let him closer to her than she had ever let anyone before.

"I had a baby when I was seventeen. Does that bother you?"

"No, I want to know all about you that I can. I know that you have been hurt deeply. I want to protect you. I want to see you develop your potential. You're bright and beautiful. You can be whatever you want to be. I just hope your future has a place for me."

"Oh, it does, Jay."

Karen told him about her wild youth and her losing her virginity to an older man. "Everybody was talking about sex. I just wanted to see what all the fuss was about. I used to skip school and drive out into the country. I drove for hours over the country roads just trying to get my mind straight."

Then she told him a little of some of her problems that led to her pregnancy. She told him also of the other men with whom she had had relationships. John felt that he was special, that he had reached a part of Karen that nobody had touched before, but he began to see that Karen was driven by feelings that were difficult for her to control.

Jaykyll felt a need to tell her secrets equally intimate, so he created one for the occasion. "I had an older lover once. She was one of my professors. She liked to play the dominating role. Handcuffed me. Tied me up.

Does that bother you?"

"You don't have an older lover now, do you?"

"No, that was ten years ago. Jaykyll found himself slipping into one of his recurrent daydreams, but there had been a strange alteration in the vision that had come upon him—

The young cub follows its mother toward the bee gum, a large tulip poplar with a bee hive in a hollow limb about fifty feet up from the ground. Weighing four pounds and measuring almost a foot long, he receives some of his first lessons in obedience and survival by means of growls and cuffs of his mother's paw as he too eagerly attacks the honey that has dripped from the tree to the shrubs below. The cub had learned to eat almost anything—acorns and beechnuts, ants, blackberries, blueberries, cherries, young buds and leaves, insects, lemmings, mice, muskrats, rabbits, shrews, and snakes. In the fall he would learn to eat grapes, paw paws, and other fruits until the mast fell again and the bear mother forces her cub to leave her before they found dens. In the base of a black gum or other large tree, they would line a snug place with pine needles and other leaves in preparation for a long winter of sleep. For the time being, though, the cub's first winter is part of the unknown and unknowable future. Now he is happy licking the sweet honey from the shrubs of the spring forest while his mother climbs the tree to rob the bees. Later he will learn to climb the tree himself and lick the honeycomb from the honey despite the annoying stings of the bees—

Because John felt protective of Karen and wished to shield her from the world's harsh blows, he felt a fatherly affection for her that baffled him. The difference in their ages was only a couple of years. He knew that, although he might feel like a father to her, in many ways Karen was far older than Jaykyll could ever imagine being. In a way," he thought, "Karen is my mother; she has brought me to new birth." Jaykyll contemplated the images of Inanna and Dumuzi, the mother goddess and her lover. He and Karen were enacting the age-old drama of fertility, and for him the bed of his grandfather was the ritual bed of the mother goddess and her consort. New life surged through him. He felt the potent lover, not a man who could date a woman for a year without intimacy.

Galvanized into new delight by this thought, Jaykyll jumped up in bed and saluted Karen with a half-mocking, half-serious salaam.

"Hail goddess! Welcome Inanna-Astarte-Aphrodite! I kiss your lips, your breasts, your belly, your loins, and your vulva, the gate of life!"

Karen laughed as he showered kisses over her body. "For crying out lound! Have you gone crazy, Jay? Lie down here beside me and behave."

Jaykyll and Karen kept talking late into the morning before they finally fell asleep. When he awoke much later and looked at her cradled in his arms, it was as if a new world had dawned for him. He could never be quite the same again, he felt. She was the goddess of fertility who had brought live-giving forces into his world. The prayer of Sumer, the sacred prayer for the marriage of Dumuzi and Inanna ran through his mind: "The people come to the palace/where the king and queen/sit together in the throne place/to care for the life of the land./On the day of the sleeping moon/the rites of New Year's Day/are woven in thread on her loom/while their bed is prepared./The queen washes her holy loins/and those of Dumuzi she bathes/to ready him for the holy dawn/when he enters her sacred vulva./The king embraces his bride/Inanna, who shines like daylight,/and her love shines at her side/Giving light to the world./The people of the goddess/sing praises to the holy pair./She shines. In his caresses/the holy Inanna is radiant." He could not help hugging and kissing Karen. The goddess awoke, sleepy and querulous, complaining that he had not let her sleep, but her complaints grew less as he began to run his hands over her body, lingering here and there, and kissing her passionately. Jaykyll's body was weary from the night before, but his passion for Karen was so great that he ignored whatever weariness he felt. Once Karen began to return his caresses, his weariness was forgotten as their embrace recaptured the state of ecstasy that they had experienced just a few hours before. Dumuzi and Inanna appeared again in the morning brilliance.

The sunlight streaming in through the window added blinding brightness to the room. The golden light made Karen seem to Jakyll the reincarnation of Inanna, and the beauty that dazzled his senses transformed him into the young shepherd from the steppes, Dumuzi, who came to plow the fertile fields of the goddess of the rivers.

"Lord. I can't believe that you have this much energy this early in the morning, especially after last night."

"You are responsible, not me. You've rejuvenated me."

"Come off of it!"

"It's true. I feel reborn. You are the elixir of love."

Karen laughed. "Maybe I can find a way to bottle it and sell it."

For breakfast Jakyll fixed hotcakes and basked in Karen's praises of his culinary abilities. Interspersing bites of hotcakes with kisses, Jaykyll could not remember having enjoyed breakfast this much ever before, even though they had to rush because both of them had to get to school.

Two hours later, Karen breezed into Jaykyll's office and smiled at him beatifically. Pretending that they were meeting for the first time that day, she offered the standard inquiry, "How are you this morning, John?"

Taking her lead, Jay responded, "I'm doing rather well, actually, Karen. Are you going to substitute for Dr. Peale today?"

"Two classes, but his door is locked. I don't want to walk back over to my office. May I work in here until he comes back?"

"Of course."

With more alacrity than care, Jaykyll quickly cleared a space on a cluttered desk for Karen to work.

As she graded papers, Karen kept up a constant stream of chatter that both amused and amazed Jaykyll. She seemed to be able to work and talk full speed at the same time.

When a janitor finally arrived and opened Peale's door, Karen moved to his office to continue grading papers, but it was not long before she popped back in to ask Jaykyll if he would like for her to fix him a cup of tea.

"I have some herb teas with me. Would you like some?"

"Yes, I'd like that. But you don't have to go to all that trouble."

"I know, but I want to."

"Well, if you insist, Miss Cleaver."

When she returned with the tea, Karen sat down to talk. She and Jaykyll had no trouble talking. In fact, Karen overwhelmed him with the sheer amount of verbiage that she could splatter against any kind of audience. The two of them could communicate now, Jekyll thought as he gazed into Karen's eyes, almost without the necessity of words.

"When can we see each other again?" Jaykyll asked.

"Whenever you want."

"What about this weekend? Would you come over Friday evening?"

"Let me cook dinner for you. I want to have something special. Come to my place Friday night."

"All right. What time?"

"Well, after dark—I think that would be best."

That evening after eating supper, Jaykyll called Karen and they had a long talk on the telephone, a fact that surprised Jaykyll, who had never before been able to talk easily on the telephone. It seemed strange to him that he was actually enjoying talking to Karen by telephone.

Friday he could hardly wait until time to go to Karen's. She let him in quickly and then they embraced. After he had kissed her deeply several times, she broke away to run to the kitchen to check on the meal that she was preparing, fish stuffed with shrimp bathed in a cream sauce.

"I love you, Karen," he said as he grabbed her around the waist and kissed her again.

"I love you, too Jay."

Karen's stove was not the most efficient, so that she had to give constant attention to the meal to make certain that it did not burn or otherwise go amiss. John could not help smiling as he watched her efforts. He could hardly believe that the Karen Cleaver that he had come to love could conjure up so much domesticity.

Karen set the table in the living room in a joyously haphazard manner, careening back and forth to the kitchen. When they finally sat at the table to eat, John was amazed at how delicious the food was. Memories of his mother's family dinners came flooding in on him. Like Karen, his mother had been disorganized, making the preparation of a meal an adventure, the outcome of which was always in doubt, though the final product was—more often than not—delightful to the eye and palate. Karen seemed to have the same ability to excite his palate and his mind at the same time. As she beamed in triumph at him from across the table, Jaykyll felt an uncontrollable urge to hold her close and kiss her. Acting on impulse, he stood up and moved around the table. Bending down, he kissed her between mouthfuls of fish and shrimp.

"You are a marvelous cook, Miss Cleaver. My compliments to the chef!"

"I don't do this very often. You should be flattered."

"I am. I'll eat enough to prove that I am."

When dinner was over and the table cleared, Jaykyll pulled Karen close to him and kissed her again. "I can't seem to get enough of kissing and hugging you, you beautiful cook. I like your cooking, but I like your kissing even more."

Karen closed the blinds, and they sat and talked while the classical music that Karen had put on set the background.

"I wish this moment could last forever," Jaykyll told her as he ran his hands over her breasts and thighs. "You're beautiful."

"You think so?"

"I know so. You fed me well, but my hunger for you can't be satisfied by that kind of food, even when it tastes so good."

Karen ran her hands through his hair and suggested that they move to the bedroom and get comfortable. As they undressed each other, they stopped to kiss and fondle. As Jaykyll looked into Karen's eyes, they turned from the blue of the sky on a clear summer evening to a gray that reminded him of his mother's eyes....

A voice interrupted. "What happened between you and Karen Cleaver," Dr. Philwaggen asked Jay when he had brought him back to the present. Jay was covered with perspiration. "Did you continue the relationship?"

"Yes, we continued the relationship for almost three years, but Karen had an excellent offer at another school, and our relationship soured when we were separated by seven hundred miles. It was a long drive, and we couldn't afford many plane tickets on our salaries. Karen couldn't remain celibate for long. We fought. We began to say harsh things to each other. We ended bitterly—nasty words ended our affair. After my experience with her, I found it difficult to form another attachment for a long time. Until I met Sarah, I couldn't enter another romantic relationship."

"No doubt that relationship with Karen was a pivotal experience for you. We'll definitely need to explore that relationship some more, but that's all we have time for today. Keep up the good fight with President Malmuth. You need to practice confrontation."

"Thanks. I will."

Malmuth Schemes

Malmuth and Melissa: Memphis

Malmuth and Missy had returned from their visit to Louisville together in a glow of excitement. That trip had gone well to Jason's thinking. He thought another trip would be very helpful in his campaign to marry Melissa Becker. Just now he was far more interested in this personal capital campaign that he was in Pine Montain College's Move to Olympus capital campaign. He had discovered that Missy was very fond of blues music. Why not offer her a trip to Memphis and to Beale Street to see the home of the blues. They could visit Graceland as well as take part in the annual Blues Festival. He was not much enamored of Elvis, but he knew that Missy was. Malmuth made plans to make another trip as soon as possible.

When Jason proposed the trip to Missy, she agreed immediately—but with conditions. She must drive and she must be in charge of making their reservations. Surprised but agreeable, Jason told her that he'd leave the arrangements to her. They agreed she should pick him up at the College about eleven-thirty. At the appointed time, the sporty red Mercedes pulled into the parking lot at the administration building again. Again Jason threw his bag in the trunk and hopped in the passenger's seat. Again Sherri Whetman watched disconsolately from the window in Malmuth's office, but this time she was even more perturbed because she did not know the destination of the Mercedes.

Down to Cookeville the couple sped over winding roads and from there on to I-40 west at greater speeds. A little after nine o'clock that night they reached the Peabody Memphis. They had made only a few stops along the way. Missy had packed sandwiches and drinks so that they could reduce their stops to a minimum. Their room was not entirely different from the one they had had in Louisville. It had a Jacuzzi. There the resemblance ended. Here they had only one room and one king-sized bed.

Missy hung up her clothes while Jason mixed gin-and-tonics. "I'm going to use the Jacuzzi," Missy announced as Malmuth handed her a drink. "Will you join me?"

"Give me some time to drink this and mix another."

Missy undressed and put on a robe with a beautiful floral print that suggested a Japanese kimono. Entering the Jacuzzi room, she set the tub to medium, took off her robe, set her drink on the edge of the tub, and got in. She sat down and closed her eyes, reveling in the warm water massaging her. It was almost ten minutes before Jason, also wearing a robe, joined her. When he hung up his robe, Missy saw that he had not worn his bathing trunks.

"Good to see you, Jason—all of you."

Malmuth set his glass beside hers, but before he got in the tub, he pulled something from the pocket of his robe. It was a small case. Opening it, he took out a diamond ring. Sitting down beside Missy, he asked her whether she would wear this engagement ring. "Perhaps you need to think about this before you answer."

"No," Missy said, taking the ring and slipping it on. "I'll wear it, but I'm still considering your marriage proposal. Maybe this ring will help me think better." She leaned over and kissed him. They stayed in the jacuzzi for an hour. Then they dried and put on their robes. Sitting on the sofa, they had a nightcap before going to bed.

"Jason, you've been married, haven't you?"

"Yes, but my wife died in an automobile accident two years ago. We didn't have any children."

"Did you love your wife?"

"Of course, what a strange question."

"I don't think it's so strange. You've proposed marriage to me. You've given me an engagement ring. Yet you've never uttered the word love in connection with our relationship. In fact, you've never even indicated that you lust for me, much less love me. Now that we're engaged, I think we might at least embark upon a little heavy petting."

"Is sex that important to you?"

"If your prick gets hard while you're kissing me, it would certainly suggest at least one reason I can understand why you want to marry me." She grabbed him and thrust her tongue deep into his mouth.

In bed Missy continued her deep kisses. She encouraged Jason to reciprocate.

When Jason had obliged her sufficiently to put her doubts to rest, she wrapped her arms around him and drifted off to sleep. Malmuth lay awake for awhile. He congratulated himself on his continuing success and that Melissa Becker could so easily be satisfied.

Saturday they helped to celebrate the birth of the blues at Beale Street and in W. C. Handy Park. They watched the river pageant in honor of King Cotton as well as a parade in his name. Then they took a riverboat tour down the Mississippi that ended with a dinner on board the boat after dark. Even Jason expressed delight at the fireworks display that ended the boat tour. That night they watched Saturday Night Live while sipping their nightcaps and engaging in the petting that Missy expected. In bed she repeated her actions of the night before and achieved a similar result.

Sunday they took an early tour of Graceland and then returned to Pine Mountain. Malmuth did not seem to Missy to be very enthusiastic about setting footsteps on the hallowed ground of Elvis, but he accompanied her without complaint. They had lunch in a little Italian restaurant where they served a very elegant eggplant parmegiana and veal marsala. They had a wine with the meal that Jason termed acceptable. All in all, it was a weekend that Missy enjoyed even though Jason's lack of passion concerned her. Warning bells should have been ringing for Missy, but she was too smitten with the Jason of her creation to hear anything but the sound of wedding bells. She decided that he was simply shy about engaging in pre-marital sex.

Belle Pumps Hiram

Late in the afternoon of the Friday that Malmuth and Melissa traveled to Memphis, Hiram Grudger received a telephone call from Belle. He was quite pleased by what she told him. He looked forward to seeing his beautiful young wife that evening.

"You're cooking Chinese stir-fry tonight." Grudger understood the message. He agreed with alacrity. In their secret code Belle was telling him that she wanted to engage in sex games that night. Grudger cleared his desk promptly at four o'clock, left the campus early, and went to the grocery to buy ingredients for the meal. By the time Belle arrived home, Grudger had the stir-fry ready. Clothed only in an apron, he greeted her at the door with a deep bow, "Empress Wu-fang, your meal is ready. Please sit and eat."

"Lowly slave, this meal had best be superior."

"I have spared nothing, your highness."

"We shall see."

The Empress Wu-fang ate a helping of the stir-fry and washed it down with the hot green tea her slave had prepared for her. "It is passable, slave, but I have eaten better."

When the meal was completed, Wu-fang ordered the slave to clear the table and put the dishes in the dishwasher. While the slave carried out her orders, the Empress went to her bedroom, showered, and changed her outfit. When the slave knocked upon her door, she ordered him in. She was dressed in black leather boots reaching above her knees, black panties with an opening in the crotch, a black brassiere with openings for her nipples, and an open black vest. Her hair was pulled back in a bun and she wore a black mask. Hiram stood gazing at her longingly. "Down on your knees, slave. Come to me on your hands and knees." When the slave reached her, the Empress spread her legs apart. "Kneel before me, slave."

The slave complied with that and further commands of the Empress Wu-fang sufficiently to receive a mild compliment.

"You have done well slave, but you must have more punishment to reach the proper state." Ordering him to lie face down upon her bed, the Empress tied his hands and feet to the bedposts. Then she brought forth a black whip and began to ply it across his buttocks. With each lash of the whip the slave groaned and the Empress asked, "Slave, will you tell me the truth when I ask a question?"

"Yes, Empress."

When the Empress found the slave's condition appropriate, she untied the bonds that held him, Then she ordered the slave over on his back as she re-tied his limbs. As she moved over him, she demanded that he tell her all that she desired.

"Yes, Empress. What would you like to know?'

"Who is the most desirable woman in the world?"

"You are, Empress Wu-fang."

"Are you happy in your slavery? Do your deserve your punishment."

"Very happy, Empress. I deserve all the punishment you exact."

"Will you tell me the truth?"

"Yes, Empress."

"Now, tell me, slave, what do you know about misuse of the College's funds. You cannot refuse me."

"I know only that I'm not involved."

"Slave, are you telling truth?"

"Yes, Empress, but if I were searching, I would look at the travel records and other items on the unbudgeted expense accounts of the College's top administrators. Perhaps they have been charging their personal expenses to the College. Perhaps you should look for a particular item, say a diamond ring."

"Slave, I am pleased. I will untie you." After the Empress had untied her slave, he performed other tasks to her satisfaction. They spent the rest of the evening in establishing the boundaries of and reconnoitering the pleasures to be obtained in the empire of the Empress Wu-fang.

Administrative Changes

When Sherri finally saw Melissa Becker after she and Malmuth returned from their trip to Memphis, the secretary could not help but notice the huge diamond on Melissa's hand. Malmuth had not told her, but Sherri deduced without difficulty that it was an egagement ring. When Malmuth was alone and she was called in for dictation, Sherri demanded that Malmuth tell her where Melissa had acquired the diamond. "Did you give her that ring this past weekend?"

"What if I did? I can give people what I want."

"By all rights, you should have given that ring to me. Maybe you bought it for me originally."

"You take too much for granted. You flatter yourself."

"I know what sort of relationship we had before you met Melissa Becker. You gave me reason to expect you to marry me after my divorce was final. You did everything but propose to me."

"Did I ever ask you to marry me?"

"No. But you certainly implied it a number of times."

"If I didn't propose to you, then I haven't breached any contracts."

"Not legally. But ethically and morally speaking you're a lying bastard."

"I don't think we should continue this conversation. I'll dictate later after you've calmed down."

"I'm warning you, Jason Malmuth, If you dump me for her, you'll regret ever having knowm me. I'm not going to accept your fickleness like a schoolgirl."

Malmuth could not think of an answer to the anger in her voice and eyes. He retreated into his office. In the next hour, he made a couple of phone calls on his private line as he thought about how to avoid seeing and hearing Sherri's accusatory face and voice. Shortly afterwards he left his office and went to that of Jeremy Bottleby. "Jeremy, I have a favor to ask."

"What's that Jason?"

"I need to trade secretaries. For personal reasons. As you no doubt have observed, Sherri Whetman does an excellent job. But the way things have worked out, I need another secretary. Your Ann Page is almost as good as Sherri. I thought you might be willing to trade since you'd get the better of the deal."

"Ann's very capable, but Sherri would do just as well. Consider it a deal. When should we switch?"

"Tomorrow morning, if it's possible."

"That's all right with me."

The next morning Ann Page expressed her considerable surprise when Jeremy Bottleby told her that the President had requested her services and that he had agreed to let her go. "I hate to lose you, Ann, but the President's wish is my command. I hope you like working in the President's office."

"What about Sherri? What's happened to her?"

"She's to be my new secretary." Ann Page raised her eyebrows but said nothing else. After all, it was her good fortune, she felt.

Sherri Whetman reacted differently. She was enraged when Malmuth told her that Bottleby had requested her services.

"I'll bet. He came to you and said that he couldn't get by without me. Was that the way it was? In a pig's eye it was. You asked him to make the switch. You made him an offer he couldn't refuse."

"I'm sure you'll be very happy working for Jeremy."

Rauncibelle Grudger had decided that it was time for another interview with Provost Bottleby. In preparation, she had done some redecorating of Belle's Bottom. It had taken on a more sinister appearance. In a passing conversation with Katy Carlyle, Belle had indicated that she felt a need to change the atmosphere of her office to something more in keeping with the current campus malaise.

"I could lend you the skull I use when I'm teaching *Hamlet*."

"That would add a very nice touch. Do you have anything else?"

"What about the wall hanging I use when we're doing the mad scene in *Lear*?"

"Great. Those ought to give just the added touch I'm looking for."

Her decorations in place and her resolve to gain more information firm, Rauncibelle arranged another tryst with Jeremy Bottleby. She had decided to use her powers of persuasion to obtain some concrete evidence of his complicity with Malmuth in misusing the college's funds. Double agent Belle called Bottleby and asked if he could find time in his schedule to meet with her in her office some afternoon that week. "I would like to discuss some assessment matters with you."

"How about tomorrow afternoon, Belle."

"Great. Would five o'clock suit you, Jeremy."

"That would be fine. See you then."

Belle spent the rest of the afternoon making sure that her camcorder and other equipment were all in good working order. The next day, she brought a little bourbon and some Coca Cola to the office for the occasion. She had observed at some faculty gatherings that Bottleby favored Bourbon and Coke. She thought it very appropriate for a man who wished to conceal his alcohol consumption just as he concealed so many other activities. Perhaps conditioned by her upbringing, Belle thought a real man would drink his bourbon straight.

A few minutes before five, Jeremy Bottleby knocked on Belle's door. She opened it to let him in and locked it behind them. Music was playing softly and the only light in the office, as usual, beamed upon the couch. "Jeremy," she asked, "would you care for a bourbon and coke?"

"That would be splendid. It's my favorite drink."

"Yes, but I'm fond of it also."

Bottleby sensed that something about Belle's Bottom was different, but he could not decide what caused him to feel this way, "Have you made some changes in your office, Belle?"

"Nothing major, Jeremy. Just a few tweaks here and there. How do you like the new look?"

"I really can't say. The place seems ever more erotic than before, but at the same time there's something eerie. I can't decide what it is."

"Don't worry about it, Jeremy. We have other matters to discuss, and I have to fix our drinks." After she had fixed their drinks, Belle sat beside Bottleby on the sofa. "Let's get to business. Have you looked at those assessment reports of the Appalachian program that I sent you and President Malmuth?"

Bottleby removed his coat and tie to make himself comfortable as he answered her. "I have. They certainly are helpful. The trend as you have presented it is in the right direction, but we need an even more negative report for Duvant."

"As I've told you, there would be easier ways to deal with Roger."

"Maybe you ought to use them then. Malmuth demands progress on getting rid of him. Of course, whoever has been trying to kill him may save us a great deal of trouble. We probably shouldn't be too hasty."

As Belle listened, she began to unbutton Bottleby's shirt.

"What if he were found misusing college funds?"

"That would be serious. We could get rid of him easily."

"How would be the best way to do this, Jeremy? How would you do it?

"Well, you would need to see that he has an account with some unbudgeted funds. That would make it easier. Then you must see that he uses some of the unbudgeted funds for personal purchases."

Belle told Jeremy to remove his clothes and then to help her undress. As they were disrobing, she asked whether he could arrange for her to have an unbudgeted account for herself as well as one for Roger. "You have an unbudgeted account. You must enjoy using it. I think it would be fun to have one." Belle underlined her desire by moving her hands over Bottleby, who sighed with pleasure as her fingers moved over him with a delicate but erotic purpose.

"Yes, I have found my fund very useful. The credit card that goes with it can be especially handy for buying knick-knacks and tickets to Europe. Am I deserving enough?"

"Yes, Belle, I believe you are."

Continuing her fondling, Belle asked if he bought tickets for himself or for others.

"Both, both," Bottleby muttered.

Writhing in pleasure, Jeremy agreed that she should have an account as soon as he could arrange it. "Yes, yes. Oh, Belle, you have convinced me that you are very deserving."

Belle comported herself expertly in her colleague's embrace as she asked Jeremy for an unbudgeted account of her own. "Am I deserving enough to have an account large enough to buy a set of lingerie to wear for you, Jeremy? Am I deserving enough to have sufficient funds to pay for a trip to Europe?"

"Yes, Belle, you deserve that and more." As Jeremy continued to mutter his pleasure, Belle smiled a smile of victory. "I must have proved very deserving, Jeremy."

"Yes Belle. There's no doubt you deserve that account."

"Sit down on the couch, Jeremy, and I'll show you that I am even more deserving." She fixed them another round of bourbon and coke. As they drank these, Belle began fondling him again. "Jeremy, am I deserving enough to have five thousand dollars in my account?"

As he slipped into her, Bottleby agreed that she was that deserving. "You may be even more deserving than that," he added.

"Be careful, Jeremy, you need to treat a deserving woman with care. I have to admit, Jeremy, that a relationship with you can give a girl a very full feeling—a very full filling," Belle laughed.

A week later, when a memorandum came through campus mail indicating that an unbudgeted account of eight thousand dollars had been set up for Rauncibelle Grudger, Director of Assessment, Belle laughed to herself and reached for her telephone.

"Have you received a memo announcing that you have an unbudgeted account, Roger?"

"Yes, it just arrived."

"Don't use the account, but keep the memo. It's evidence. The screws are tightening on the rat trap."

Roger could not helping thanking the power that guided his destiny that Belle had decided to help him. He couldn't believe that God or whatever power moved the universe approved of his trysts with Belle, but he couldn't help joking to himself that the Lord works in mysterious ways. This affair had developed differently from that with Melda Gilpin. He had engaged in his relationship with Belle in full control of his emotions. He had not chosen freely, though. He had seen no other alternative than looking for a position at another school. His feelings of guilt were always diminished by the knowledge that, ironically, he had done what was best for Betty and the boys. In lighter moments he could even see the comedy of his being Belle's love toy to keep the bread on his family's table. He had to admit that his prostitution had enjoyable elements, yet he also resolved to end it as soon as he safely could. He was hopeful that Belle would grow tired of him and that she would end their relationship amicably before it caused damage to his marriage.

Last Session

Philwaggen greeted Jay cheerily. "I've some good news for you. I believe that this might well be our last session."

Jay was surprised. "I didn't realize I'd been making that much progress."

"Yes, reviewing my notes, I find the Karen Cleaver episode to be pivotal. You have been suppressing that episode and others because of the hurt they gave you. I think your affair with Karen was a shattering experience. Now that we have that out in the open, I believe that you will find that your problem will gradually subside if you practice effective confrontation as I have advised."

"You think that my talking about these experiences will suffice?"

"Yes. I think you brought many experiences to your consciousness that you have tried to suppress. Your childhood experiences and your early experiences with lovers all have led you to have an unusually great fear of losing the things and people you love. That causes you to avoid conflict. I wouldn't be surprised if this didn't have an effect on your relationship with your wife, although we haven't gone into that fully. We could take more time to explore that, but I don't believe it's necessary. Just as a guess, I'd say that you keep a lot of things to yourself rather than discussing them openly with her. Bring disagreements with her out in the open. At any rate, you need to be more assertive in that and all your other relationships. Your spells have been coming on primarily in situations where you need to be assertive but fear to be because you are afraid of losing a relationship with someone or afraid of losing something more tangible. If you will begin speaking up when these conflicts arise, you'll find that your trances will disappear. It's possible that your daydreams may reoccur, but as long as you keep them under control, they'll do no great damage. It's healthy enough to daydream.

"What if I offend people by speaking up?"

"By all means offend some people. I want you to offend. You need to be somewhat offensive to a few people, especially Jason Malmuth. That's the medicine I prescribe. Should your problem not disappear, I'll be glad to see you again to give you encouragement—but only for that."

"All right, Dr. Philwaggen, I'll go out and be as nasty as I can."

"Good, good."

"And if I ever see you again, you owl-eyed shrink, it'll be too soon."

"Wonderful. Keep up the good work. Give Malmuth hell."

Malmuth Wins and Loses

Sherri's Evidence

Late one night, John Jaykyll was called to the telephone by Sarah. "It's Sherri Widderbe Whetman, she says it's important."

"Hello, Jay here."

"Jay, can you meet me somewhere to talk. My place would suit me. Or I could come to your place. I have some information that I don't want to mention over the telephone."

"Does this have something to do with the administration?"

"Yes." Jaykyll thought he heard Sherri crying.

"Then I'll be right over." Jay told Sarah where he was going and instructed her not to reveal his destination to anyone. "Take a number and tell them I'll call back tomorrow."

On the drive to Sherri's, Jay wondered what information would be forthcoming. As Malmuth's secretary, Sherri had access to a great deal of information that would be helpful to RAU. What could have prompted her to reveal Malmuth's secrets—that is, assuming she planned to reveal any secrets.

When he rang the doorbell to Sherri's apartment, he could hear sobbing inside. His suspicions were confirmed as the door opened. Sherri's red and swollen eyes revealed that she had been crying a great deal.

Sherri Whetman had moved from the huge mansion her husband had provided to a small two-bedroom townhouse. As Jaykyll entered, he saw a room that served as the great room, the kitchen, the bar, and an eating area on the other side of the bar—all open to one another, not separated by any load-bearing wall. The cathedral ceiling over the portion that served as a great room lent a sense of spaciousness to what was in fact a very small area. Sherri had managed to give her space a modernistic yet warm, snug, very feminine atomosphere. It suggested sophistication and femininity. Jaykyll could see why Malmuth had found Sherri attractive. This place was an extension of her—efficient and svelte, yet nevertheless voluptuous and enticing. What a cold fish Malmuth must be to be able to throw all this away as soon as another, more lucrative dish presented itself to him. Evidently his desire to climb socially dominated his decisions, and that climb demanded money. His sexual desire must be under the complete control of his acquisitive impulses, Jaykyll thought, or as Philwaggen might put it, Malmuth's Id was completely dominated by his Ego. Jaykyll could not help feeling a brief pang of admiration for someone who could so completely control his Id. He himself had had great difficulties in achieving control of his impulses. He was thankful that Philwaggen was helping him gain more control. Still, Malmuth's control had cost him his humanity. A person so enamored of social status and image could not be a complete human being.

"Better an Id a little rowdy than one that has become completely attenuated," Jaykyll concluded before offering solace to the weeping woman in front of him.

"What's the matter Sherri?"

"Jason has left for a week in Galveston with Melissa Becker. If they aren't married now, they will be when they get back. I know. I saw the receipt for the diamond ring. The second one. A huge one. He already had bought a big one for an engagement ring."

"But that's not a crime, Sherri."

"No, but using College funds to do it is."

"Can you prove that?"

"Here's copies of the credit card receipts. Those receipts are for the credit card to his unbudgeted fund."

"Sherri, did you make other copies? For safety's sake there should be other copies."

"Don't worry. I have two other sets of copies. You can make more from those. I hope you can nail the bastard. After all I did for him. The worst of it is that I think I still love him."

"You love the Jason Malmuth that you created. That Malmuth doesn't really exist. The real Malmuth is a cold-hearted, conniving crook. He doesn't deserve you, Sherri. If I weren't a married man, I'd propose to you here and now." Jay hugged her and kissed her on the cheek.

In spite of herself, Sherri smiled a little. "Thanks, Jay. Please put those to good use. I have some coffee brewing. Would you stay and have a cup with me. I could use a little male companionship just now, and you know how to make a girl feel desirable."

"I could use some coffee. Do you have a little whiskey to put in it? I think I could use a bit?"

"Of course. I'll give you a little of Jason's favorite brand."

Over coffee, Jay told her that there were many wheels in motion, all moving toward the removal of Malmuth and Bottleby. "They don't know it yet, but their days at Pine Mountain College are dwindling fast."

"That might be a great help. I would feel better if I didn't have to look at him every day. I just can't help going ballistic every time I see him. I can't understand it. I didn't feel this strongly about my husband. We just ended our marriage. It was almost amicable. We were really tired of each other. I didn't and don't feel the overpowering anger toward him that Jason brings out."

"You obviously fell in love with a Jason Malmuth that doesn't exist. He has an undeniable surface charm. You're bitter because your Sir Galahad turned into the Black Knight. He destroyed your dream."

After lingering over a couple of cups of Irish coffee, Jay told Sherri that he had to get back home while he could still drive safely. As she saw him out, Jay kissed her on the cheek and gave her an avuncular hug. "You are extremely desirable, don't forget that, Sherri."

As he drove home, Jay could not restrain feelings of triumph. It would be Malmuth and Bottleby who would be cast into the outer world, not Roger Duvant. It would not be long before Malmuth would receive the fate he deserved, banishment from Pine Mountain, maybe even a jail term. "He might even wish he had taken me up on my offer to spend some time at the funny farm with him," Jaykyll thought. "He may end up on a prison farm instead." Though not an unduly vindictive person, Jaykyll could not resist a broad grin at that prospect.

Malmuth and Melissa: Galveston

To complete his plan to convince Melissa Becker to marry him, Jason asked her to go with him to Galveston. They would leave on a Monday and return on the following Saturday. That would give them almost six days in Texas. Melissa readily agreed when Jason accepted her stipulation that their room have only one bed. They drove to Knoxville to catch their flight to Hobby Airport in Houston, where they rented a car to drive to Galveston.

Along I-45 Melissa could hardly believe the flatness of the countryside. As they crossed Galveston Bay on the causeway, she saw gulls and other birds.

"Look at the pelicans, Jason. They're funny."

When I-45 turned into a city street, Melissa admired the palm trees and live oaks that lined the Boulevard. The large houses impressed her also, especially the Bishop's Palace. "I'd like to tour some of these old homes that are open to the public, Jason." He agreed that they would.

The sunshine on the beach at Galveston warmed Melissa and Jason. They stayed at the Hotel Galvez, an imposing old structure overlooking the Seawall, the structure built after the great hurricane of 1900 to protect the city. Their room overlooked the Gulf, so they could look down on the beach when they were not bathing. The food at the Galvez whetted their appetites so much that even Jason ate more than he should. They also visited some of the other good restaurants in the city. In turn they visited Gaido's, Landry's, and the Captain's Table. They took in every store on the Strand and ate at the Brewery. They took the tour of the sailing ship Elissa and visited the railroad museum. There was hardly an old home they did not enter. In short, they occupied their time so fully that the five days they had in Galveston seemed like a short weekend.

Their days were so long that they were ready for sleep when they had had their dinner and returned to their room. They were usually quite tired after a long day of sightseeing and surfing in the waves on the beach. Always Jason prepared a nightcap for them-always gin-and-tonic. Melissa contented herself with the heavy petting that they had begun in Memphis until their next-to-last night. After dinner, while they were having their nightcap, Malmuth drew a small object from his briefcase and opened it. In it lay cushioned a huge diamond ring. Getting down on his knees, he presented it to Missy and again requested that she marry him.

"I hope I'm not rushing you, Missy, but will you marry me before we go back to Kentucky? If you agree, we'll find a justice of the peace tomorrow and get married. We can have a big church wedding later, back in Kentucky."

Missy had given a great deal of thought to the idea of marrying Jason. She was still dubious about whether or not he possessed enough passion for her to produce a satisfactory marriage partner. She was certainly interested in many things other than sex, but she had a healthy interest in having a satisfactory sex life. She wanted to have a family. She wanted a man who would demand her attention, not just acquiesce when she expressed her desire.

"Jason, I've given this lots of thought. I think you're a swell guy. I want to be your wife, but I'm afraid you don't love me. You never seem passionate. I don't want to be raped, but a little aggressive love-making once in a while wouldn't be unpleasant. Are you sure you want to marry me."

"Of course I'm sure, Missy. It's been my number one priority for some time. I'm afraid my job's been neglected because of my pursuing you."

"All right. I'll agree to marry you tomorrow, but you have to promise one thing."

"What's that?"

"That we'll consummate the marriage tomorrow night."

"I promise."

"Then I'll marry you tomorrow."

The next day Missy turned down Jason's offers to take her sight seeing again. They found a justice of the peace after breakfast and were married before noon. During the afternoon they spent several hours on the beach. Then they showered and had an early dinner at the Galvez. Back in their room, drinking the by-now ritualistic gin-and-tonics, Missy told Jason it was time for him to make good on his promise. Undressing in front of him, she announced that she was ready for bed and ready to be bedded. Down to her bra and panties, Missy began undressing Jason. She unbuttoned his shirt and unbuckled his pants. "Now do the rest yourself," she told him as she lay down upon the bed and waited to be taken.

"Jason, I want you now."

"I have to put something on first, Missy. We're not ready to start a family." Despite Missy's protests, Jason insisted on the soundness of his decision.

Jason did fulfill his bargain that night, but Missy was not entirely satisfied. She didn't like his arguments about why they shouldn't risk pregnancy just yet. She still detected a lack of passion in Jason's approach to her. His actions and his words seemed perfunctory. As they flew back to Kentucky, she wondered how long this marriage would last unless Jason developed more desire for her. He seemed very reluctant to have children. Unless things changed, she was not sure she wanted to continue the marriage.

They saw the headlines in the newspapers at the airport. FOUNDATION ANNOUNCES GRANT. Reading the article, Malmuth amazed Missy with the vehemence of his curses. Their volume attracted a great deal of attention. Embarassed, Missy pleaded with Jason to control himself. "People are staring at you, Jason." At her urging, he began to display outward calm although inwardly he continued seething with anger. The Davy Crockett Foundation for Appalachian Studies had announced its grant to Pine Mountain College while Jason Malmuth and Melissa Becker enjoyed the sunshine on Galveston's beaches. Dr. Daniel Crockett had called a press conference. He had no doubt enlisted Sherri Whetman's help in contacting all the local newspapers and television stations as well as those in Lexington. Thus there had been a large media presence in the convocation hall when Crockett made his announcements. One of these announcements was that Daniel Crockett had been appointed the first Director of the Davy Crockett Foundation and that future behests to Pine Mountain College might well occur should the Foundation be pleased with the way its first behest was used.

There were also certain stipulations about how the College must use this ten-million-dollar grant. First, the College must use the funds to build the Melissa Becker Center for Appalachian Studies on the College's campus. There must also be a Rob Taylor Chair of Appalachian Studies and the first recipient of this chair must be Dr. Roger Duvant. He would have control of a special account into which would be placed the funds remaining after the building of the Center and the endowing of the Chair of Appalachian Studies had been accomplished. After he had outlined the terms of the grant, Dr. Crockett had opened the floor for questions from the media. He had said that he would answer any question concerning the Foundation's bequest. There had been many.

"What does the Foundation hope will result from this donation?"

"The Foundation hopes that through its bequest Pine Mountain College can become a leader in the field of Appalachian studies. Already the College possesses a highly trained and dedicated group of professors who have devoted their research time to dealing with Appalachian issues. The Foundation hopes that the College will build on this strong base."

"When did this Foundation come into being?"

"A few months ago. Its Board of Directors consists of a number of prominent Kentuckians."

"How does President Malmuth feel about this bequest?"

"The Directors have told me that President Malmuth had pressed them for some time to make a donation to the College."

"Does this mean that President Malmuth has changed his attitude about the Appalachian Studies program at Pine Mountain College."

"I believe the facts speak for themselves. Evidently he has."

"Does this mean that he has abandoned his anti-rusticity campaign?"

"I can think of no other interpretation of these events."

All the faculty teaching in the Appalachian Studies program had been present. They had not completely contained their glee during the questions from the press. Jay had not needed to combat the grayness at all during the proceedings. As he read the account, Malmuth recognized that he had been greeted with a *fait accompli* upon his return from what he had considered his great success at Galveston. He would have been even more angry had he heard John Jaykyll's telephone call to Sarah after the meeting. "Be sure not to miss the evening news, honey. You'll find it very interesting."

Sarah turned on the television and sat down. She laughed all the way through that segment of the news.

The Shooting

Sherri Widderbee did not wait for Monday to see Jason. Her despair had grown into a cold anger. She was determined to make Jason Malmuth pay for his duplicity. She drove by the President's mansion several times Sunday evening. When she finally found the lights on, she parked her car at the head of the tree-lined lane and walked the rest of the way to the house. She wanted to make certain that he was alone. Peering through the windows, Sherri could see nobody but her false lover. After she had surveyed the scene completely and was fairly sure that he was alone, she went to the front door, took her key to the house and her revolver from her purse, and opened the door.

She knew the house quite well. So she checked Malmuth's bedroom to make certain Melissa was not there. Then she walked to the den, where she expected to find him. The door was open. She eased up to the doorway and peered in. Jason was alone at his desk going through mail and memos. For a time, Sherri stood silently contemplating the object of her revenge. He was handsome, she noted with a pang that increased her anger. She had to fight for control of her emotions. Finally she spoke in a low voice. "Hello, Jason, welcome home." At the sound, Malmuth swung around in his chair. She did not try to conceal her anger. "Did you marry Melissa?"

"Yes. We married in Galveston."

"Why isn't she here?"

"She thought it best to go to her father's to tell him. She'll be here day after tomorrow."

"Jason, you are a two-timing bastard. I gave you my complete support. I was loyal even when I knew you were wrong. I loved you. You led me to believe that you loved me and wanted to marry me. Somebody needs to mete out some punishment to you. You shouldn't be allowed to treat people so callously without paying some penalty." Sherri brought forth her gun from behind her back where she had been concealing it.

Seeing the revolver in her hand, he became frightened. "Don't do something you'll regret, Sherri. I'm not worth it."

"I know that." She aimed the revolver carefully. Malmuth heard the gun go off and felt a throbbing in the inner part of his thigh. He bent over in pain. Grasping at his thigh, he fell to the floor. Walking over to the writhing man, his attacker examined his wound. "You'll live. If my aim had been better, you never would have had any children. But I missed." Malmuth cowered before his attacker, moaning his pain. Quickly Sherri tied his hands and feet with rope she had brought with her. Moving over to the telephone, she called the local newspaper to add the final touch to her revenge. "I thought you'd like the story. President Malmuth of Pine Mountain College has just been shot by a jealous woman." Next, she called the Pine Mountain police and repeated her statement. Then she stripped her victim's pants down to his ank;es and applied a tourniquet to stop the bleeding of his wound. Next she took out a lipstick from her purse and wrote "Here lies a two-timing liar" on his white shirt. Finally she tied Malmuth's pantless legs together below the knees with his pants and walked out of the house and down the tree-lined lane to her car.

Feeling better than she had for weeks, Sherri drove home and had a whiskey and soda nightcap before going to bed and sleeping peacefully. It was her first good sleep in weeks. Monday morning she was at her desk bright and early. She wanted to make certain she was there to greet President Malmuth whenever he chose to appear. About eleven o'clock, he appeared limping into Bottleby's office looking very haggard. An expression of shocked surprise spread across his face when he saw Sherri at her desk.

"Good morning, President Malmuth. How are you this morning."

"All right. Little thanks to you. I'm surprised you showed up this morning."

"Why not? If you had any sense, you didn't tell the police or the reporters who shot you. I know you for a two-timing louse, but I didn't think you'd do something so stupid that it was bound to finish you as president of this college. Did you?"

"No. I'm not quite that stupid."

"Well, there you are, honey. I can't afford to lose a day's pay just because my former boss is a little the worse for wear and doesn't particularly like me any more. After all, I'm not rich like your new wife."

Messerand Strikes

Several weeks passed after Roger Duvant escaped the rifle shots during his evening jog. His attacker had spent the intervening time cursing his ill luck. Jacques Messerand could no longer contain his hatred of Roger Duvant. His desire to strike down the man he had marked as his most grievous enemy began to drive all other thoughts from his head. Messerand decided that he must strike a lethal blow at close quarters. His hatred demanded the satisfaction of thrusting a weapon into his tormentor's body. He went shopping for a hunting knife. He would confront the man who had bedeviled the majority of his waking moments since he had come to Pine Mountain. As he sat in the living room of their house sharpening the knife, Simone asked him what he intended to do with it. Messerand looked up and gave her an evil smile. "They call these pig-stickers. I bought it to stick a pig with, cheri."

Simone looked on apprehensively, but she did not dare to ask any more questions. She suspected what Jacques had in mind. For days he had been accusing her of having made love with Roger Duvant and speaking of his desire for revenge on the man he termed her backwoods Apollo. Simone had told Betty Duvant of her fear that Jacques planned to attack Roger with the knife, but there was little that could be done. Roger simply laughed off the danger. "If automobiles, arrows, bullets, and poison didn't work, a knife could be next," he told Betty, "but I'll deal with it when it comes. I can't live my life hiding from the man."

Roger was much more worried than he allowed Betty to see. Several nights he had imagined he heard a dog howl—more than once. He attributed these imagined howls to an overly active imagination, but he still thought he needed to keep alert. He felt sure that Messerand had bought that knife for him, but he had no evidence to offer the police. At least a knife would have to be delivered at close range. Messerand could not avoid being seen if he used that. The main thing, Roger thought, was for him to be prepared for the attempt. He tried to remain alert.

Three weeks after his revenge on Samp, Messerand decided that the time to strike again against Duvant had arrived. That night, after dark, he tied Simone to a chair and gagged her once again. Then he donned a symbolic outfit of black—a black face mask, black shirt and pants, and a black cape. Before he left with his pig-sticker in hand, he modeled his outfit in front of his captive wife and told Simone that the black avenger was about to strike. "The black avenger attacks under the new moon. Adulterous lovers of Jacques Messerand's wife should beware the time when the new moon graces the sky. *Au revoir, cheri.*"

Roger had become suspicious of all unexpected knocks at the door after dark, and he did not let Betty respond to them any more. So it was Roger who answered the knock at the door that night. As he peered into the dark he imagined that he heard a dog howl. Instead of a person at the door, he saw in the outside light a letter on the stoop. As he carefully opened the screen door to pick it up, a figure dressed all in black leapt at him from the dark. Just in time, Roger saw the huge knife in the upraised hand. He managed to partially ward off the blow, but the knife blade reached his chest. Luckily it hit the medallion that Belle had given him. Roger felt the blow as he grabbed the arm of the knife wielder and twisted it, throwing the dark figure to the ground. The black figure quickly recovered and came at Roger once more. "Call the police, Betty. We have the killer," Duvant yelled as grabbed the attacker's uplifted arm and shook the knife from the hand of his assailant. Then he tackled him, knocking him to the ground.

Quickly Roger retrieved the knife, jumped astride his assailant, and pulled the face mask off of Messerand. "You murderous bastard, I have you now. It'll be a pleasure to hand you over to the police." Then he sat on Messerand and waited.

The campus police arrived in a few minutes. They took Messerand into custody and called Sheriff Mullgrab. A police car with two sheriff's deputies soon pulled up to the Duvant's. "I guess you'll feel a lot more comfortable without this man next door," a deputy told Roger as he pushed Messerand into his police car.

"I couldn't be any happier if pigs could fly," Roger answered.

When the police had finished their work and hauled Messerand off to jail, Betty thought about Simone. "We'd better check their house, Roger. God knows what he did to Simone before he came to attack you." They went to the door of the Messerand house and found it ajar. Entering, they called Simone's name. Then they saw her tied in the chair next to the kitchen table. She was trying to talk. Loosening the gag, Betty untied her as she babbled about Jacques, the black avenger, and the pig-sticker. "It's all right, Simone," Betty assured her. "Roger survived the attack. He's not hurt at all. The police have Jacques in custody and have taken him to jail. I don't think you have to worry about him for awhile."

No Confidence

The Faculty Senate of Pine Mountain College met at the request of Jonathan Large to decide whether or not to have a meeting of the entire faculty.

In requesting the meeting, Large had told the Chair of the Senate, Harlis Williams, that evidence would be presented that would prove the misuse of college funds by Provost Bottleby and President Malmuth beyond any doubt. Roger Duvant took the lead in presenting their case to the Senate.

"We have copies of his credit card forms showing that Malmuth bought two diamond rings with College funds. We have copies of records from the business office showing the same thing and showing no reimbursement. We have videotape of Bottleby telling in his own words of using College funds for personal purchases. We have witnesses that will testify that Bottleby and Malmuth suborned perjury in an effort to destroy the careers of faculty whom they disliked. We have all this besides Malmuth's intemperate remarks and actions at the faculty meeting. You all know, I think, that Malmuth and Bottleby tried to persuade John Jaykyll to take treatment at a mental institution. Certainly everyone knows of the damage that Malmuth has done to the College with his so-called campaign against rusticity. Given all this evidence of the unfitness of Bottleby and Malmuth, I don't see how you could give them anything other than a vote of no confidence. We request that you call a meeting of the whole faculty to consider having such a vote."

The Faculty Senate voted unanimously to call a meeting to discuss a proposal to censure the President and Provost. Without a dissenting vote and only one abstention, the Senate agreed to call this special meeting immediately. They allowed two days for the notices to be distributed. Almost all the faculty attended meeting that Thursday. Roger Duvant repeated his speech to the Faculty Senate, adding that the evidence of criminal conduct had been forwarded to the

Governor and the state police. This time the vote was not unanimous. Jacques Messerand and Ichabod Balboa voted against the motions of no confidence and censure. A few other faculty members that had been favored by Bottleby and Malmuth abstained. Despite these few dissenters, over ninety-five per cent of the faculty voted that they had no confidence in the administration and voted to censure Bottleby and Malmuth for misuse of the College's funds.

"Victory is sweet," Lavender Large told Pauline Hauptman.

"Yes, Lavender, but in this case revenge is just as sweet."

Melissa Dumps Malmuth

Ernest Becker had never liked Jason Malmuth very well though he had agreed with Melissa that Jason was a catch. He was after all a Harvard graduate and a college president. Becker knew better than to argue with his daughter about her personal life. Although he grudgingly had accepted Melissa's choice, Becker had not dropped his dislike for Malmuth's elitism. "That damn fellow may be good lookin', but he's a damn snob. He's just a piss-ant mountain boy who's got above his raisin.' Besides that he cheats at golf."

Melissa had laughed at her father. "You don't like him because he doesn't drink bourbon straight and cuss."

She paid more attention to her father's objections than she let him see. Her father's dislike of Jason had been very much on Missy's mind after she and Jason had married. On the flight from Houston to Tri-Cities airport in Tennessee, Missy had already been having second thoughts about marrying Jason. She decided to stay with her parents a few extra days rather than joining Jason immediately in Pine Mountain as she had planned. After learning of Sherri Whetman's shooting Malmuth and the vote of no confidence that the faculty of Pine Mountain College had given Jason, Melissa began to have very serious doubts about her choice. She had gone home only to inform her parents about her marriage to Jason, but as the bad news poured in she decided not to go back to her husband before thinking long and hard about her course of action. She even asked her father for advice. It was no surprise that her father was not pleased with the marriage. He had attempted to dissuade her from continuing her engagement to Jason Malmuth. He was even more eager to dissuade her from continuing the marriage. When she showed him the marriage ring, he pointed out that she probably could have had any man she wanted. "You're bright. You're beautiful. You have a glowing personality. You're goin' to inherit a fortune. Why waste all that on that prig. What about that young geologist you met at that party Malmuth threw. Daniel Crockett. He's got a doctorate. He's good looking. And he's the son of a friend of mine. Now that boy has brains. He's educated and he has common sense. He knows geology, too. That boy could take over Becker Enterprises when I retire. And anybody at that party could plainly see that he was smitten with you. Why, if he'd been a pet dog, he would've been licking your hand. And he's a handsome boy."

"He is really good-looking. He called me a couple of times after the party, but I was already going with Jason."

Melissa spent the next few days thinking about little else than her relationship with Jason. When he called, she told him that she was upset by what she had been hearing about him and needed time to think. His protestations of undying affection for her rang hollow to her ears, which listened to him now with greater acuity.

Later, she approached her father and asked him if he held firm in his opinion of what she should do about Jason.

"Yes, Missy. I think you'd be wise to abandon that ship. He's been shot by a jealous lover and his faculty have saddled him with a vote of no confidence. I'm told by Davy Crockett that evidence of his misuse of the College's funds has been gathered and is being sent to the Governor and the State Police. If you stick with him, you'll probably have to visit him in jail. I'll be happy to have your wedding annulled. I'll foot the whole bill for an annulment. I don't want to tell you what to do, but I think you should know that I'd be more inclined to give you my money if you married Daniel Crockett than if you persist in your marriage to that prissy crook, Jason Malmuth."

"Daddy, I'll have to admit that you've been right about Jason. I've been thinking about it ever since I married him. He has always been so interested in your success. I guess he married me for your money. He never did show much passion toward me, anyway. I barely got him to consummate the marriage, and he wore a condom to make certain I didn't get pregnant. He said he didn't think we ought to have children right away. You go ahead and get the annulment process started. I was a sap to marry him."

Jaykyll Emerges Victorious

RAU confronts Malmuth and Bottleby

Having presented their information to the Faculty Senate and the full faculty, the members of RAU now demanded a meeting with the Provost and the President to confront them with the evidence. They marched to Malmuth's office and told Ann Page that they wished to speak with the President.

"I'll ask whether he can see you now. He's in conference with Provost Bottleby."

"That's not necessary. What we have to say concerns both of them," John Jaykyll told her.

Without saying anything more, the group marched past Ann's desk, opened Malmuth's door and walked in. Bottleby and Malmuth looked up in surprise.

"Who told you that you could barge in here like this?" Malmuth asked.

"Nobody. We did it on our own authority. We've just come from a meeting of the entire faculty. They have conducted a vote concerning the effectiveness of this administration. Over ninety per cent of them have voted no confidence in the administration and have voted to censure you two for misuse of College funds." Jaykyll spoke without having any problem with the grayness that had bedeviled him. He was taking considerable delight in this confrontation, he decided.

Roger added to what Jaykyll had said. "You two also ought to know that we have sent the Governor and the State Police evidence of your misuse of College funds."

"What are you raving about? What evidence?"

"Oh, we have the goods on you two. You've been using College money to finance your personal purchases. Part of your high life style has been at the expense of College programs—especially the Appalachian program, no doubt.

Have you bought any diamond rings lately, President Malmuth? How have you financed you and your wife's trips abroad, Provost Bottleby?" Roger rested his case there.

"You're bluffing. You couldn't have evidence that would harm us." Bottleby was defiant.

"Yes, we do," said Jaykyll. "Many people have spent time compiling it. And the Governor and police have what we have. I think you ought to be thinking about getting out of Dodge. Maybe if you resign and offer some restitution for the funds you've misused, they'll let you go without prosecuting you for grand larceny. Roger will provide you with a view of the evidence, if you wish."

Bottleby and Malmuth looked at each other for a long time. Finally, Malmuth spoke. "We'll talk it over and let you know. Whom should we contact if we decide to resign?"

"Hiram Grudger is the next highest figure in the administration. Tell him and he'll arrange a press conference for you." Jaykyll had the satisfaction of the last word.

Roger stayed for the promised show-and-tell. Besides the other evidence amassed against the two, Roger had Belle's tapes. He had made copies of the appropriate audio portions of Belle's sessions with Bottleby. Having seen and heard the evidence against them, the Provost and President could hardly bring themselves to speak. Of course, the tapes that Belle had handed over to Roger had been suitably edited by him so that only the parts pertinent to Bottleby's malfesance were left on the audio and the video had been eliminated entirely, though Roger promised to make it available if necessary. The two malefactors were even more cowed when Roger again assured them that the evidence had been sent on to the Governor and the State Police. After the two had deliberated briefly, Malmuth telephoned Hiram Grudger, who had been prepared for the call by Belle.

"Hiram, Jeremy and I have decided to resign our posts at the College. Would you please arrange a press conference in the convocation hall so that we can announce our resignations to the media. We'll have our letters of resignation on your desk before the day is out. We'll leave it to you to pass them on to the College's Board."

"All right, President Malmuth. I'll do as you ask. Would three in the afternoon tomorrow be all right with you and the Provost?"

"Certainly. Thank you."

Roger could imagine the other end of the conversation. He left Malmuth's office glowing with RAU's victory. "*Sic semper tyrannis*," Roger told Ann Page, pointing to the Virginia state flag as he left. She followed him with puzzled eyes as he departed down the hall whistling *Bonaparte's Retreat*.

Duvant and Belle

After the faculty meeting where the no-confidence vote had occurred, Roger had walked Belle to her office. They had agreed to talk about what was to happen next once Malmuth and Bottleby were gone. The sun was shining. There was hardly a cloud in the sky.

"Belle, I really appreciate your letting me have those tapes—not only the ones we needed to deal with Bottleby but those others of us."

"A gift of friendship."

"You really are a friend, Belle."

"Roger, I'm so glad that your would-be killer has been brought into the open. I really had begun to fear losing you."

"You know your amulet is what saved me, Belle. If I hadn't been wearing that, he would have killed me. Or at least wounded me severely."

"Maybe I am a good angel."

Roger agreed to come back to talk about the future after he and others had faced down the President and Provost. Then he went to find Jaykyll and the rest of the group that was to confront Malmuth and Bottleby.

Later, when Roger returned and knocked on Belle's door, she opened it, pulled him in and locked the door behind them. That accomplished, she turned and hugged Roger as hard as she could and kissed him. "Man, you're so handsome I can't keep my hands off you. If that crazy Frenchman had killed you, I would have seen to it that he never left Pine Mountain alive. Now, sit down on the couch and let's have a cup of tea."

While Belle heated the water for tea and put on Beethoven and Mozart, Roger talked about the possibilities for interim management at Pine Mountain College. "I think the powers in Lexington and Frankfort will heed the recommendations of those of us in the Appalachian program, especially if you and Hiram concur in our recommendations."

"What do you propose to recommend?"

"We have agreed to recommend Hiram for Acting President, Jonathan Large for Acting Provost, and John Jaykyll for Acting Dean. The faculty won't object to any of them. Hiram doesn't have much more than a year to retirement, and Jonathan and John have no aspirations for high administrative posts. They'll be only too happy to resume full-time teaching after a search has produced replacements. How would you feel about being the spouse of a president?"

"I hope it wouldn't cramp my style too much. I'd have to be very careful. If Sherri Whetman agrees to stay on as president's secretary and continues organizing the social events, I don't think I'd mind too much."

"You could do it for just a year, Belle. You don't have to give up your office and assessment job."

"In that case, I'll lead the chorus of Hiram Grudger for President. Now, honey, I want a reward for all the help I've given you." Without waiting for an answer, Belle drew him down to her and kissed him—rather tenderly Roger thought. When he had provided Belle with the requested reward and as soon afterward as they were able to move, Belle got up and fixed them some more tea.

"I don't know whether Sardel's love potion works, Roger, but I do know that I feel more for you more than I ever felt for anyone before. Not that I don't have a very warm affection for Hiram, and I must admit I have enjoyed sex with other men, but my feelings for you are different. I have a lust for you almost beyond my control, but there's something more. For lack of another name, I call it love."

"I guess I know what you mean, Belle. I love Betty passionately, but I feel more for you than simple lust. There's something between us now that goes beyond lust. Remember, though, it's our secret. If poetic justice were served, you and I would be punished along with Bottleby and Malmuth."

"It's our secret. I certainly wouldn't want the truth about you to be widely known, you gorgeous hunk. I'll never have enough of you, Roger. Never."

"Belle, it's a cliché, but I think we have to stop meeting like this."

"I know you're right, Roger, but I'm not ready yet. I'm afraid I'm addicted to you—maybe it's that love potion of Sardel's. I can't give you up cold turkey.

We'll have to talk some more about this. I'll have to undergo gradual withdrawal."

"Then I had better see Sardel about an antidote."

RAU Parties

Three weeks later, the evening news announced the appointments by the Board of Regents of Pine Mountain College of the people whom the faculty had recommended to replace President Jason Malmuth and Provost Jeremy Bottleby. Pending a nationwide search, Hiram Grudger would become Acting President of Pine Mountain College. Jonathan Large would be Acting Provost and John Jaykyll Acting Dean.

The celebration had been planned ever since it became apparent that Jason Malmuth and Jeremy Bottleby did not have long to stay at Pine Mountain College. The group included all of the Appalachian Studies faculty, Sherri Whetman, and the Pore Folks Frolic members. Virgie Jones and the rest of the Chalbotfest Committee received invitations also. Belle and Hiram Grudger were the hosts at the President's Mansion at Roger Duvant's request. As Roger had promised Belle, Sherri Whetman took care of all the arrangements. Money for the event came out of the President's unbudgeted account and was listed as a contribution to college-community relations.

The invitations requested that everyone come dressed as much like rustics as they thought fit. Roger suggested to Belle that she and Hiram should wear Indian war paint covering their bodies except for Indian warbonnets and bathing suits. He and Betty would do the same. He begged Daniel to come and bring an escort dressed as their ancestors would have been—Dan in a deerskin suit and coonskin cap, and his date in a calico dress. The others he left to their own devices.

Over the doorway to the entrance hung a sign that read, "True Education. Substance, Not Image." Lavender Large came in a revealing lavender dress with an extremely short skirt with RUS and TIC emblazoned across the front and back. Jonathan wore short pants and a tee shirt proclaiming him HISTORIAN OF THE RUSTICS. Pauline Hauptman came in a skirt that had a johnny-house emblazoned on its rear. Her date, Nathaniel Boone, wore blue jeans and a tee shirt that proclaimed RUSTIC LEAVES RUSTLE.

In keeping with the rusticity of the event, several kegs of beer were on hand. Nobody was allowed to drink anything else except water or moonshine.

When Belle greeted Betty and Roger at the door, he noted that Belle had added to her outfit two hairpieces hanging down her back. These were labeled J.B. and J.M.

When she saw Roger eying them, she told him that she had been a brave warrior and had taken scalps. He asked her whether she had adjusted to life in the mansion. "It takes getting used to, Roger, but I think I'll adjust. Hiram doesn't seem to like it much, though. He says he's more comfortable in our smaller place. I'm glad you suggested this outfit, Roger. It really shows off my figure. Yours is gorgeous, too, Betty."

"Why thank you, Belle. I believe it caught Roger's attention."

"Betty, this is the woman who saved my life. Belle gave me that amulet for good luck after the third attempt on my life. If I hadn't been wearing it when Messerand attacked me with that hunting knife, I'd be dead."

"I guess you're Roger's good angel, Belle."

"I hope so, Betty. I'm certainly glad we didn't lose him to that crazy's Frenchman's murderous attempts. For some reason not entirely clear to me, I know you and I have a great deal in common. You must come by and have tea with me some afternoon."

"Thanks for the invitation, Belle. I just wish we could do something for that poor Simone. Her life has been a living hell. Now her husband is going to be allowed out of jail on the condition that he go back to France. I wish she didn't have to go back to France with him."

"According to what I've seen in the assessments, she has worked wonders tutoring students in French. Maybe we could find enough money to keep her here in some sort of capacity. We could let her stay at our place and housesit for a year while we are in this mansion."

"Belle, that would be wonderful. That way almost everyone who deserves it can have a happy outcome to this Malmuth mess."

"I'll get to work on Hiram. There are times when he cannot refuse me anything I ask. Maybe I'll have some good news for you soon. I'll let you know when and you can come by my office to discuss the arrangements."

Dressed in buckskin and a coonskin cap to honor Roger's request, Daniel Crockett brought along Melissa Becker Malmuth in calico as his date and introduced her as Missy, the woman for whom the new Appalachian Studies Center was named. He was obviously very happy about his prize. He could not keep his eyes off of her. "She's getting an annulment of her marriage to Malmuth," he announced to everybody he saw. Missy smiled benignly at Dan and told those who asked her about Malmuth that she felt she was lucky to be able to escape with an annulment.

"I married somebody that I had created in my mind, not the real Jason Malmuth."

The Flowerpiercers arrived in straw hats and bib overalls. MALMUTH: ONCE'T WAR ENUFF was emblazoned on the bibs. Gentry claimed that he had sent a going-away present to Jason Malmuth: a tape of his students whose mountain dialect was the most pronounced.

Virgie Jones and other members of the Chalbotfest Committee came dressed as country singers and musicians. Their group's name, Sourwood Mountain, was emblazoned on their shirts and blouses. They promised to provide an evening consisting of traditional mountain music except for one new tune created especially for the occasion: *The Hanging of Jason Malmuth*.

John and Sarah Jaykyll came dressed in hobo outfits sporting the message JACK KILLED THE GIANT. Jay took particular care to speak to Sherri Whetman, who came dressed in an eye-catching western outfit and dragging along Rufus Webbot in jeans, a cowboy hat, and cowboy boots. Sherri's skirt stopped well short of her knee boots. She had a holstered six gun on either hip, and SHERRI SHOT HER MAN painted on a tee-shirt that displayed her cleavage quite effectively.

"Sherri, why don't you apply for the secretary's job at the Appalachian Studies Center. I'm sure you'd find the job pleasant and you'd be among friends. After all, you're the woman who shot Jason Malmuth. Maybe they'll make a movie starring you. It'll rival that great film starring Jimmy Stewart and John Wayne, *The Man Who Shot Liberty Valance*."

Sherri laughed. "Thanks, Jay, I'll think about it. I hear you've completely gotten over your psychiatric problems. Congratulations."

Before he moved away, Jaykyll told her, "From now on, honey, call me Jack."

0-595-26710-6

Printed in the United States
1248300005B/60